Tremolo

cry of the loon

by Aaron Paul Lazar

Twilight Times Books
Kingsport Tennessee

Tremolo: cry of the loon

This is a work of fiction. All concepts, characters and events portrayed in this book are used fictitiously and any resemblance to real people or events is purely coincidental.

Copyright © 2006 by Aaron Paul Lazar.

All rights reserved. No part of this book may be reproduced, stored in a retrieval system or transmitted in any form by any means electronic, mechanical, photocopying, recording or otherwise, except brief extracts for the purpose of review, without the permission of the publisher and copyright owner.

Twilight Times Books
P O Box 3340
Kingsport, TN 37664
www.twilighttimesbooks.com/

First paperback printing: November 2007

Library of Congress Cataloging-in-Publication Data

Lazar, Aaron Paul.
  Tremolo : cry of the loon / by Aaron Paul Lazar.
     p. cm.
  ISBN-13: 978-1-933353-08-1 (trade pbk. : alk. paper)
  ISBN-10: 1-933353-08-2 (trade pbk. : alk. paper)
  1. Teenage boys--Fiction. 2. Camps--Fiction. 3. Maine--Fiction. I. Title.
  PS3612.A97T74 2007
  813'.6--dc22

                                                    2007040992

Photo credit Aaron Lazar

Printed in the United States of America

*This book is dedicated to
My beloved grandparents
I love you and miss you.
'Til we meet again.*

Tremolo: cry of the loon

Preface

If you've ever stayed at a lakeside camp, you'll understand my fascination for the Belgrade Lakes of Maine, where I spent many childhood vacations. *Tremolo* whirls with nostalgic memories from that era, based on some of the happiest times of my youth.

The word "tremolo" describes the laughter of loons. It's a lovely yodel that cascades over the lake, rippling the waves with enchanted song. But the bewitching loon's laugh is actually a *distress* call, often heard if humans come too close to their nests. Danger stalks young Gus and his friends in this novel; thus, *Tremolo: cry of the loon* seemed an appropriate title for this lakeside coming-of-age mystery.

Tremolo's mysteries are founded in pure fantasy. Thank God. I wouldn't have enjoyed being chased through the woods by a drunken murderer at age eleven, or at any age. And wouldn't my life be a rather fearsome thing, if all my fictional villains were based on reality?

There are some events, however, that jump right from my childhood—such as the "bat" scene. I'll always remember my dad running around the living room in his boxers with a butterfly net, chasing a trapped and confused bat while I cowered behind my bedroom door. Or the time he took me to see "To Kill a Mockingbird." I distinctly remember sitting in the dining room after the movie, when he turned his forearm in the sunlight and said how lovely it would be to have golden brown skin, like Tom Robinson.

Dad was like that. Passionate and liberated, he embraced all people and welcomed life's full gamut of experiences. And guess what? He was quite a bit like the man Gus becomes in the LeGarde Mystery Series.

The lake, cabins, buildings, boats, loons, and the swing were real. The horses I knew as a child, but not in Maine. That's one of

Aaron Paul Lazar

the attractions of writing fiction—to be able to summon sublime scenes from childhood, decorate them, combine them in any fashion, and populate one's books with them.

The words from Oscar Stone's slide show in chapter thirty-nine are based on writings found in my maternal grandfather's papers, the man who inspired Oscar's character. In addition to being a fine pianist and devoted husband, he was a gifted photographer.

I'll never forget those sun-drenched days in Maine. I still dream about them and summon the memories when life gets tough. Magic was there, and although the camp has long been torn down and replaced with condos, it remains alive and will forever endure in my mind.

Thanks for listening. I hope you enjoy this romp through Gus's childhood.

Aaron Paul Lazar
November 2007

Tremolo: cry of the loon

Acknowledgments

Special thanks to my critique partners who helped along the way:

Sonya Bateman, Jeanne Fielding, Nancy Luckhurst, and Lesia Valentine.

Thanks to my family, friends, and "inner circle" of advanced readers who provided insight and encouragement:

Lorraine Anderson, Sue Clark, Sherrie Coleman, Eva Douglas, Anne K. Edwards, Don Harman, Jason Jarvis, Dale Lazar, Mum, Pete Pellissier, Rik Lennox, Ken Ramirez, Bobbi Scranton, Linda Slade, Scott Slattery, Mina Sniderhan, and Jane Soan.

Many thanks to my astute editor: Leslie Holman-Anderson.

Heartfelt gratitude to my German language advisors: Matthias Regelsberger and Melissa Ingersoll.

Finally, deepest thanks to my publisher, Lida Quillen, for her undying patience and for believing in *Tremolo*.

Tremolo: cry of the loon

One

We're not gonna make it.

I looked across the darkened lake and pulled hard on the oars in the direction of home. Feathers of fog slipped over the glassy water, whispering moist threats.

Siegfried shrugged out of his sweatshirt and handed it to his sister, who shivered in the stern of the old skiff. She tossed him an uneasy smile and put it on.

I took a deep breath and nodded to the ten-year-old twins with more confidence than I felt.

"Don't worry. We'll make it. We're almost to Moose Point."

Elsbeth drew the sweatshirt around her. The sleeves, six inches too long, dangled like limp shrouds. She slid them up to free her hands and peered at me through a mass of dark curls, moving closer to her brother.

"What's happening, Gus? Why is it so dark?"

I cast my eyes around the lake and up to the sky. It had been sunny when we set out for Horsehead Island. Now a thick fog bank obliterated the sun. I answered carefully, feeling responsible for the two since I was a full year older.

"It's just the fog. Don't worry. I'll row to shore and we'll wait it out, okay?"

Elsbeth nodded and yanked the hem of the sweatshirt over her legs. Her eyes darted with apprehension. I broke into a cold sweat and wrenched harder on the oars. They creaked in the damp silence. Siegfried turned and looked toward the disappearing shoreline, wrinkling his brow.

"You'll row to shore? *What shore?*"

The land had vanished.

Returning his somber gaze, I set the oars in the boat. Water dripped from the wooden paddles and pooled below and the fog enveloped the boat in a ghostly mist. I shifted on the vinyl seat cushion to avoid the cracks that chafed my legs. A loon warbled in the distance, his cry distorted to a hysterical giggle. Blind, we sat in the rocking boat and waited.

"Well," I said, "we can sit here 'til it clears. We'll be safe. If we hear someone coming, we'll just make a bunch of noise."

Siegfried nodded, running his fingers through his long blond hair. It had grown over the tops of his ears since his last haircut and each day he looked more and more like the lead singer in Herman's Hermits. I was envious and begged my parents to let me skip my weekly trim at the barbershop. So far, they hadn't surrendered.

"Good idea. *Gut*," he said. Although the twins had been in the States for six years, they still harbored traces of a German accent. Siegfried, in particular, often combined phrases from both languages in the same sentence.

Elsbeth stiffened, staring across the bow.

"Listen."

The faint drone of a motorboat purred in the distance. Motionless, we strained to hear. It grew louder, heading toward us. Siegfried's blue eyes widened in alarm.

"Schnell!" he shouted, pointing to the oars.

I picked them up and spun the boat around. Pulling with all my strength, I maneuvered the boat across the water. The thrum of the motorboat escalated as it bore down on us. We shouted, trying to warn them. Our voices combined in a triad of shrieks.

Shrill laughter echoed as the driver gunned the engine. My heart sank to my bare feet as I realized he must be either drunk or insane. I dragged harder on the oars until my arms burned, propelling the skiff forward into the mist.

A dark shape emerged from the fog and scraped against our stern. Barely avoiding a collision, he swerved away, accelerating into the mist. His passengers shrieked with laughter and the wake from their boat rocked us violently, causing our craft to skitter forward.

Without warning, a crash jolted us from our seats.

Siegfried pointed toward the bow.

"*Gluck mal!* (Look!)"

Water gushed through a ragged tear in the bottom of the boat. I spun around to inspect the damage. It was bad. Very bad.

A glistening turquoise reflection loomed large and sullen beneath the surface.

"Oh, crap," I yelled. "We hit Big Blue."

Elsbeth and Siegfried scuttled to the front of the boat, gaping at the monstrous boulder. Water swirled around our ankles.

"*Mein Gott,* (My God,)" screeched Elsbeth. Her hands fluttered to her mouth and she stared at the deepening water. Siegfried grabbed her cushion and forced her hands through the loops.

"Hold this, Elsbeth. Hold it tight."

The water bubbled higher and the boat listed to the bow, throwing us off balance. Siegfried snatched his cushion and motioned for me to grab mine. It floated beside my legs. I shook myself out of the stupor and followed his lead.

"Come on," I said. "Let's get out and stand on the rock."

I set one foot on the slimy boulder. It was slick beneath my toes, but I found my balance, threw my other leg over the bow, and reached back to help Elsbeth. Siegfried followed. Within seconds, the boat disappeared.

"My father's gonna kill me," I whispered. I'd cared for the boat for the past three summers with the understanding that I'd return it to my grandfather in good shape at the end of the season.

Elsbeth said, "It wasn't your fault the fog came in. He'll understand, won't he?"

I hoped she was right.

We shivered knee deep in the water of the Belgrade Lakes, clutching the cushions to our chests.

The voices of our parents echoed across the lake. Their words traveled through the fog in muted, garbled waves.

"Gus! Elsbeth! Siegfried! Where are you?"

We shouted back in vain, yelling until we were hoarse, with cries gobbled by the fog. After fifteen minutes, we gave up.

"Shoot," I said, trying to hide the cold fear rumbling in my stomach.

"Scheisse," muttered Siegfried, surprising us with the German profanity. He shuddered suddenly, staring down at a two-foot lake turtle that brushed against him. Elsbeth screeched and jumped in the water, arms churning as she splashed away from the snapper. Siegfried shouted to her, then dove for her cushion bobbing in the opposite direction. Fearing we'd be separated in the fog, I yelled and plunged after them.

"Wait up. We've gotta stick together!"

Elsbeth and Siegfried joined together as I swam toward them. We linked our arms above the triangle of floating cushions and treaded water as the light dimmed and the fog thickened. I gripped their hands and waited for the air to clear.

Two

The fog condensed and settled in for the night, thick and impenetrable. Our parents' voices warbled through the mist, becoming fainter as we drifted away.

The lake water grew warmer than the air. We reconnected our grip beneath the cushions, looping them through the handles and grasping each other's prune-wrinkled fingers.

Elsbeth began to weep, her breath hitching with each sob.

"Don't cry," I said. "It'll just make you tired. You've gotta save your strength."

I could barely see the outline of her head in the darkness. She sniffled and nodded. "Okay. I'll... I'll try."

Siegfried used a firm voice. "Elsbeth Marggrander. You *must* be strong. As long as we are together, we will be okay, *nicht wahr?* (right?)"

"*Ja,*" she said, pressing our hands beneath the water.

The hours passed and we struggled to avoid sleep, singing "I Wanna Hold Your Hand," "Can't Buy Me Love," and "Please, Please Me," until our throats grew sore. The camp waitresses in the little red cabin had blasted the songs the last few weeks. We knew them by heart.

The tunes billowed in the night, punctuating our bizarre watery world with lost love and youthful yearning. My voice rasped as we sang, becoming weaker. I laid my head on the cushion. Exhaustion took hold. My eyes closed and I slurred the words to "A Hard Day's Night."

A faint sound of splashing washed in syncopated rhythm with our voices. Reluctantly, I raised my head from the cushion. The soft sound of water lapped the shore nearby. I squeezed the twins' hands.

"Which way is it?" Siegfried whispered.

Elsbeth pointed toward the noise. "It's over there. That way. Come on. *Auf geht's.* (Let's go.)"

We paddled toward the welcome sound. When our feet touched soft sandy bottom, we hurried toward the shore, climbing on a granite boulder hidden under a canopy of white birches.

"Where are the cabins?" Elsbeth asked.

I strained to see in the pitch-black. No lights shone through the fog. No aromas of grilling burgers wafted on the air. And no sounds of scampering children met our ears.

I sputtered with frustration against a chorus of crickets and peepers. "We're probably on the West end. We'll have to walk a ways to find someone. Come on."

We picked our way along the narrow shore trail, occasionally stepping over fallen trees. When we'd walked in the fog for about twenty minutes, we paused to catch our breath. Shivering, we stood barefoot on the pine needles that softened the path.

A flashlight glimmered on the trail ahead. Someone skittered toward us, racing away from the light. A wisp of a girl with long blond hair came toward us.

The light bobbed as its owner approached.

"Sharon!" a man's voice roared. "Sharon, where are you?"

The girl nearly collided with me. Staring with huge eyes, she covered a trickle of blood in the corner of her mouth. She trembled and breathed hard, silhouetted by the eerie glow of the light, clutching her torn blouse where two buttons were missing. Her palpable terror raised goose bumps on my arms.

Before we could speak, she panicked and hopped off the trail into the woods.

A flicker of fear passed through me. Siegfried sensed the danger and pulled us into the woods just before the man lurched past. The stench of whisky and sweat filled the air. He thundered on the trail, bellowing like a man on fire.

"Sharon! God damn it, girl. Where are you?"

Sharon had disappeared. After a few moments of tense silence, we chanced it and returned to the track, tearing away from the drunk. The office of The Willows campground came into view. A pale orange light glowed above the door of the camp store, enveloped in a festival of fluttering moths. We opened the screen door and fell into dry warmth. The woman behind the counter nearly dropped the half-gallon of milk she was ringing up for the customer at the cash register.

"Well, my heavens. What have we here?"

We babbled about the fog and the capsized boat and were soon surrounded by caring adults who wrapped us in blankets. Our parents were called. We told the storekeeper about the girl and the man who'd been chasing her. Within an hour, a deputy arrived. He drove us through the dense fog to Loon Harbor, my grandparents' fishing camp, where our parents descended on us with relief and hot cocoa.

When I finally crawled under the woolen blankets in my bedroom over the lake, Sharon's face floated before me, sending shivers down my back. I had shared her fear as we stood side by side in the dark woods. She was terrified. And hurt. The lout had hit her. I knew it.

I closed my eyes tighter and prayed she escaped his grasp. After a half hour of tossing and turning, I drifted off into fitful dreams.

Three

My cold feet woke me. They dangled over the side of the bed, almost numb. I drew them back under the blankets, rubbed my legs together to generate heat, and snuggled deeper into the feather pillow. The morning breeze lapped lake water against the rocks beneath my room with a rhythmic, soothing sound. It almost lulled me back to sleep, but the aroma of bacon and eggs wafted into my room, making my stomach rumble. Shadow poked his beagle snout out of the covers and sniffed, allowing cold to invade the warm pocket beneath the blanket. I pushed him out and re-tucked it around my legs, cocooning inside. He tried to nose back in.

"Shadow, stop it."

He whined and scooted up to my pillow, licking my face.

"Cut it out!" I laughed as he stuck his cold nose against my neck. I grabbed the blankets and pulled them over my head just as my mother called from the kitchen.

"You up, Gus? Breakfast is ready."

I freed my head and shouted.

"Yup. Be there in a sec."

This time, Shadow snaked his head under my armpit and nuzzled me. I patted his head and made a fuss over him, telling him what a good dog he was. His eyes closed in ecstasy as my fingers ran down his floppy ears, stroking them. They were soft and silky and I loved the feel of them.

"Okay, boy. Time to get up."

Throwing back the covers, I slid onto the cold wooden floor and reached to pick up the socks I'd worn for the past two days. I sniffed them and shrugged. "Good enough. They're not walking on their own yet."

Shadow followed me to the dresser, wagging his tail. I pulled out a fresh shirt, jumped into the jeans that hung over the top of the chair, and laced up my once-white Keds. My big toe almost poked through the right shoe. I threw on a flannel shirt and buttoned it up, then trotted to the kitchen where my mother stood stirring eggs in bacon fat in a cast iron skillet. Raisin toast had just popped out of the toaster.

"I'm starving," I said, reaching for the toast.

She tapped the back of my hand. "Hold on a minute, young man. Just look at those grimy paws."

I flipped them over and shrugged. She ruffled my hair and leaned down to hug me.

"You had quite an adventure last night, didn't you?" Her voice quavered and she squeezed me tight, comforting me with her warm embrace. After a few seconds, she let go, wiping her eyes with the corner of her apron.

"Now go wash up and comb your hair." She flipped the eggs in the skillet and added, "Your father started a fire. You can eat breakfast beside it, if you want."

I nodded and walked into the new bathroom installed just last year. It was located behind the kitchen and beside the big bedroom my parents shared. The addition was a welcome replacement for the outhouse, in spite of the fact that it didn't always function as it should. A bucket of water stood beside the toilet, ready for the next flush. I used the toilet and dumped the water into the bowl. It gurgled down the drain. The tap worked, so I lathered my hands with a sliver of Ivory soap, splashed cold water on my face, and ran a wet comb through my hair.

"Don't forget to fill the bucket," my mother called.

It was too big to fit under the faucet in the sink, so filling it up meant a trip to the water pump behind the cabin. I carried it into the kitchen.

"I won't," I said. "I'll do it after I eat, okay?"

She smiled indulgently and filled my plate with fried eggs, bacon, and buttered raisin toast.

"All right, just this once."

Grinning, I took the food and a hot mug of Ovaltine into the living room. Perching on the side of the high hearth, I soaked in the warmth of the fire. My father entered with an armful of firewood.

"Mornin,' Son." He unloaded the logs onto the hearth beside me.

"Mornin', Dad," I mumbled through a mouthful of bacon.

He smiled at me with a familiar tolerance. "Don't speak with your mouth full, Gus," he said, turning toward the kitchen. "Is the coffee ready, Gloria?"

Throwing another log on the fire, he leaned down to pat Shadow. He stroked his long ears and made a fuss over him, just like I had. Shadow, in his glory, whipped his tail back and forth in delight. The flames licked higher, glowing red-gold on the rough pine walls.

"Yes, dear. Come sit with me and have some."

My father cupped his hand beneath my chin and raised my face to his. To my horror, he leaned down to kiss me on the forehead, then casually walked into the kitchen for his coffee.

"Dad!" I hissed, mortified someone might have seen.

I spun toward the door to be sure no one was walking past the cabin. The front door to the Marggrander cabin was closed with its shade drawn. Elsbeth and Siegfried were still in bed. Relieved, I returned to my breakfast and devoured it.

Casting a furtive glance toward the kitchen to be certain my parents weren't watching, I laid my plate on the ground. Shadow licked the buttery remains from the china, his tail wagging rapidly. As I leaned over to pick it up, Oscar Stone knocked twice on the screen door. He raised one scraggly blond eyebrow in surprise when Shadow slurped the dinner plate.

"Good morning, everyone." He worked his way into the kitchen and sat down for his usual cup of coffee. Feeling guilty, I followed him and put my plate in the sink, shaking some Borax powder on it. I used a sponge to scrub it extra clean and rinsed it with hot water from the teapot. Oscar noticed and nodded with approval.

"Is Millie still in bed?" my mother asked.

Oscar looked in my direction, unwilling to share the difficulties of caring for his wife in front of me. The Stones had been family friends since before I was born and frequently joined the Marggrander family and ours for their summer vacation at Loon Harbor. Millie suffered from severe rheumatoid arthritis. William, their fifteen-year-old son, worked as a cabin boy during the day. He slept in the bunkhouse at the top of the hill next to the icehouse. I couldn't wait for the day when I held the job myself, and envied his pine-walled bunkroom.

Oscar lowered his voice to a whisper. "I'm afraid so. The poor dear had trouble sleeping last night, so she's resting. Thought I'd come by to see if you'd heard."

My father put down his white china mug and looked directly into Oscar's blue eyes.

"Heard? Heard what?"

Oscar shot me a glance. I knew in an instant what he meant. "This is adult talk. Vamoose."

I slunk back into the living room and plopped on the couch next to Shadow, who'd curled into a ball in the corner. Running my hands down his smooth coat, I listened closely.

"A ten-year-old girl's missing. Near Black Bear Point."

I bolted straight up.

My father asked, "What happened?"

Oscar looked at me, still reluctant to speak. I rose from the couch and moved out of sight around the corner. In spite of the fact that he whispered, his words were still clear.

"Name's Sharon Adamski. Her father called the police station last night around midnight. Folks have been searching since dawn. They need more volunteers, which is why I came to get you, André."

I drifted back into the kitchen. "That's the girl—"

"Dear Lord!" my mother said, covering her mouth with her hand.

My father scraped his chair back on the linoleum, suddenly all business.

"Of course I'll help." He took a final swig of coffee and reached for his sailcloth jacket. "Let's go."

I raised my eyes to his. "But—"

"Later, son. This is important."

They strode out the door, leaving me behind to consider the ungodly possibilities of Sharon's fate.

Is she still hiding in the woods? Did he find her and beat her? I shuddered inside.

Heavy-hearted, I pressed my nose to the screen and watched Oscar and my father disappear over the hill.

Four

My mother rested her hands on my shoulders as I stared out the screen door. She leaned down and kissed my cheek. This time, I didn't care. I looked up at her, full of concern.

"We saw her last night, Mum. We saw the girl."

She squeezed my shoulders. A furrow creased her brow. With a sigh, she smoothed my hair and sank to her haunches, pale blue eyes level with mine.

"I know, honey. I know. I'm sure they'll find her. Try not to think about it, okay?" Her worried eyes searched mine. "Why don't you run up and see if you can help your grandparents?"

I nodded and glanced at the Marggranders' cabin.

"Okay. I guess the twins aren't up yet, anyway."

I pocketed my concerns and whistled to Shadow as my mother disappeared into the kitchen. He sped to my side and tap-danced beside me, ready to rocket out the door.

"C'mon boy. Let's go."

I pushed out the screen door and leapt from the porch onto the pine needle pathway.

"Don't slam the door!" she called just as the door swung shut and banged against the doorframe.

I raced across the dirt pathway with Shadow close behind, calling over my shoulder.

"Sorry, Mum."

After passing the Marggranders' cabin, I bounded up the stairs onto the boardwalk that fronted the lakeside bungalows. My feet thumped rhythmically on the gray painted boards. I passed three docks and pounded along, waving to fishermen returning from dawn expeditions.

A hand-fashioned railing edged the porch. I leaned against it to catch my breath. As was my habit, I peeled off a strip of stringy bark from the pine sapling, rolling it into a small ball that emitted a strong clean scent. I lifted the bark to my face and inhaled, then called to Mr. Baker whose boat cuddled the dock.

"Mornin'. Catch anything?"

He brandished a string of glistening pickerel. "Ayah! Some good 'uns."

I flew across the vacant porch of the communal "living room," past the glider, the Coke machine, and the water dispenser. Shadow followed close behind as I skidded around the ping-pong table and bounded up the sandy pathway. I leapt over buried logs that doubled as steps and erosion deterrents and swooped past cabins sitting under aromatic pines, past the shower building, and up the office steps.

The long one-story building sported white clapboards with red shutters. One end housed a small office. The opposite end featured a cavernous kitchen where my grandfather and the waitresses prepared breakfast for the Loon Harbor guests. The knotty pine dining area sat in the middle of the building where guests ate three hearty meals a day.

"Gus? Is that you?"

My grandmother opened the office screen door and peered at me over her bifocals.

"Time to ring the bell. Would you like to do it this morning?"

I grinned and jumped onto the porch.

She smiled and handed me the heavy brass bell. I hurried to the top of the pathway to summon the guests. Planting my feet firmly apart, I held the wooden handle with both hands. I raised it high above my head, then let it fall, repeating the action until the sound of ringing filled the woods.

The bell rang clear and loud. I continued to swing it until my grandmother poked her head out of the door once more.

"Thank-you, Gustave. You're a good boy."

I handed it back to her. She shuffled the papers on the desk. "The Johnsons are leaving this morning. Will you help see them off around ten o'clock?"

I nodded and scanned the parking area filled with two-hundred-year-old pines.

"Sure, Gram."

The Johnsons' car sat beside their cabin with its trunk open, already stuffed with several suitcases and hatboxes.

The office phone rang. My grandmother answered in her usual musical phone-voice.

"Loon Harbor Resort, Odette LeGarde speaking. How may I help you?"

Shadow found a scent and ran in circles with his snout to the ground. His white-tipped tail wagged furiously.

"Looks like that little hound of yours is onto something."

My grandfather smiled and emerged from the dining room screen door. He adjusted his chef's hat and retied a white apron around his waist. Shadow bayed and ran into the woods with his nose pressed to the ground. I ran to him and threw my arms around him. He squeezed me to him, nearly knocking the air from my lungs.

"Mornin', buddy."

"Mornin'." I inhaled the scent of fresh starched linen and waffles, then stepped back. Guests began to straggle in from all directions, looking hungry.

"Wanna help in the kitchen, Sport?"

I skipped beside him and answered with a smile.

"Sure."

We walked through the dining room and into the fray.

Five

I followed my grandfather into the noisy room smelling of toast and warm soapy water. The waitresses hovered over a black and white enamel table, giggling and sighing over the latest issue of *Teen Scene* magazine. It featured a full-page spread of Paul McCartney.

"Oh, I could just *die*. Look at those long lashes! Isn't he dreamy?" Annabel sighed and feigned a swoon.

June and Betsy held each other's shoulders and hopped up and down, singing the refrain from "Love Me Do."

Betsy spotted me standing beside my grandfather and smiled. She grabbed a frilly apron, placed it against her flat midriff, and spun around.

"Gus, honey? Would you please tie my apron?"

She looked over her shoulder at me with a glance that melted my insides. My heart flip-flopped and turned to soft taffy. I took the silky ties with trembling hands. Carefully, I made a tight bow in the back of her smooth, white uniform. She turned around and brushed her lips against my cheek, smelling of Jean Naté bath powder. Her ponytail whispered against my face.

"Thank you, sweetie pie," she said.

I blushed and looked at my sneakers. My grandfather clapped his hands and walked to the black stove that spread across one wall. With multiple gas burners and two sizzling grills, it was perfect for cooking breakfast, lunch, and dinner for the two dozen guests.

"Leave the boy alone, Betsy. We've got work to do. Come on, now. Let's take orders."

The kitchen staff snapped to attention. For the next hour, I helped butter stacks of toast, mix pancake batter, and pour juice into small glasses. Later, when the last of the satisfied diners strolled back to their cabins, I helped clear dishes, hefting loads of china to June, who washed them in the arm-deep metal sink.

Annabel dried the plates and cups while I hauled trays of wet silverware to the table, where Betsy polished fistfuls of spoons with a linen dishtowel.

I watched her as she worked, unable to take my eyes off her. She joked with her friends while her fingers flew rapidly over the silver.

Something had happened to me over the past few weeks—and it knocked me for a loop. When Betsy leaned over to deposit a handful of forks into the drawer, my knees weakened. My jaw dropped and my heart beat like Ringo Starr gone wild.

Her uniform rustled when she bent over the table, sliding over her skin with intense intimacy. My eyes locked onto every move and I blanched each time she tossed a glance in my direction. Although painful and embarrassing, I still longed for her company.

"So…" she said, turning to me, "Who's your favorite Beatle, little man?"

I stammered, and to my horror, my voice cracked.

"John," I said. "He's a card."

She nodded in agreement, ignoring the vocal anomaly.

"Yeah. He's a riot. But I'm stuck on Paul."

June wandered over and passed her hand in front of Betsy's eyes as if to bring her back to earth.

"Betsy's gonna marry Paul. She's got it all planned."

The girls joked around until Grandpa removed his chef's hat and laid it on the table with a look of finality. He squeezed my shoulder and turned to address the girls.

"Betsy, you'd better wait 'til fall to marry that long-haired renegade. We need you in the kitchen." He winked at me, then barked instructions, sounding like a drill sergeant. "We've got cabins to clean. June? I need you down in Number Fifteen. Spruce it up real good. We've got a special guest arriving today. Annabel? Betsy? Go see Mrs. LeGarde. She'll have the schedule for you. The Johnsons are leaving at ten, so be ready to join us for a big send-off."

The girls nodded obediently and skittered away.

I looked expectantly at my grandfather as he untied his apron and tossed it in the dirty linen basket. He reached inside his pocket for his pipe and tobacco and began to pack the bowl. Slowly and purposefully, he grabbed a stick match from the black dispenser on the wall. He struck it twice before it flared into an orange-blue ball. Lifting it to the bowl, he puffed on the stem. I kept an eager expression on my face as I followed his movements.

Finally, he slid the pipe over to the corner of his mouth and leaned toward me. "Okay. Go ahead, Sport. You earned it."

I darted into the back storage room, kneeling beside shelves loaded with oversized jars of food. The maraschino cherries sat on the bottom shelf. I lugged the two-gallon jar onto the counter and unscrewed the lid, rolling up my sleeve and plunging my fingers into the sticky red syrup. With a flourish, I brandished a fistful of plump cherries. Nectar streamed down to my elbow and I popped the cherries in my mouth. After demolishing the fruit, I sucked on the stems to be sure I'd consumed every bit of sweetness, then screwed on the lid and tossed the stems into the garbage. Wiping my face with the back of my sleeve, I returned to the kitchen.

"Thanks, Grandpa."

"You're welcome," he chuckled. "Just don't tell your grandmother."

Six

When I emerged from the kitchen, I spied William hauling a heavy canvas bag to the Johnsons' car. I hurried to his side to help rearrange the suitcases in the trunk so the bag would fit.

"Thanks, Squirt." He faked a punch and laughed when I flinched, ruffling my hair.

I grinned, basking in the attention. William, tall and lanky for fifteen, scratched his beak-like nose and waited for the Johnsons to emerge to deliver his long-awaited tip. I eyed the bowie knife on his belt. It had been purchased courtesy of the tip he'd received from the Murphys last week. He'd practiced throwing the knife like Daniel Boone and was getting quite good at hitting the same spot on the target on the wall of the icehouse.

When I watched him throw the knife I'd always say the same thing.

"You're *so* lucky."

He'd scoff, looking down his nose at me.

"It's not luck. It's skill."

I kicked the dirt near the tire, making a dust cloud, then squinted at William.

"Did you really eat nine hamburgers?"

He looked at me and laughed.

"Who told you that?"

I answered readily.

"Your mother. She said you did. Did you really?"

He smiled. Mr. Johnson emerged from the cabin.

"I guess I did. Did she tell you I had a hollow leg, too?"

"Yeah." I backed away when Mr. Johnson approached and headed for the rope swing hanging from colossal twin pines in the center of the dirt parking area. I grabbed the thick rope and jumped on the shiny wooden seat, pushing off from the flat rock beneath my feet. Watching Mr. Johnson take a green bill from his wallet and press it into William's hand, I pulled hard and soared into the air, inhaling the scent of balsam and pine. The wind whistled as I flew higher and my Keds pointed straight up to the blue sky.

"Hey, Squirt," hollered William. "Come on down."

I nodded, allowing the swing to slow down. At just the right moment, I launched myself into the air, landing lightly on my feet. I beamed at William.

"Nice job," he said. "That's farther than last time."

He dragged his heel across the ground, making a line to mark the spot.

"Thanks." I stared at his hand. "How much did you get this time?"

He showed me a crisp five-dollar bill.

"Holy smokes. Five whole dollars!" I yelled. "What are you gonna buy with it?"

He covered my mouth with his hand.

"Not so loud. If my parents hear you, they'll make me put it in the bank. I've got my eye on this Thunderbird model with green metallic paint at Anderson's. Wanna walk up with me later?"

I nodded and he uncovered my mouth.

Mr. and Mrs. Johnson descended the cabin steps with final armloads of clothes on hangers and the birdcage with their pet cockatiel, Lilly Belle. The waitresses grabbed pots and long metal spoons. My grandmother handed me the brass bell. William and Grandpa each ran to parked cars and opened the drivers' doors. When the Johnsons started up their Chevy Bel Air and headed out, it was to the tune of honking horns, ringing bells, and rattling pots and pans. I thrilled to the traditional send-off and rang the bell long and hard until their car disappeared.

Seven

June, Annabel, and Betsy emerged from the laundry building balancing stacks of clean linen. Their carts overflowed with dusters, rags, Pinesol, and Comet Cleanser. At the top of the path, they separated—Betsy and Annabel walked briskly to the cabin just vacated by the Johnsons, and June headed down to Number Fifteen. I idly wondered about the guest due later in the day. My grandfather usually treated everyone equally, so it was unusual for him to give such special instructions.

William burst from the icehouse with a large ice block balanced on his shoulder. He wore leather gloves used ice tongs to hold it. The burlap bag on his shoulder insulated the cold and helped maintain friction.

"Wanna help?" he asked.

I ran to his side.

"Sure."

He glanced back at the icehouse.

"Close the door for me, will ya?"

I scooted behind him and latched the heavy door with a thud. He'd already started down the path toward the lake when I ran to catch up.

"Who's getting ice so early, William? Don't you usually do the ice at three o'clock? Why are you–"

He grunted and repositioned the block on his shoulder.

"A new guest is coming into Number Fifteen. Your grandmother wants everything to be all set for them."

Cabin Fifteen sat back on the wooded lot fifty feet from its neighbors on the back trail, a hundred feet up from Wee Castle, the lakefront cabin we lived in all summer. Number Fifteen was constructed of whole logs stripped of bark and it sported a full porch with a view of the lake. One of the better cabins, it boasted a sink, stove, and small bathroom with its own bathtub and shower.

I raced up the steps to open the lid of the green wood icebox beside the door. Just before William dropped the ice, I plucked the ice pick from the box, then closed the lid and jabbed the pick into the pitted surface.

"Thanks," William said.

He drew a red bandana from his dungarees and wiped it across his brow, then sprawled on the top step. I sat beside him, listening to Annabel's transistor radio blaring, "The Girl from Ipanema," inside the cabin. The sun warmed the air, chasing away the morning chill. I rolled up my sleeves and pulled out my shirttails, thinking about the loss of our boat.

As if reading my mind, William asked, "Did you get in trouble last night? For wrecking the boat?"

"Nah. They weren't mad. They know how fast that fog can come in. My dad said it happened to him once when he was courting my mother. They got stuck on the lake for hours."

"Were you scared?"

I hesitated, but told the truth. "Sure I was. I mean, we hit Big Blue an' all. Made a huge hole in the skiff. It went down wicked fast."

"Wow. And you saw that missing girl? Running away or something?"

I studied him. I'd wanted to confide in him all morning, but didn't know how to broach the subject.

"Yeah. I did. She was running away from *someone*, not something. He was a big guy. Really drunk, too. He almost saw us."

"Her father?"

"I guess so. But..."

"What?"

"I think she was running because he hit her. Her mouth was bloody."

He stared at me with his slate blue eyes, clearly upset. Before he was able to respond, my grandmother appeared at the top of the hill with a tray of drinking glasses and a fresh flower arrangement from her cutting garden. William and I ran to help her. I grabbed the flower vase and William commandeered the glasses.

"Thank you, boys." She leaned on the porch railing and caught her breath. "It was heavier than I thought." She ran her hands over her fine gray curls and patted them into place.

"Flowers, Gram?" I asked, confused by the flustered look on her face. She was going through a lot of trouble for this particular guest.

She smiled at me indulgently and patted my arm.

"Yes, honey. Just want the place to look nice. Now you run along. I'm sure William has plenty of work to do. Why don't you see if the twins are awake?"

I shrugged and nodded. William jogged up the hill to attend to his next chore.

"Okay, Gram."

I wandered down the hill toward Wee Castle, whistling the tune from "The Girl from Ipanema." Shadow had returned from his woodland hunt and was snoozing on the porch. He raised his head and stretched before trotting over to greet me. I sat on my heels and rubbed his soft ears, singing snippets from the song and trying hard to forget the haunting face of Sharon Adamski.

The Marggranders' shades were up. Mr. Marggrander came to the door before I could knock. Dark circles swam beneath his eyes.

"The twins left a few minutes ago. They went that way."

Before I could thank him, he went back inside and shut the door. Feeling unsettled, I headed onto the lake path, figuring he was probably mad at me for nearly drowning his children last night. A pang of guilt washed through me as I retraced my steps to the living room, jumping over the roots criss-crossing the trail. I was relieved to see Siegfried sitting on the porch glider. The sounds of a Bach fugue floated on the air, a testimony to Elsbeth's hard work over the past year. Although we both took piano lessons from the same octogenarian in East Goodland, New York, she rapidly surpassed me and already had decided her only path to happiness was through the career of a concert pianist. Her fingers flew as she coaxed the music from the old spinet my grandparents had bought at an auction the year before.

Her brother sat with his head down, pushing a stubby pencil over a booklet on his lap. I plopped beside him.

"Hey, Sig."

He looked up at me and flashed a tired half-smile, then turned back to his booklet.

"Hello."

We sat on the glider in silence for a few minutes. I waited for him to look up again.

"Doing more math?"

"*Ja.* Derivatives. If I want to get into advanced calculus next year, I need to master this material."

I nodded, totally confused by the exotic math topic. While I struggled with fractions in fifth grade, he had been placed in math classes with high school kids. The teachers whispered, "genius" when I walked down the halls with him. I was proud of my friend, but wondered where it all would end. Would he graduate early and leave me behind? The thought scared me.

Elsbeth's playing speeded up and the notes exploded from her fingers. Siegfried finally put the booklet away and looked over the lake. He ran his fingers through his long blond locks and groaned.

"What's wrong?"

He shrugged. "When we got home last night we were in big trouble. Papa hit us. Then Mama went crazy. You know how she does sometimes."

My insides dropped. It was my fault. I took them to Horsehead Island and didn't pay attention to the weather. I should've rowed home at the first sign of the darkening sky. A sick feeling pooled in my stomach.

"Geez, Sig. I'm really sorry. It was all my fault."

He looked at me through his long forelock.

"No, it was not. It was no one's fault. *Kein Problem.* (No Problem.)"

I reached into my pocket for a sticky roll of cherry Lifesavers, offering him one of the last two in the roll.

"*Danke,*" he said.

"Is your mother okay? Was it about the war again?"

"*Ja.* Buchenwald. The camps. She has nightmares, you know?"

I nodded. Brigit Marggrander was held in the Buchenwald concentration camps as a young child during World War II. She lost her entire family to cruel violence and disease, emerging in 1945 to be raised by her aunt, Mrs. Frieda Hirsch. She met and married Mr. Marggrander eight years later. They were smuggled from behind the Wall in East Germany in 1959 with their two four-year-old twins and settled in the farmhouse just down the road from our place. We'd been inseparable ever since.

"Will she be okay?" I repeated.

Siegfried got up and walked to the porch railing. He leaned over and stared at the water lapping the granite boulder below.

"I hope so."

The music stopped. Elsbeth came out and sat beside me. Her shoulders slumped and she kicked her feet without saying a word. I offered her the last Lifesaver and was rewarded with a puzzled smile.

"But it's your last one," she said.

"Go ahead. I saved it for you."

She reached over and daintily picked it up, tossing it into her mouth.

"Mmm, cherry. Thanks."

Eight

We chatted on the glider for another half hour, then moved to the dock to lie in the sun.

"Wanna go for a dip?" I asked.

I sprawled on my back with knees up and hands laced behind my neck. Shadow snoozed beside me, his head flopped on my belly. I reached down to stroke his ears, listening to a motorboat purring in the distance. The gray dock boards felt rough beneath my skin. I kicked off my sneakers, rolled up my jeans, and unbuttoned my shirt. The heat became unbearable.

"Okay." The twins answered in unison. Their voices were laced with molasses, sweet sticky stuff that held them motionless beneath the sun.

They didn't budge. Elsbeth lay on her stomach with her arms dangling over the dock. She tickled the placid surface with her fingers. Siegfried sprawled with a boat cushion under his cheek and his eyes closed.

A blue dragonfly buzzed overhead and landed beside me. I leaned on one elbow and studied its dazzling metallic wings. They quivered and winked in the sunlight. Shadow repositioned his head on his paws, deep in dog dreams.

Elsbeth looked up with an impish expression. Peering from her mass of mahogany curls, she smiled innocently, then cupped a handful of water. Carefully lifting it, she shot water through the air toward me. It landed on my bare chest with a splat.

Galvanized into action, I ran to the end of the dock and picked up a small metal pail, scooping it full of lake water. I laughed when she jumped to her feet and grabbed Siegfried's hand, dragging him toward the shore.

Uncontrollable laughter bubbled from my lips as I chased her with the pail. The water sloshed onto my legs when I ran over the bumpy trail. She and Siegfried made the turn, leapt up the wooden stairs to the living room porch, bolted across the boardwalk, and started down the path, hopping over the roots like sure-footed gazelles.

I raced behind them and lost half of the water.

They reached the porch of their cabin, winded and laughing. Just before she slammed the screen door behind her, Elsbeth hollered over her shoulder. "Meet you in ten minutes back at the dock."

Shadow and I arrived seconds later. He trotted to Wee Castle as I dashed the contents of the pail against a large fern.

I smiled and headed home to get changed.

It's gonna to be a great summer.

Nine

I darted into my room and stripped off my shirt. It landed on the chair by the door where I tossed the rest of my clothes before slipping into my blue bathing suit. It was still damp. Kneeling on the floorboards, I poked my head under the bed. There were my sandals, swim fins, and mask. I reached in among the dust bunnies and dragged them out, then slid into the green flip-flops and raced out of the cabin, shouting as I leapt from the porch.

"Goin' swimmin' with the twins."

My mother waved to me from the clothesline in the back. The white sheets billowed around her, flowing and ebbing in the hot breeze. I grabbed my towel from the porch railing and raced to the Marggranders' cabin. Siegfried and Elsbeth emerged just as I arrived. Siegfried looked tall and skinny in his bright red trunks. He towered over Elsbeth, petite in her yellow-peach colored suit with ruffles and her pink flip-flops. They carried masks and well-worn towels.

Siegfried shouted and raced toward the dock with his towel snapping behind him in the breeze. "Last one in is a rotten egg!"

His long legs ate up the ground, leaving us in the dust. Elsbeth and I rose to the challenge, laughing as we streaked along the path and up the stairs to the boardwalk. He earned a ten-foot lead by the time we reached the living room porch. The closest dock afforded the best swimming; the bottom shimmered clear, layered with golden sand.

I noticed with satisfaction that all of the boats had been rented for the day. The dock was wide open. For the time being, it was ours.

Siegfried rounded the corner and flew down the dock. Elsbeth and I pounded along the porch, closing in on him. We reached the dock seconds behind him. I tossed my towel, mask, and fins and kicked off my flip-flops, scarcely missing a beat. Siegfried jumped in, then Elsbeth and I followed, flying side by side into the clear green water. I held my nose and opened my eyes, watching Elsbeth's hair billow around her head like curly dark seaweed. She smiled behind a screen of bouncing yellow bubbles. A sunfish swished between us, his blue and gold scales glistening dully. I reached to touch him, but he darted away. Siegfried made a kooky face, then pushed himself back to the surface, thrilled he had beaten us once again. My feet touched the soft sandy bottom and I pushed up, rising through the cool liquid and into the sunlight. Elsbeth appeared beside me.

"You're a rotten egg," Siegfried taunted.

Elsbeth stuck out her tongue. "You smell like rotten eggs."

I stroked toward the dock. "We're both rotten eggs. We jumped in at the same time."

Elsbeth shot me a grateful look and dog-paddled to the ladder. I reached for my mask. After rinsing the lens, I positioning it snugly over my face, took a deep breath, and ducked back under the water. I pushed past the slimy green post and swam under the dock, examining small rocks that shimmered on the sandy lakebed. I emerged on the other side. Shafts of sunlight filtered through the water, dancing in the sandy ripples. I swam lazily to the bottom and poked around at a mussel. A muddy cloud swirled above it as I plucked it out of the sand. Almost out of breath, I stood up in the chest-deep water and inhaled a lungful of air. As if I were skipping stones, I chucked the mussel into deeper waters, knowing its sharp-edged shell wouldn't cut anyone's feet at that depth.

Stretching out my arms, I lay back in the water, floating on my back with the mask still in place. The sky grew distorted through the foggy lens. Breathing gently through my mouth, I retreated into the private floating world that was mine, thinking of lost boats, penny candy, and Sharon Adamski.

Aside from the times the twins' stern father punished them, I'd never been exposed to a child hurt by a parent. Hurt so badly that they bled. I'd seen handprints on Siegfried's thigh after a particularly bad swat, but it had always been swiftly administered. He was never chased by a drunken father through the woods.

Sharon's face loomed in the clouds that raced across the sky. Her blond hair trailed behind her, wispy and wild. Her wide, frightened eyes called to me. I yearned to talk to the twins about it, but didn't want to frighten them. Especially Elsbeth. It wasn't that she was weak or needed coddling. She was a strong girl. Strong willed. Strong headed. But the urge to stand between her and danger hit me frequently.

My reveries were interrupted by a swirl of water currents as something swam beneath me. I righted myself, touching bottom. Siegfried surfaced with a smirk. I pushed the mask up and grinned back at him. He swept his hand over the water's surface, catching me in the face. I returned the favor, and we repeated the game a dozen times.

"Gus?" Elsbeth called from the other side of the dock.

"Yeah?" I answered, still laughing.

"May I use your fins?"

"Sure. Just tighten the straps a little on the back, otherwise they'll fall off."

I was about to swim under the dock to show her what I meant when my grandfather appeared at the shoreline, holding a push broom. His curved pipe rode his lips and he strode toward us with purpose. I swam to the ladder and waited for him.

Elsbeth and Siegfried joined me, their faces bright with expectation. Grandpa always had a treat or a story to share and had practically adopted the twins as his own grandchildren.

"Havin' a good swim, kids?" He laid the broom down and sat on the edge of the dock to light his pipe. The bottoms of his heavy black shoes almost touched the water.

We nodded eagerly and crowded around him. He puffed on the pipe to get it going, and looked out across the lake.

"I was just about to sweep the porch and the sundeck when I had a vision," he said. A mischievous glint washed over his face.

"What was it, Mr. LeGarde?" asked Siegfried.

He puffed again on the pipe, closed his eyes halfway, and raised one hand to the horizon, as if looking at a mirage.

"I saw three young pups with brooms, sweeping the sundeck and porches every day. I saw them digging night crawlers for guests, and catching crayfish for bait. They worked awfully hard to earn the right to use my Starcraft." He smiled and looked down at us, as if sharing a sweet conspiracy.

My mouth dropped open. I gawked at his aluminum boat moored to the next dock over.

Elsbeth spoke up first. "Was it two boys and a girl you saw, Mr. LeGarde?"

He winked at me. I returned a broad grin.

"Yep," he tamped his pipe again and then relit it. "It was you three, all right. Think you're up for it?"

We began chattering about digging the most worms he'd ever seen. We'd bring buckets of crayfish back from the stream by Anderson's store and sweep every single pine needle from the decks.

"Okay, then." He grunted when he stood and put weight on his bad knee. "Promise to come directly home if the weather turns and wear one of those life jackets whenever you're out. If you can do that, we've got a deal."

He pointed to the orange life vests hanging on nails beneath the porch roof. We nodded gravely, promising to follow the rules, elated that our lakeside grounding had been revoked in this most surprising manner. He propped the broom against the side of the sundeck, then called back over his shoulder to me.

"Gus?"

I pulled myself up the ladder. "Yes, Grandpa?"

"Your mother says lunch in twenty minutes, son. Don't keep her waiting."

"Okay. I won't. Thanks, Grandpa."

I grabbed my towel and started to dry off. I wanted to be first to sweep the sun deck.

Ten

"Another sandwich, Gus?" my mother asked.

We sat on the Wee Castle porch at the picnic table. I'd wolfed down two grilled cheese and tomato sandwiches and drained two glasses of chocolate milk. My father sat across from me, lost in a world of his own, staring across the lake. He absent-mindedly wiped a crumb from the corner of his mouth and sighed. He and Oscar Stone had spent the morning with the rest of the volunteers searching for Sharon Adamski. They hadn't found her.

"No thanks, Ma. I'm stuffed."

I belched loudly and received a raised eyebrow from her.

"Excuse me."

My father continued to look into the distance. I wondered if he was thinking about Sharon.

"Dad?"

He refocused, looked at me, and smiled with his eyes.

"Yes, son?"

"Is it okay if I go to Andersons' with William at one o'clock?"

He looked at my mother, who nodded her assent.

"I guess so, Gus. Be careful, though. There are lots of folks out there looking for that little girl. Stick close to William."

I nodded.

"The twins are going, too, Dad. We'll all stay together."

I reached over the table for the pitcher of milk and poured another half glass, swirling the dregs of the chocolate until it turned pinkish brown.

"Dad? Can I have my allowance?"

My father straightened and reached in his pocket to pull out fifteen cents.

"It's 'May I,' Gus. And yes, you may have it. Here you go, don't spend it all in one place. By the way, we're going to Oakland

Monday. Your mother needs some fabric, and there's a movie I'd like to see."

I looked at my mother, then back at my father. Excitement welled inside me.

"Really?"

The last time we'd gone to see a movie had been Disney's "Sleeping Beauty" several years ago.

"Really," my mother answered. She smiled indulgently.

"That's fab!" I said, mimicking the language the waitresses used during breakfast.

My father raised his eyebrows and exchanged glances with my mother.

"Fab?"

I jumped from my chair as the twins emerged from their cabin.

"Bring your dishes inside first," he said.

I'd nearly escaped. I stopped dead, ran back to collect my plate, glass and the pitcher of milk, and then scurried around the table and into the kitchen to dump them in the sink. I slid the pitcher onto the top shelf of the Frigidaire. Without missing a beat, I flew out of the cabin just in time to meet the twins halfway, whistling to Shadow as the screen door slammed behind me.

Eleven

We walked four abreast, swinging our arms and chattering about Sharon, the mysterious guest, and William's big tip. William found us walking sticks, and mine was an old dried pine branch with a knob at the top for easy gripping. I jabbed it into the dirt and propelled myself forward with each step.

Elsbeth wore white shorts and a yellow and white striped shirt; a turquoise bandana covered her curls, tied behind her neck under her hair.

She looked at me with mischievous eyes. "Let's… do… William."

Without hesitation, Siegfried and I joined the game as William looked on indulgently.

"William, William, bo billiam. Banana panna po pilliam. Fee fie mo milliam… William."

William screwed up his face and laughed.

"It's much better with Bill," he said. "Let's do Bill."

We nodded and followed his lead.

"Bill, Bill, bo Bill. Banana panna po pill. Fee fie, mo mill, Bill."

Siegfried shouted, "Let's do Gus."

I knew this was his favorite and chimed in with him, emphasizing the best words as we skipped along the dirt road.

"Gus, Gus, bo bus. Banana panna, po PUS. Fee fie, mo mus, Gus," we shrieked.

Elsbeth laughed, covering her mouth with one small hand. Her brown eyes sparkled beneath long lashes.

"Gross," she laughed. "Pus."

We'd walked for about fifteen minutes when we came to the blueberry farm. Although the woods were filled with wild berries, the large, easy-to-pick cultivated berries were quite popular with the locals. A number of cars had parked in the field by the gray shed.

William stroked his thumb and forefinger along his chin and looked into the field.

"Hmmm," he said, eyeing the berries growing on the other side of the stone wall. "There's nothing like those big warm berries, fresh from the bush... they just about melt in your mouth."

We looked over to the field and then back at him.

"Doesn't it cost a lot?" I asked.

My parents would never pay for berries when they could send me to the woods behind Wee Castle to gather those that grew free.

"Yeah. It's way too much," he said. "But I have an idea. Who's up for an adventure?"

His eyes glinted conspiratorially and looked down at us from his height of five feet, ten inches. Grinning, he explained the plan swinging his gawky arms.

"One of these nights, we'll get up after everyone's asleep. We'll sneak up here and help ourselves to some of these berries. They won't miss 'em, I guarantee ya."

My heart beat faster as he described the plan. Sneaking out without permission, violating the No Trespassing sign, and stealing. It felt so foreign—yet there was a strangely appealing element to it. I exchanged glances with the twins. An atmosphere of anticipation hung between us as we marched in the hot air.

We continued past the blueberry farm and plunged back into the pine woods that flanked the rutted dirt road. Shadow ran before us with his nose to the dust.

"William, tell us again about the model you're going to buy," Elsbeth said when the conversation waned.

A dreamy look stole across his face. He put one hand on her shoulder and waved the other across the sky while describing the car of his dreams.

"It's a 1955 Ford Thunderbird. Convertible. I'm going to paint it metallic green."

We looked at William in admiration.

"Metallic green?" I repeated. "Keen."

William nodded in self-satisfaction. The crunch of tires around the bend warned us of oncoming cars. We jumped to the side and leaned against a two-ton granite boulder as the vehicles approached. I ran forward, grabbed Shadow's collar, and squatted beside him. The lead car was a dark, late model Oldsmobile. When they passed, I noted the occupants were dressed in dark suits. The middle car was an older model Packard, its gleaming paint muted with road dust. The driver nodded politely to us when we waved. Because of the tinted rear windows, it was impossible to see who sat in the back seat. Another dark sedan followed close behind.

William leapt back into the road and turned to watch the procession. He lifted his wristwatch to his face, frowning.

"If that's who I think it is," he said. "They're early. "It's only one-thirty. Your grandmother's gonna have a fit. She was expecting them at three."

We looked up at William expectantly.

"Oh, I don't know who it is," he said. "But it's someone very important. It's all very hush-hush."

We stood watching for a long time, contemplating the possibilities. I suggested that it might be the Beatles, and Siegfried guessed Queen Elizabeth.

Shadow followed close behind as we neared Mr. Anderson's farmhouse. The white A-frame was well kept. Mrs. Anderson's nasturtiums tumbled from flower boxes lining the small porch, and the lawn had just been mowed. The small green barn and post-and-board paddock was home to two horses. I craned my neck to see if they were still there. I couldn't see them and guessed they must be inside the barn. Last summer Mr. Anderson let us exercise them and we had a fantastic time, riding bareback through the logging roads and along the lake trails. I'd seen him twice since we'd arrived, anxious for another invitation to ride, but he'd been busy with customers each time, and hadn't yet breathed a word about the horses.

We cut across the grassy meadow bordering the Andersons' field. Elsbeth stopped along the way to pick handfuls of wildflowers. Siegfried and I helped her, finding Queen Anne's lace, black-eyed Susans, and daisies. She picked tall fuzzy-stemmed flowers that resembled dandelions. I never knew what they were called. They grew in clumps of yellow, rust, and orange. As we walked through the meadow, a large monarch butterfly floated and circled around us, flitting from flower to flower. The afternoon sun shone on our heads with pleasant warmth and we chatted amiably about what we planned to purchase with the coins jingling in our pockets.

When we finally reached the store, our thirst drove us to the stools lining the ice cream counter. Shadow sneaked inside the screen door just before it slammed shut. His toenails clicked across the wide wooden floorboards and followed us across the room. The overhead fan circulated the air blowing gently across our shoulders and faces.

William pulled the five-dollar bill from his leather-tooled wallet and plunked it down on the counter. Mr. Anderson finished ringing up the lady at the cash register and finally wandered over to us.

"Well, well, well. Lookee here! If it's not the Loon Harbor gang."

He wiped his hands on a white apron and looked down at the five-dollar bill.

"Hi, Mr. A," said William. "Four sodas, please. It's on me today. I got a heck of a tip this morning."

We looked at William in shock. I quickly calculated I'd be able to buy candy *and* comic books if William paid the five cents for my orangeade. Elsbeth ordered a grape soda. Siegfried stuck to his usual root beer, and William got his customary Coca Cola.

"That'll be twenty cents."

We sat on the stools drinking soda and watched a group of men come through the front door. I called Shadow and held his collar. His nose twitched in the air, sniffing the men who milled around, discussing the search for Sharon Adamski. As they spoke of the search area, I realized they hadn't yet begun to check the west side of the lake where we had seen her the night before. I hailed Mr. Anderson and whispered in his ear, telling him what we'd seen. He nodded, and spoke to the man who appeared to be the leader. He shook his head, looked over at us, and then said something to Mr. Anderson. They left after a few minutes, purchasing a case of soda, flashlight batteries, and cigarettes.

"Seems Mr. Adamski says she went missing over by their cabin. It's not where you kids say you saw her. They've been going by the police report, Gus. They're searching around Black Bear Point first."

I looked up in shock, exchanging glances with Elsbeth and Siegfried.

"But they'll never find her there," I said slowly.

Mr. Anderson scratched a bald spot on the top of his head and adjusted his apron straps.

"I'll have a talk with the sheriff when he comes in later, son. I'm sure they'll find her soon."

Elsbeth piped up, looking very serious.

"What happens to her when they *do* find her, Mr. Anderson?"

Siegfried echoed her question.

"*Ja*, what happens to her?"

Mr. Anderson picked up a damp rag and wiped down the counter as he spoke.

"Well, I imagine she'll be returned to her family. That would seem to be the right thing now, wouldn't it?"

We all exchanged worried glances. She'd been running from Mr. Adamski as if from the devil himself.

"Don't you kids go worrying about this, now. Why don't you stop by one of these days and take the ponies out? They're getting too fat."

"Really?" I said, thrilled he'd finally offered.

"Ayah. You kids are welcome to come over and take them out anytime."

The mood lightened as Siegfried, Elsbeth and I exchanged excited glances. I tilted my bottle of orange soda and downed the last of it. The cold fizz trickled down my throat, quenching my thirst. Setting the bottle on the counter, I hopped from the stool and walked to the penny candy counter, followed closely by the twins. I chose a string of rock candy, a pack of Teaberry gum, two fireballs, and a stick of licorice. The twins picked out their own selections of penny candy and I wandered over to the comics to find the newest editions of Richie Rich and Superman. Toying with both of them, I finally picked the former, knowing that Elsbeth enjoyed it as much as I did.

William picked out his model kit, had it wrapped in brown paper, and we headed home with Shadow close behind.

Twelve

I savored the string of rock candy as it melted, then bit off one of the crystals from the end and worked on it until it dissolved into sweet nectar. Shadow stopped to drink from a puddle, then cantered to catch up.

"William?" Elsbeth asked through a mouthful of bubble gum.

He cocked his head in her direction.

"Can we go back the long way? By the hill?"

He gazed longingly at the package under his arm, then back at our expectant faces. Finally, he shrugged and smiled.

"Okay. I guess it would be okay."

Behind the Anderson's farm was a thin copse hiding three rolling fields lined with stonewalls. Beyond the hills lay a network of logging trails that ultimately led to the lake.

We walked back through the meadow of wildflowers and reached the wooded hedgerow. William led the way and we followed the path single file, emerging into a protected glen. We deposited our packages beside the stone wall, then raced to the top of our favorite hill while William settled in the shade to watch.

Panting from the ascent, I lay on the crest beside my friends and crossed my arms tightly in front of my chest. With a slight push to overcome inertia, I log-rolled down the hill, lifting my face with each revolution to avoid smashing my nose against the turf. I rolled faster and faster as the hill steepened. The course of my direction changed. In an instant, I made a large semi-circle, heading straight for Siegfried. We crashed, laughed hysterically, and raced up the hill to do it again. Shadow followed me each time, barking with delirium.

ಬಂಡ

After we enjoyed a dozen spins down the hill, William stood and motioned for us to rejoin him. I popped an Atomic Fireball into my mouth and dusted wispy grass from my clothes and hair.

Shadow bounced behind us and we headed home through the logging roads that eventually joined up with camp. The walk took ten minutes longer than the main route, but there was rarely any traffic. The trails eventually skirted along the sparsely settled west side of the lake where Sharon Adamski had been chased by her drunken father. I shivered when I remembered his craggy face and the smell of him as he'd passed so close.

We'd settled down to a good pace when I offered to trade Elsbeth a fireball for a piece of her bubble gum. She agreed immediately. She'd watched me with envy as I sucked on the first one for a long time, exclaiming over its fiery properties and frequently taking it out of my mouth for a break.

We swapped candies. I pocketed the gum, deciding to save it for later. William and Siegfried had taken the lead on the two-abreast trail. Elsbeth trotted to catch up to her brother and I lagged behind, thinking of Sharon.

Why aren't they searching in this area?

We'd told the sheriff last night, our parents, and the men in the store that we saw her and her attacker in these woods along the shoreline.

Don't they believe us?

The cold truth hit me.

They don't. They believe her father... the liar who claimed to have lost her around Black Bear Point.

I shook my head in disbelief, unable to accept the fact that the authorities believed a drunken adult over three kids. I fell further behind my friends and puzzled over Sharon and her plight, kicking a small round stone. The sunlight dimmed and sketchy gray clouds slowly rolled overhead. I shivered, thinking of the poor girl alone in the woods.

She'd been outside since last night with no breakfast and no lunch. She'd probably frozen during the evening.

Where will she go tonight? How will she survive?

I looked at the darkening woods and pictured myself in the same situation. I could pick blueberries and drink water from the lake. That would take care of the hunger and thirst. I might find an abandoned jacket, or get brave and steal an old blanket from someone's barn. In her situation, I guessed that staying away from her tormentor was more important than abiding by the law. When they found her, they'd most likely return her to her father and not believe her claims of… whatever it was he did to her.

I sighed, wishing I'd joined the Scouts like my friends at home instead of the 4-H club. Maybe I would've learned more about survival in the woods instead of how to clean out horses' hooves. I slowed a little more, glancing around as I walked. There were probably dozens of edible things right under my nose.

Can you eat pinecones?

Shadow took off down the path. He bayed along the lakeside in the distance. Something white flitted behind the trees to my right. I spun, stared into the woods, and stopped dead. Within seconds, I saw it again, but further back this time. It flashed quickly, as the fabric of a dress might do when a woman flounces along a street. Or perhaps the tail of a blouse might flap in the breeze as a frightened girl runs through the woods. I hesitated. My friends disappeared around the corner. If I ran to catch up to them around the bend, I'd lose my chance to identify the apparition. I plunged rapidly into the pines in the direction of the white blur.

"Sharon!" I called. "Stop. I won't hurt you."

I ran for fifty yards or so and then stopped and listened. The sound of someone running rustled to the right. I jumped over a fallen log to follow the sound. Another blurry spray of white flashed behind the brush. I was after it in a second, flying through the woods.

"Sharon! I have something for you!"

After five minutes of the chase, I stopped for a moment to catch my breath and to listen for the sound of her feet. I heard nothing except the ragged sound of my own breathing and the faint baying yip of Shadow in the distance. She stopped, too. Perhaps she was watching me.

"Sharon! Look. I'm leaving this for you."

I dug out the piece of bubble gum and the licorice stick and tossed them onto a large, flat boulder.

"I can come back tomorrow, Sharon. I'll bring food, and clothes. If you take these today, I'll know you're here… and you'll know I'm not going to hurt you. I know why you're running. I saw him chasing you."

I sat down on the boulder, looking hard into the woods. My heart hammered against my chest. A tiny chickadee landed on the ground ten feet away. He hopped three times in my direction, cocked his head to the side, and took off in flight, landing on the branch of a nearby sapling. He continued to watch, safer in his new position in the tree. Except for the gentle swaying of the branches overhead, all was still.

"Okay, then," I called hesitantly. "I'll come back in the morning. Good luck."

I turned to retrace my steps and walked for a few minutes in the general direction from which I'd come, breaking branches as I went so that I could find the boulder again in the morning. After several minutes, I stopped and looked around. Nothing looked familiar. I quickly swiveled from right to left, then turned in a full circle. Pine trees with pillows of moss at their bases waved crisscrossed branches overhead like geisha girls fanning their lords. Two red squirrels scampered across the pine-needled floor, chirping and tumbling over each other as they frolicked. The birdsongs quieted as I tromped through the underbrush and startled them. A trickle of perspiration ran down my neck. I looked around in alarm.

Which way had I come?

I rubbed my hands nervously against my jeans. Panic rose in my throat.

A sudden breeze lifted the curly fronds of the ferns carpeting the forest floor. Black clouds piled overhead and fat drops of rain splashed on my cheeks. I looked back from where I'd come; thinking about Sharon in the dark, wet forest. Perhaps I should follow the broken branches back to the boulder and wait for her?

I shook my head and rejected the idea. My parents would go berserk with worry and I'd caused enough trouble last night. The fear began to well inside me again, swelling to tall waves that swamped my reason as the panic took hold.

I ran.

After ten minutes, a queasy feeling rolled in my stomach. I raced blindly, pushing through the wet branches that slapped against my bare arms and face. I ran until I slipped on a decaying wet log and went down hard on my side. My ribs throbbed as I lay on the wet woodland floor and cried. I cried for the pain in my side, for the girl whose bloody, frightened face I couldn't forget, and for the feelings of intense fear swelling in my heart.

Finally, the sobs stopped and I sat up, wiping tears from my face with my shirttail. After chastising myself for acting like a baby, I got up again, straightened my shoulders, and chose a direction.

I walked a little more in what I thought might be a northern course, then looked frantically around for a familiar tree or boulder. The rain soaked my clothing. I stopped and turned quickly in a circle, searching again for a familiar sight. My throat tightened when I realized the unbearable truth. I had to face it.

I'm lost.

I sat down on a small flat rock and hugged my arms to my chest, trying not to cry.

"Think."

With hands face down on the lichen-covered rock, I suddenly pushed back up to a standing position. I looked at the moss on the base of the trees. Wasn't it supposed to grow on the north side? If it were true, at least I could walk north for a while. It should connect with the lake eventually. I used the technique and walked for about ten minutes in the same direction, breaking branches along the way. The rain finally let up. The sun returned, shining through moisture raining from the overhead leaves. Suddenly, I stopped and stared in horror at a shrub. I was about to snap the branch of a bush that flaunted a freshly broken twig.

Already broken.

Somehow, I'd come full circle.

Fear bubbled in my throat. I stopped and took a deep breath, forcing myself to relax. Closing my eyes, I listened. The faint drone of a motorboat purred in the distance. I listened harder and heard the laughing squeal of children at play on the shore. Opening my eyes, I searched for the source of the sounds. A silver ribbon glistened beyond the pine branches. Relief flooded through me; it was the shimmer of the lake.

I walked toward it. There was no path, but I made my way around large boulders, through patches of ferns and wildflowers, and past trunks of massive pines, breaking branches as I went along to make a clear trail for tomorrow. I needed to get back to that boulder. After five minutes of tromping in the general direction of the lake, I heard William calling. I shouted back and started to run in the direction of the calls. Within seconds, I heard Elsbeth and Siegfried as well. I called louder, waved my hands, and scrambled toward my friends.

When I burst out of the woods onto the trail, they fell around me, bubbling with concern and questions. I stood among them while they patted my back with relief. William tousled my hair.

"What the heck happened to you, Gus? You scared us to death."

I looked at them one by one, then spoke in a shaky voice.

"I saw her. I saw Sharon."

They stared with wide eyes. Elsbeth spoke first.

"You *saw* her?"

I nodded, lifted my hand to my face, and rubbed at a spot that hurt.

Concern flooded Williams's lean face. "Are you sure it was her, Gus? Did you actually see her?"

I looked back at the woods and thought for a moment.

"Well, someone was out there. They ran from me. I chased them. It was white and…"

William swatted a mosquito on his forearm. I did the same. In seconds, all four of us slapped at our bodies as the blood-sucking insects swarmed around in their usual post-rain shower fury.

Siegfried grabbed my arm and yelled. "Let's get out of here!"

We dashed down the path toward the lake, trying to escape the cloud of hungry mosquitoes. We were bitten a dozen times each and scratched furiously all the way home.

Thirteen

"Where'd you get those scratches, son?"

My father passed the baked beans. I scooped out a large spoonful and plopped it on my plate beside two hot dogs, trying to decide how much to tell him.

"Umm. I kinda ran through the woods today, Dad. We took the long way home."

When I washed my face before supper I'd noticed a scrape on my face as well as several on my arms. I'd stuffed my filthy shirt under my bed and put on a white tee shirt instead.

My mother sliced a piece of brown bread baked in a tin can and handed me a warm aromatic disc.

"Well, you be careful out there, honey," she said.

I nodded. "I will." I picked up a hot dog with my hand and bit off a huge chunk. "So, who moved into Number Fifteen?"

"Gus!" my mother said. Her eyes flared in horror. "For goodness sake, use your fork and knife. We don't live in a barn."

My father's mouth twitched when he stole a glance at me.

"Sorry, Mum," I mumbled with my mouth full. I swallowed, picked up the fork, shoveled in a pile of beans, and asked again. "You didn't answer. Who's in Number Fifteen?"

My father stiffened and exchanged glances with my mother.

"No one you need to be concerned with, son. She needs her privacy and is here for a rest. We want you to stay away from the cabin. Is that clear?"

He knew full well I'd pester them until I discovered something more useful about the woman.

"But what's her name? Can't you even tell me that?"

He tried to give me his stern look, but it dissolved into a smile and he shook his head. "Son, I really can't say. She's an old woman with a cat who needs some time to mourn. She recently lost a family member and is very sad. Can you try to understand that? She needs quiet, Gus. Peace and quiet."

I searched his eyes, realizing he was serious. "Oh. Okay."

After gulping down the second hotdog, I asked for more bread.

"Can I…May I have more bread, Mum? And can Siegfried sleep over tonight?"

I looked at my mother for this one. She pursed her lips, tilted her head to the side, and pondered the question.

"Please, Mum?" I begged. "We'll go to bed early, I promise."

She smiled and patted my arm.

"I guess so, honey. If you feed Shadow right after supper."

I smiled at her and dropped a hunk of bread to Shadow under the table. I'd been feeding him plenty already. He gobbled it up and waited for more.

Fourteen

One hour later, Siegfried flicked his pole and cast over the calm lake. The water surged gently and golden-red wisps of color laced the horizon as a copper ball of the sun sizzled into the dark tree line on the opposite shore.

"So, she said it's okay?" he asked.

I nodded and reeled in my fishless line. "Yup. Long as we go to sleep early."

Elsbeth pouted on the dock beside us. Her dark curls hung loosely around her heart-shaped face.

"I don't see why I can't come. What's the big deal?"

I looked guiltily at Siegfried, then back at the lake. Casting my line sideways, I shot the hook and sinker beyond the end of the dock.

"I'm sorry, Elsbeth. You're a girl. Boys can't have girls sleep over, that's all."

Her face crumpled again. "It's not fair. I *hate* being a girl."

She looked so sad. The guilt grew heavier.

"Maybe you can come over to toast marshmallows in a while. What do you say, Ellie?"

She looked at me and stuck out her tongue.

"Okay, but don't call me that. You know I *hate* that."

I smiled; glad we'd made it through the awkward moment. Balancing two best friends could be a challenge, especially when one was a girl.

"Right, *Elsbeth*. Sorry. I forgot."

She smiled back and tossed her hair with an air of victory.

The sky darkened to indigo blue as we cast and recast our lines over the glassy lake. Siegfried caught a small yellow perch and had just released it into the still water when Elsbeth screamed.

"*Mein Gott!*" she wailed, waving her hands around her head. "*Eine Fledermaus!* (a bat!)"

Siegfried and I dropped our poles and ran to her side. The bats had begun their nighttime diving ritual, swooping through the air searching for juicy mosquito snacks.

Siegfried grabbed his sister and held her, ducking down low to avoid them.

"Is it in my hair?" she screamed.

She'd repeated stories of bats getting tangled in people's hair and was petrified of the possibility. Siegfried checked her hair and assured her she was free from varmints. I walked back to reel in my line, grabbed both poles and the bucket of worms, and followed them to the porch.

"What's wrong, kids?" my mother asked, poking her head out the door.

"It's okay, Ma, it's just the bats."

My mother looked at the darkening sky and frowned. I stacked the poles and bait on the porch.

"They won't hurt you, Ma," I said, echoing my father's words, "they eat up the mosquitoes. They're good little bug catchers."

She nodded, still nervous.

"Mum?" I asked before she could retreat entirely indoors.

She looked out at me from the other side of the screen door.

"Yes, honey?"

"Can we toast marshmallows tonight?"

"Sure you can. I'll have your father start the fire. It's getting a little chilly in here, anyway."

She crossed her arms and hugged herself, shivering in the cool night air. She wore a short-sleeved white cotton blouse and plaid shorts. Her hair was in its usual high ponytail. I watched her stand in the doorway and thought was the prettiest woman in the whole world.

Fifteen

I stuffed two more marshmallows on my willow branch and wedged in between Siegfried and Elsbeth to hold it in the flames.

"Gus," my mother reprimanded, "hold it *over* the coals so it'll melt. See how Elsbeth does it?"

Elsbeth looked pleased that she noticed.

My marshmallows burst into a flaming ball of confection. I smiled. "I like it burnt, Mum. It's okay."

I turned them around carefully so they'd be cooked equally on all sides, and then carefully pulled the stick from the fire to blow out the flames. My father watched behind his Life magazine; probably afraid I'd set the place on fire. The marshmallow bag was almost empty. I lost count of how many I ate and was stuffed. Overstuffed. But I forged onward. I removed the crispy black layer and popped it in my mouth. After crunching up the charcoal sugary coating, I went after the sticky soft insides, chewing and licking them from the branch. Siegfried sat beside me. He'd devoured his last marshmallow moments earlier and looked rather gray.

My mother finally put an end to the party. Elsbeth went home, slightly mollified, and Siegfried and I prepared for bed. We changed into our pajamas and brushed our teeth, then braved the night, creeping outside to the well pump to refill the bucket in the bathroom.

Finally, we settled into bed with Shadow snuggled between us. I gave Siegfried the good pillow and took the flat one for myself, doubling it up under my head to provide some height for talking. A gentle wind blew waves against the rocks beneath the floorboards.

"Gus?" he whispered.

"Yeah?"

"Was it scary out in the woods today?"

I stayed silent under the blankets for a few minutes, recalling the chilled fear.

"Yeah, it was. I kinda panicked, I guess. I was lost, and then I fell, and it was raining."

He lay quiet, imagining the scene.

"I didn't want to ask you in front of the others. But you looked pretty scared when we found you."

"Thanks," I whispered. I meant it. I changed the topic to the thoughts uppermost in my brain. "What do you think Sharon's doing now?"

Siegfried rolled onto his side and leaned on one elbow, scratching at a mosquito bite on his arm.

"I don't know. Maybe sleeping under a pile of leaves?"

I lay on my back and pictured her with her long, wispy blond hair and frightened eyes.

"Do you think she built a shelter? Maybe out of branches and sticks? She could weave them together and make a roof."

Shadow wiggled closer and laid his head on my arm. I automatically stroked his smooth coat.

"*Ja*. She could make a bed of grass and ferns. Maybe pile them up really high. It might be comfortable."

I pictured her lying beside the big boulder under a tent of branches on a soft bed of ferns. She was eating the licorice stick and snuggling under a sleeping bag she'd found in someone's barn. My eyes grew heavy as I comforted myself with the image. The first sensation of drowsiness washed over me. I fought it hard.

"Tomorrow we'll bring her some real food," I said with conviction.

Siegfried responded, his voice thick with fatigue. "Okay. Maybe we can take the ponies out. Elsbeth wants to ride again."

Siegfried lay down on his pillow. His right arm twitched in a pre-sleep spasm; his eyes closed and his mouth fell partially open.

"Good idea," I whispered as I drifted off to sleep.

Sixteen

I ran through the grassy field with arms outstretched. A familiar sensation hit me: weightlessness. It blossomed through my body, filling me with euphoria unparalleled in waking hours. I leaned forward, my feet lifted off the ground, and I glided over the earth, toes brushing against tips of timothy. The earth rushed beneath me. Willing myself higher and higher, I flew through the air, circling my friends while they gazed up at me in wonder. The breeze fluttered on my face and I closed my eyes in exhilaration.

I stirred, still feeling the wind on my face. I figured the feeling must have lingered from sleep and crept into reality. Shrugging inwardly, I tried to force myself to return to the recurring flying dream. It didn't work.

I reached for Shadow, who slept under the covers to my left. Siegfried's gentle snoring created a syncopated rhythm with the waves beneath the bedroom. I smiled, pleased that I remembered the term that Mr. Olsen had taught me during my spring term of piano lessons.

A gentle scrabbling whispered against the side of my face. Puzzled, I opened one eye in the pinkish-gray predawn light.

Something moved on the headboard.

I froze.

"Siegfried," I said.

He didn't move. I shoved him with my right foot. He stirred, but didn't wake. I kicked him harder and yelled, "Siegfried, wake up!"

He didn't open his eyes, but mumbled under the blankets.

I couldn't move, afraid to disturb whatever it was on the headboard. I hoped it was a bird that had flown down the chimney, but had a sinking feeling I was wrong.

"What *is* that?" I whispered.

He finally raised unfocused eyes to mine. Suddenly they widened in fear as he sat up and jumped from the bed, gesturing frantically toward my face.

"*Mein Gott! Eine Fledermaus!* (A bat!)"

No longer immobile, I turned to see the small wings of the bat fluttering beside me. I leapt from the bed and jumped onto the cold floor beside Siegfried. Shadow raised his head beneath the covers and started to bark. Caught under the blankets, he became a comical canine lump, circling and barking on my bed.

The springs creaked as my father jumped out of bed. His footsteps pounded across the floorboards as he ran into the room.

"Boys? What's wrong?"

He stood before us in red-and-white polka dotted under shorts and a v-neck tee shirt. We darted behind him, yelling and pointing at the headboard.

"Over there! It's a bat!"

He flipped on the light switch and backed up a step when he saw it.

"Where's your butterfly net, son?" he asked softly.

I answered in a whisper.

"On the porch."

Without waiting to be asked, Siegfried and I ran to the porch to find the net. The screen door slammed and I tossed the net to my father. My mother appeared in the bedroom door, wearing her white slip. She slid into a flannel shirt and buttoned it around her.

"What is it, André?"

I handed the net to my father, who ducked as the bat flew past him into the living room. Siegfried hollered. We ran toward my mother, who yelped in surprise and shoved us into the bedroom behind her. She slammed the door and we leaned against it, crouching behind her and breathing hard. My father cursed. It sounded as if he collided with a piece of furniture. My mother raised an eyebrow and called through the door.

"André? Are you okay?"

His footsteps echoed as he ran across the room.

"Hold on a minute, Gloria. I almost got him."

I trembled behind my mother and exchanged a wide-eyed glance with Siegfried. The bravado I showed earlier in the face of distant bats evaporated. Shadow's barking grew louder. I guessed that he'd escaped from the blankets.

"Gosh darn it!" my father yelled. It sounded as if he tripped and went down hard.

She opened the door a crack and peered into the living room.

"André?" she asked timidly.

He didn't answer immediately.

She opened the door another inch.

"André? Are you all right?"

"It's okay, Gloria. I've got him. You can come out now."

She opened the door slowly. We peered around her. Dad lay in a heap on the floor, the net grasped firmly in his hands. The bat wiggled inside the mesh. Dad's feet were tangled in my bed sheet. Beneath him, Shadow circled and plaintively bayed beneath the sheet, resembling a beagle-ghost. He poked his nose against the fabric and tried to bulldoze his way out.

A laugh gurgled in my throat. My mother raised a hand to her mouth. She tried to control herself, but couldn't do it and burst into laughter, leaning against the doorframe. Siegfried and I joined in, holding our stomachs and wiping the tears from our eyes as we whooped and hollered. My father's mouth twitched.

"What? What's so funny?" he asked, rearranging his polka dotted shorts to a more seemly position.

He leaned over and released Shadow from the sheet. The dog burst out and raced around the room in circles, yapping happily. I ran to him and shushed him, remembering that the rest of the world was probably still asleep.

Dad got up slowly, holding the net carefully so that the bat wouldn't escape.

"Do you wanna see the little fella, boys? Before I release him?"

I looked at Siegfried. He nodded nervously. We crept forward and peered at the net.

The bat was the size of a mouse with short gray fur. His legs and arms were tiny matchsticks, attached in multiple places to a fine, black material spread between them. It reminded me of my mother's nylons she hung over the shower rod at home. He wiggled inside the net. Siegfried and I jumped back.

"See, boys? He's really harmless. Gloria? Do you want to take a look?"

My mother shook her head.

"No thanks, honey. Not this time."

She closed the bedroom door firmly.

My father smiled, shrugged, and walked out to the porch. He spread the ends of the net open so that the bat could fly away. We watched through the screen door as he jiggled it a little to encourage the bat to release his hold.

"Come on, little fella. You're free now. Go on. That's right."

I watched my father standing in his bare feet and underwear and marveled at his bravery. Finally, the bat flew away, swooping off into the treetops. I looked at my Mickey Mouse watch. It was four forty-five in the morning.

"Okay, boys. It's all over. Back to bed with you, now."

We scrambled back to the bedroom with frozen bare feet. Dad picked up the sheet and remade the bed. Siegfried and I helped him with the corners, then we climbed back in and snuggled under the covers. My father leaned over, about to kiss my forehead. I shot him a mortified look, stopping him in his tracks. He smiled and ruffled my hair instead.

"Night, boys. See you in a few hours."

Seventeen

The next day, I slapped the fifth peanut butter and jelly sandwich together and cut it in half with a butter knife. Oscar Stone sat in his usual kitchen chair with my parents.

"So, have you seen much of our new guest, Oscar?" my mother asked. Her voice was soft and muted, almost a whisper.

Oscar lifted his coffee mug to his lips and looked at me over the rim. His eyes followed as I stuffed food into my father's old canvas rucksack. I packed enough for our lunch and extra for Sharon.

He raised his eyebrows, looked at me, and lowered his voice while turning back to my parents.

"She sat on her porch last night with Odette. They talked for a long time."

My father took a sip of coffee. "They go back a long way, Oscar. Childhood friends."

Oscar glanced at me and continued in a soft voice.

"Her, ah, her guardians are staying in the little cabin right beside us. They take eight hour shifts."

I looked up with interest.

"Guardians?" I asked.

My mother shot Oscar a warning glance and rose quickly from her chair.

"Oh, honey, don't you worry about that stuff. Have you got enough food for lunch? How about some apples? I have a new box of Twinkies, too."

It worked. The mention of Twinkies distracted me from the topic of the mysterious guest and I happily dumped half the box into the sack.

"Planning a long day in the wild?" asked Oscar. His bright blue eyes twinkled and he smoothed back a stray lock of pale blond hair.

My father smiled at him over the Sunday paper, rustling it as he turned the page and answered for me.

"The children are going riding today. Mr. Anderson has offered his horses again for the summer. Isn't that grand?"

My mother took her seat and briskly buttered her toast. "Don't forget to sweep today, Gus… if you expect to borrow Grandpa's boat."

"I won't, Mum. We're gonna do it this afternoon when we get back."

She nodded approval and took a crunchy bite.

"Would you like a ride to the Andersons' barn? Millie and I are heading up to church in a little bit," Oscar offered as he peered out the window toward Number Fifteen. His attention wasn't on me, or the kitchen, or my parents. He stared as if he couldn't tear his eyes from the cabin next door.

I nodded, noting he sported his Sunday best suit and polished shoes.

"That would be swell, Mr. Stone. Thanks."

Tightening the cap on the thermos full of cherry Kool-Aid, I slid it into the sack and swung the bag over my shoulder. The Marggranders' cabin door slammed shut, signaling the imminent arrival of the twins.

"We'll meet you at the top of the hill," I shouted, and flew out of the house.

Eighteen

Siegfried and Elsbeth leapt from their porch and ran to greet me. Siegfried carried a bulging leather bag with a long shoulder strap. We linked arms and started up the hill.

"Did you bring the blanket?" I asked. We trotted up the rooted path in tandem.

"*Ja,*" Siegfried answered.

He seemed distracted. I followed his gaze - he was staring into Number Fifteen.

"It's just an old lady and her cat, according to my parents. Nothin' too exciting. She's an old friend of my grandmother's."

Elsbeth pointed to one of the front windows. "Look!"

A colossal cream-colored Persian cat slept on the windowsill inside the house. He watched us with round copper eyes and reminded me of the Cheshire cat in Alice in Wonderland. As I watched him watching us, I decided the similarity had to do with the self-satisfied glint in his eyes.

We reached the top of the hill, piling our knapsacks into the back seat of the Stones' car. The oversized sedan easily fit three in front and four in back. William and Oscar arrived, supporting Millie between them. She walked slowly, smiling as she approached.

I opened the front door for her. William helped her slide onto the seat as the twins climbed in back. She wore a pastel flowered dress, white gloves, white shoes, and a hat decorated with dried flowers and berries. A long hatpin fastened it to her tight black curls.

"Thank you, Gus," she said as she settled in the seat.

The aroma of roses filled the air from her favorite scent, Summer Rose. We'd given her a large powder box last Christmas. I closed the door carefully after she pulled her dress inside.

"Hello, twins... how are you? You haven't come to visit in a while."

Elsbeth piped up, "We thought you didn't feel well, Mrs. Stone."

Her brother jabbed her with his elbow. She frowned and rubbed her ribs, whispering fiercely, "Well... *it's true.*"

I slid in beside William. Millie slowly swiveled in her seat. "You're right, sweetheart. I did have a few bad days, but I'm feeling much better now and I'd love to see you."

Siegfried leaned forward. "How about tomorrow?"

Millie smoothed her gloves and nodded her head.

"That would be just fine. Why don't you three come for lunch?"

"I'm sorry, I can't. I'm going to Oakland with my folks," I said.

"That's okay, honey. We'll do it another time. Meanwhile, the twins will keep me company."

William tugged at his starched collar and tie. His slicked back hair smelled of spicy hair tonic and he looked quite spiffy in his shined Sunday shoes. Although we attended the East Goodland Methodist church quite regularly during the school year, my parents took the summer off when we stayed at Loon Harbor. I hadn't been to church in weeks.

The back seat, deep and roomy, enfolded us in comfort and we barely felt the bumps in the road when Oscar drove us to the Andersons' barn.

Nineteen

The cavernous white barn needed a paint job, but was in good condition. Rows of cow stands ran along either side of the aisle. I pictured the dairy cows of yesteryear tethered for their morning milking and almost smelled their aroma in the cool barn. The Andersons gave up the dairy farm for their small country store long ago. Two box stalls stood on the far end of the aisle for the "ponies," as Mr. Anderson called them. With doors that opened into the pasture, the horses were able to seek shelter at will. Mr. Anderson fed them by tossing their hay over the stall walls and dumping the scoop of grain into buckets hanging inside. A short hose ran from the spigot to the stalls, which made filling the water buckets easy, a very practical set-up.

We set the bags on the floor and reached for two lead ropes hanging on nails near the stalls. Elsbeth grabbed the braided leather lead and I took the frayed white rope. We headed into the field through one of the stall doors.

Although Mr. Anderson referred to his pets as ponies, they were actually full-sized horses. The Count of Monte Cristo, or Monty, as we called him, was a black-and-white pinto with a thick black mane and wide-set eyes. He stood at fifteen hands, a full two inches taller than official pony dimensions and the size of most average pleasure horses. The twins usually rode him. His docile personality and gentle gaits were his most noteworthy features. When Siegfried and Elsbeth approached him, he raised his head from the pasture.

My faithful steed, Sir Galahad, was a palomino with a wide blaze, four white socks, and a white mane and tail. He stood at fifteen and a half hands and was a bit more spirited than Monty. Both animals were well nourished. Their coats shone in the morning sun, courtesy of the special wheat germ oil Mr. Anderson sprinkled on their grain.

Sir raised his head and stared at me. I stopped ten feet away, dug into my pocket, and pulled out one of the sugar cubes I stole from the sugar bowl at camp. I knew if I tried to catch him without bait he'd run me ragged until we both were too tired to go for a ride. He looked at me skeptically and chewed on a mouthful of pasture grass.

Monty willingly allowed himself to be captured and was on his way to the barn. I stood fast with my hand outstretched.

"Sir. Come on. Over here."

I clicked my tongue to get his attention. "Come on, boy. Come 'n get some nice sugar."

He stood still, staring. I decided to brave it and walked another step toward him. He raised his head higher and almost turned to trot away when he noticed my outstretched hand.

"Come on, Sir. We're going for a nice ride. You don't wanna be left home alone, do you?"

He took three deliberate steps toward me. I held the lead rope behind my back with one hand and jiggled the sugar cube in the other.

"Let's go, Sir. Here ya go, boy."

The gelding took another two steps forward, stopping just before he reached me. He stretched his neck as far as possible, maintaining his advantage. He couldn't reach.

"One more step, boy. That's it."

The gelding capitulated and took the step. His lips moved over my hand. The sugar cube disappeared. I reached up with my free hand and grabbed his halter, attaching the brass clip to the ring beneath his chin when he tried to pull away. Finally he stopped, lowered his head, and surrendered as I stroked his blaze and murmured to him.

"Good boy. What a good boy. You remember me, don't you Sir?"

I dug out another sugar cube and fed it to him. I hoped he would remember next time.

Tremolo: cry of the loon

Monty stood in the crossties midway down the aisle. Elsbeth ran a brush through his thick forelock. The gentle gelding lowered his head to her hands and thoroughly enjoyed the attention from his adoring fans.

I clipped Sir into his crossties and went over to the box of currycombs, brushes, and various other tools of the trade. I picked a hard stiff brush, a soft-bristled finishing brush, a rag, and a hoof pick.

There were bits of grass and leaves in his mane and tail, one burdock firmly entrenched in his forelock, and several small patches of crusty mud on his flank. I worked systematically from front to back, starting with the stiff bristled brush to dislodge the mud and loose hair, and finishing with the soft brush and a rag to polish his gleaming coat. After twenty minutes he sparkled, his mane and tail were fluffy and his hooves shone. The twins finished the same time I did, since their mount required extra care in his white patches.

Siegfried applied the hoof polish to Monty's interestingly variegated white and black hooves as I sprayed both horses with Repel-X bug spray. I wiped a rag soaked in the solution across and inside the horses' ears, around their jaws, down their blazes, and under their chests. The mosquitoes could be fierce deep in the woods, and if we ran into a patch of horseflies, we'd be miserable without protection.

Elsbeth bridled Monty with the gentle snaffle bit. I used the more traditional Pelham bit on Sir. The shank of the added curb accomplished what its name implied, curbing his more devilish instincts to bolt with an eleven-year-old on his back.

The saddles Mr. Anderson bought at auction years ago no longer fit. The horses' bellies had grown in proportion to their excellent care. We'd given up trying to make them work and had learned to enjoy riding bareback.

Elsbeth mounted first with a leg up from Sig. He handed the leather bag to her, then led Monty to the fence, who stood calmly while he climbed onto the top rail and swung over the horse's broad back behind his sister.

Sir was not as cooperative. I'd tried the fence routine last summer, but realized it would never work. He was too quick for me. To deal with his prancing side step, I learned to mount from the ground. I grabbed the reins and a large handful of mane in my left hand and tightened up the rein. If he moved, he'd be forced to walk in a small circle. I hopped on my left foot and leapt onto his back as he began, as expected, to turn in tight circles to his left. Once up, I released the tension on the left rein and sat down firmly on his back, redirecting him back to the fence to get my backpack. After three tries, I got close enough, grabbed the pack, and slid my arms through it. I let Sir canter up beside Monty and the twins, who were already loping along the fence toward the woods.

Twenty

It took an hour to find the boulder where I'd left the candy the day before. We followed broken branches in what seemed like circles until we came to a spot I recognized. Siegfried and I led the horses as Elsbeth rode astride, ducking low or breaking branches above her head to help clear a path. Siegfried carried his map and compass and assured me that once we found the boulder, he would prepare a superior exit path using his orienteering skills. I wasn't sure exactly what he meant, but had seen him striding purposefully through the woods at home with compass and map in hand. He'd never gotten us lost and I trusted his genius for the sport.

"Are you sure this is it?" Elsbeth asked, sliding off of Monty's back.

I looked around, nodding as I scratched my head. The big boulder looked familiar.

"Yeah, I'm pretty sure."

Siegfried walked to a bush and picked something up from the ground.

"You're right, Gus. Here's the wrapper from the bubble gum you left. The Bazooka Joe comic is gone, though."

I handed Sir's reins to Elsbeth and ran to Siegfried's side, taking the wrapper from his hand.

"She was here. I don't *believe* it."

We stopped and exchanged long glances, then looked carefully into the surrounding woods.

Siegfried lowered his voice. "Do you think she's watching us?"

A shiver ran down my spine.

"She might be. I think she was watching me yesterday."

Elsbeth began to call out in a low, sweet voice.

"Sharon? Shaaarrrrron!" The echo of her lilting voice traveled through the pine trees and back again. She tried again. "Sharon? We have food and a blanket for you! Sharon... Please come out!"

A cool breeze lifted the fern fronds, rippling along the forest floor. An owl hooted softly in the distance.

"She's afraid." I said softly. "She's afraid we'll capture her and bring her back to that drunk."

We called for five more minutes, trying to entice her out of hiding.

Finally, we tethered both horses to shrubs and opened the lunch bag. I unwrapped the peanut butter and jelly sandwiches and poured red Kool-Aid into three Dixie cups. Elsbeth spread the blanket on the top of the boulder and surprised us with a bag of Fritos and some carrot sticks. We lay back on the blanket and ate, wondering about Sharon.

"I wonder if she has a mother?" Elsbeth asked, taking a dainty bite of her sandwich.

"Good question," I said.

"*Ja*... What if she has brothers and sisters?" Siegfried asked.

He reached for his second Twinkie, downing it in two bites. Elsbeth refilled his cup. He drained it in one swallow. I started to take one of the carrot sticks, but Elsbeth slapped the back of my hand.

"*Nein!* Those are for the horses!"

I quickly withdrew and smiled.

"Sorry. I should've known."

She grabbed the bunch of carrots that were wrapped in an old piece of wax paper and a rubber band and carried them to her equine friends.

Both horse heads turned and persistently nudged her until she'd given them all of the treats. She brushed her hands against her jeans and walked back to the rock. Carefully, she arranged the remaining sandwiches and food on the blanket, then dug a small folded piece of paper out of her pocket, anchoring it with a rock beside the food.

"What's that?" I asked.

"A note to Sharon," she said. "It tells her who we are and that we won't hurt her."

"Do you think she'll write back?" I asked.
Siegfried pulled a short stubby pencil out of his shirt pocket.
"Not without a pencil," he said as he laid it on the blanket.
Elsbeth and I nodded in approval.

We made our way out of the woods following Siegfried and his compass. Every twenty steps or so, he blazed a tree trunk with his pocketknife. We made a trail that took us straight back to the path connecting up with the Andersons' farm. It was one o'clock by the time we arrived home. We spent a full hour sweeping the sundeck and living room porch to ensure our right to borrow Grandpa's skiff, then headed up the hill in search of William.

Twenty-one

William bent over plastic parts spread on a newspaper and adjusted his work light. The twins and I watched in his quiet bunkroom while he arranged the model pieces he'd snapped off the grid. He flattened the instruction sheet and tacked it to the paneled wall behind the desk.

"Did you kids have fun today?" he asked without taking his eyes from his project.

We nodded in unison. "Uh-huh."

William leaned forward and chose a small round piece. He held it up against another and pursed his lips. Frowning, he checked the instructions, then rearranged two pieces so they fit together perfectly. Satisfied, he reached for the model glue, unscrewed the cap, and pierced the aluminum seal with the end of a safety pin. The strong smell of toluene filled the room as he applied a dab of glue on the parts and then set them on the newspaper to dry.

Elsbeth spoke up.

"We found Gus's rock."

I shot her a warning glance. William was my hero, but if he knew we'd found Sharon, he'd tell his folks. Sharon would be forced to go back to the father who beat her and we'd all be responsible for her future pain. Until we figured out what to do, we decided to keep our discovery to ourselves.

"Gus's rock?" he asked automatically. "What's the big deal about an old rock?"

William glanced sideways at me, breathing noisily through his nose. I answered before Elsbeth could explain, afraid she'd spill the beans.

"Oh, it's just a big boulder that makes a good fort. Out in the west woods. We ate lunch on it today. It could make an excellent clipper ship, too."

He whistled through his nose, concentrating on the directions.

"Well, as long as you three don't get lost like you did yesterday. Stick together. There's an awful lot of wilderness out there, kids. You know, black bears, moose. You might wanna stay closer to camp for your next picnic."

We exchanged glances behind William's back.

"We'll be okay. We've got Siegfried's compass and the map, and usually Shadow's with us. He's a good watch dog, you know," I said.

At the mention of his name, Shadow lifted his head from his paws. He'd jumped onto the bunk bed and slept on a gray woolen blanket pulled tightly across the mattress. William told us in the navy sailors had to make their beds *just so*. He was practicing, and wanted to get a head start on the technique. He hoped to rise to the top of his class when he joined up, and to become an officer within seven years. We'd heard the story many times and listened eagerly every time William received a letter from his cousin Daniel, a five-year veteran of the navy. Postcards from every port were pinned to the wooden boards over the desk, featuring tropical seascapes and dancing hula girls.

William worked on his model, and I glanced around the small bunkroom with envy. The building housed the ice room, the laundry, a small woodshop, two bunks, and a washroom. Various pennants were pinned above the beds - mementos of past occupants. My grandparents usually hired college students as cabin boys, but this year agreed to hire William. Although he was just entering his sophomore year in high school, he was a hard worker and almost as tall as most of the college freshman. Strong, lean, and dedicated, he learned his job rapidly and became indispensable the first week. Normally Grandfather hired two cabin boys, but the boy who'd promised to come back this year from Clarkson College broke his leg while climbing in the Adirondacks. Grandfather was still searching for a suitable replacement.

After forty minutes of concentrating and piecing together tiny parts, William capped the glue and pushed back his chair. He rubbed the top of his beak nose and sighed.

"The hardest part is done. Tomorrow I can start attaching parts to the body of the car."

"Neat," I said. "Can we watch again?"

William smiled and looked at us.

"Sure, but don't you kids have anything better to do than watch me build models? Isn't it boring?"

We shook our heads, again in unison.

"Heck no, William. It is a blast," Siegfried said.

I loved it when Siegfried picked up the latest slang. It added such an interesting flavor to his potpourri of German phrases.

"*Ja*, William, it's keen," said Elsbeth, using her own favorite word.

A knock sounded on the door and we swiveled around. Betsy stood in the doorway and flashed a helpless look.

Twenty-two

"Excuse me?" Betsy's voice was small, tentative. She looked through the doorway with wide eyes.

William bolted from his chair, knocking it back in his haste. He pushed past me and strode to the door.

"Betsy?"

We followed William, crowding around him. He batted us back and moved closer to her, ogling her with a moonstruck expression. I recognized the look. A pang of jealousy hit me square in the chest. *William likes Betsy.* Although I knew it was ridiculous, I enjoyed her gentle teasing and dreamed I might earn a special place in her heart. She looked at William with interest, batting her eyes as she spoke.

"I can't seem to make this darned washing machine work. Could you help me?"

Betsy had changed from her white waitress uniform to casual Sunday clothes. Her smooth brown hair was pulled into a high ponytail, tied with a white filmy scarf. She wore turquoise pedal pushers that snugged around her rounded hips. The pant legs rode tight around her calves. A soft lavender sweater with small pearly buttons was worn backwards, in the style of the day. The buttons rippled down her spine in a gentle curve, riding the fabric as she waltzed before us. A thin strand of white pearls graced her neckline. On her feet were black Capezios, the thin leather slippers that had become so popular with the girls that year. She walked with the grace of a ballerina, placing each foot carefully before the other and skipped over the floorboards.

I followed, spellbound, and slammed into the side of the workbench. The edge of the table caught me in the ribs and my right shin scraped against the table leg. Siegfried caught me when I collapsed from the pain.

"Are you okay?" he asked as he tried to help me up.

I waved him away, mortified that Betsy might see. Elsbeth stared at me with a puzzled expression.

"Gus? Are you okay? You look weird."

My face reddened. Fortunately, neither William nor Betsy turned around. William draped his arm over her shoulder as they leaned forward to examine the machine controls. He pointed out the features. Betsy's giggle mimicked the tremolo of the loons, melodic and sweet. Confusion spun my brain in circles. That tremolo, that crystalline yodel belonged to my feathered friends on the lake, not in a flirtatious encounter in the icehouse.

She sidled up to him and batted her lashes. I clenched my fists and bit my lip. How *could* he? How could *she*?

William opened the washer door and showed her where to put the detergent. She laughed again, this time sounding like tinkling wind chimes. My insides melted as I sagged against the workbench and held my ribs. I couldn't take much more.

"Gus? What's the matter?" Elsbeth repeated.

"I'm okay," I whispered fiercely. "I just need a second to get over it."

I took a deep breath and pulled myself up, trying to regain control. The twins put their arms around my shoulders and leaned into my face.

"Gus?" Siegfried whispered.

I shrugged them off.

"I'm fine, really. I'm fine."

I managed a small smile. It worked.

"Okay," Elsbeth said hesitantly. "If you're sure?"

I nodded and smiled wider this time.

She seemed relieved. Siegfried gave me one more piercing look, then finally shrugged his shoulders and joined his sister when she headed for the door.

"We'll meet you in the living room after dinner," she called over her shoulder.

William twisted the round control knob to its appropriate position and tugged on it to start the machine. I waved to the twins and meandered over to watch as it came to life.

"Oh. So that's how it works," Betsy said, widening her eyes in admiration. She looked at me and smiled. "I'll bet you knew how to work it all along, hey, little man?"

I blushed furiously and became tongue-tied. She sashayed toward me, linking her arm in mine.

"Gus is my special friend," she said, leaning down to brush her soft lips against my cheek.

My legs wobbled, my vision grew unfocused, but it returned to normal as her warm body pressed against my side. She smiled at William, flirting with him as she ran her slim fingers through my hair.

"I think you should grow it out, Gus. Nice and long. You look a little bit like Paul, you know. Those big, long-lashed eyes... I think with long hair you'd really resemble him."

I nodded dumbly.

William punched my free arm, hard. He was pretending to fool around, but the strength with which he jabbed me was sharper than usual. He encircled my neck, tore me from Betsy's arm, and dragged me away, rubbing his knuckles hard against my scalp.

"If he grows his hair out, it'll be harder to give him noogies," he said, laughing as he scraped his knuckles over my head.

"Oh, leave him alone, William!" she pleaded as she tried to pry his arm from my neck.

He hung on, tightening his grip. My vision began to blur.

Laughing, he taunted Betsy.

"There's a price to pay for release, Mademoiselle. One kiss, and I'll let him go. But you have to promise that you'll go through with it."

She hesitated, watching me with concern. He tightened his grip and I moaned loudly.

"Okay, okay. I'll pay your price," she said, losing the alluring tone she'd used before.

He released me abruptly. I fell back, rubbing my neck and looked at him in shock. He'd never been so rough with me. I was shattered. The smile that played around his lips was almost vindictive. It hinted of malice. I took a surprised step back and knocked against the washing machine.

"Okay, Mademoiselle, time to pay up," William said, ogling Betsy.

She straightened her shoulders, pushed out her chest, and walked toward him with a new expression. His eyes closed and he lowered his face to hers. At the last moment, she spun and walked up to me.

Tilting my face up, she kissed me on the lips, then glared victoriously at William.

"There. I've paid my fee. You didn't say WHO I had to kiss, now, did you?"

She turned on her heels and pushed out of the door, trotting back to her cabin. I slumped against the wall and looked at him. He looked at me, back at the door, and then began to roar with laughter.

"I'm sorry, little buddy. I didn't mean to hurt you."

He slapped his thighs as tears of laughter ran down his face.

"She really showed me, didn't she?" he chortled.

The laughter was contagious. My mouth twitched and I felt myself being drawn into the joke. I began to laugh, forgiving him for his rather strange behavior.

Girls sure make boys act weird, I thought.

I wiped the tears from my face and rolled around on the floor, hiccupping and roaring with William as we bellowed with laughter.

When we finally quieted down, we got back to our feet and headed outside. He walked with me toward Wee Castle. I walked slowly, scuffing my feet along the sandy path.

"You like her, don't you, William?"

He looked down at me in surprise.

"What?"

I knew he was stalling.

"You like Betsy. You *like* her."

He stopped, peeled some of the bark off the fence railing that lined the pathway, and finally met my eyes.

"Aw, Geez. I like 'em all. I like June, and Alice. I like Sue from back home. Then, there's Linda, and Carol… But don't worry, buddy. She's seventeen. There's no way she'd go for a guy two years younger than her. I was just kiddin' around."

I rubbed the skin on the side of my neck, remembering how tightly he held me in his grasp. Even though we'd laughed together, the fact that he chose to hurt me to gain Betsy's attention stung.

We began to walk again, passing Number Fifteen. I looked toward the cabin and saw a face in the window. It disappeared before I could lift my hand in greeting.

"Hey, I know," William said as if struck by a great idea.

"What?" I asked, still upset with him.

"How about tonight?"

I looked at him blankly.

"Tonight?"

He nodded his head with enthusiasm.

"Yeah! Tonight's the night. We'll sneak out to the blueberry farm and pick us some big ole' blueberries."

My stomach twisted with nerves. *Stealing blueberries.* Just thinking the words made me feel guilty. I looked uncertainly at him.

"But what if we get caught?"

He started to grab me around the neck again, but stopped when I held up my hand and drew back. Instead, he punched me a few times in the arm.

"Who's up in the middle of the night? We'll wait 'til… say… two AM. Then we'll do it. Whaddya say, buddy boy?"

I looked at my shoes for a minute, then down toward my cabin. My parents were sitting on the glider, looking out over the lake. I felt guilty just talking about it, but I knew William was trying to make a special effort to apologize and repair the damage.

"What about the twins? Can they come?"

He leaned over to pick a piece of grass from a clump growing beside the fence post. Placing it between his teeth, he chewed on it for a few seconds, then looked down at the Marggranders' cabin.

"I guess. If you think they can keep their mouths shut about it. Can we trust 'em?"

I nodded. "Sure we can."

"Okay, then. I'll come down and tap on your window at two. Be dressed and ready to go. Don't bring Shadow, though. He'll give us away if he catches a scent. If the twins wanna come, tell them to be waiting beside their cabin and we'll pick 'em up, okay? Wear dark clothes. A dark sweatshirt with a hood would be best."

A thrill chased down my spine. William had lowered his voice as we approached Wee Castle. My father looked up from his mystery, waved to me, and turned back to his book. My mother's eyes were closed and her head leaned on his shoulder as they pushed slowly back and forth in the glider.

"See you at two, then," William whispered as he turned on his heels and walked back up the hill.

Twenty-three

I shone the flashlight on my Mickey Mouse watch for the tenth time.

Ten 'til two.

Shadow snored on the end of the bed and I lay fully clothed under the blankets. The rubber tips of my sneakers stuck to the bed sheets, making it hard to slide them around. They stood like twin peaks in the moonlight, poking toward the ceiling. I'd draped a hooded sweatshirt on the chair by the open window, ready to put on the minute William knocked on the window.

Water dashed against the rocks beneath my floorboards, heightening the nerves that trilled up and down my spine. Steadily, my heart slammed against my ribs, increasing in frequency as each minute passed.

What if my parents hear me leaving?

The anticipation of being caught pooled cold in my stomach.

What if Shadow barks?

I'd probably be grounded for at least a week. Maybe for the whole summer. Shuddering at the thought, I decided to slip outside before William could startle Shadow.

Slowly, I sat up and slid my feet under the covers, lowering them to the floor. Shadow raised his head from his dreams and eyed me in surprise. He yawned, then lay his head back down. I leaned over and stroked his ears, calming him until he fell back to sleep. I stuffed my pillows beneath the blankets, arranging them to look like a body. It didn't look quite right, so I reached under the bed and pulled out my baseball glove, fashioning it to look like a head. After putting on and zipping my sweatshirt, I stuffed my flashlight into a pocket. Shadow didn't wake.

I tasted the lake on the cool breeze blowing in the window and my pulse rose as I walked toward it, one squeaky step at a time.

When I reached the window, I stopped for a moment and listened, hearing nothing but water lapping on rocks below. With heart pounding, I pinched the fasteners on the bottom of the screen, making a soft screech. I froze, imagining the sound like a thousand fingernails on a chalkboard.

I raised the screen inch by inch, stopping every few seconds to listen. When it was high enough to squeeze through, I slid one leg over the sill. Quiet prevailed, so I ducked my head through the window and felt a shudder of fear when I came face to face with William. I sucked in a lungful of air, ready to yell. William pressed a finger against his lips, trying not to laugh.

"Ssshhhh," he whispered.

"You almost gave me a heart attack!" I said.

"Sorry," he whisper-laughed. "Now hurry up and get out here before your folks wake up."

Pulling my other leg through the window, I pushed down the screen until it nearly latched, leaving a two-inch gap.

William wore a dark blue watch cap with a black sweatshirt and dungarees. He held his hand up, listened for a moment, and led me over to the lake side of the porch. We crept down between crisscrossed railings and landed on the ground below. He leaned over and whispered. "Best not to take the porch. The steps creak."

I nodded, admiring his talent in the art of skulking. I wouldn't have considered sneaking out this way.

We crept around back and crawled behind a boulder, away from the view of my parents' bedroom window. A light flashed twice across the path. Elsbeth waved. I dug out my light and flashed twice in response.

William sprinted toward them, then motioned for me to follow. Heart pounding, I ran as fast as I could, bending low to avoid detection. Siegfried and Elsbeth wore dark clothes. Stifling a giggle, Elsbeth took my hand and pressed it in excitement. William used hand signs to lead us up the hill. I felt like a soldier at war, stalking the enemy.

We avoided Number Fifteen and the cabin of so-called guardians. A red glow came from the cigarette of a man smoking on the porch. I'd come to understand that the elderly woman was someone of great importance, and these men were hired to protect her. We made a wide berth around the guards' cabin and scuttled up the hill through the sheltering woods.

When we reached the dirt road, we relaxed and began to whisper.

"Whoa, that was close. Did you see that guy smoking on the porch?" I asked.

Siegfried nodded. "*Ja.* I thought he would see us."

William shushed us, pressing a finger to his lips.

"Sounds carry in the woods, especially over the water. We have to be quiet."

The crickets and peepers didn't heed his warning, chirping in the cool night air. Elsbeth linked arms with me, her eyes shining with excitement in the moonlight. She'd tied back her wayward curls in a thick ponytail and wore a kerchief over her hair. Her dark eyes flashed at me as she whispered in my ear.

"We're the Blueberry Bandits," she giggled, reminding me of the loon's tremolo. Coming from Elsbeth, it was innocent, pure. Quite different from the rendition I'd heard when Betsy flirted with William in the icehouse.

I walked close to her, shaking my head and laughing at her silly joke.

Siegfried stopped suddenly, holding out his arm. We piled into him. William looked ahead and scanned the roadside. A scrabbling sound came from the woods. We watched in silence as a wild turkey poked his head out of a clump of ferns and waddled across the road, picking at whatever gourmet bits he found along the way. His gobble sounded bizarre in the still of the night.

We exploded with laughter, clamping our hands across our mouths to minimize the ruckus. When the bird crossed the road, we resumed our march, moving briskly through the night. Within minutes, we reached the entrance to the blueberry farm.

White boards crisscrossed the driveway entrance, resting on two old milk cans. We waited for a few minutes at the edge of the woods, listening to the rhythmic chorus of the peepers.

Satisfied it was safe, William waved us on and walked boldly up to the crossed boards, stepping over the middle section with ease. We followed him timidly, looking over our shoulders as we set foot on the private property. A shiver of guilt ran down my spine when I read the large black and white sign.

"Trespassers will be prosecuted."

I hurried to catch up with William as the twins trotted behind me.

I'm trespassing. I'm going to jail.

I tried to ignore the taunting thoughts while we followed William to the back of the field. He tested a few bushes and raised his hand to beckon us into one particularly good row. We scurried after him, ducking down low in spite of the fact that it was nearly pitch black.

The berries were clustered in bunches. I reached my hand along one branch and blindly scooped off a damp handful. The heavy berries plopped into my palm. I shoved them into my mouth, tasting incredible sweetness when they burst against my tongue. They were huge, nearly as big as the concord grapes that grew wild at home. I reached my hand back into the bush.

Elsbeth stayed close at my side. "*Mein Gott.* These are so good."

Siegfried moved a few feet from us, and William stayed at the end of the row, keeping watch. After we'd gorged ourselves on berries, we sat on the wet grass between the rows and listened as William told ghost stories. We'd been there for almost forty minutes when he held his hand up in warning. We'd all heard it: the crunching of tires along the dirt road. We sat quietly, waiting for the rumbling to pass as the car drove past the field. Rather than drive by, however, it stopped. A car door clanged. Someone had parked at the entrance of the field and was removing the barricade.

The car door closed again and headlights swept across the field. It bumped down the lane in our direction.

William flapped his hands frantically toward the woods. We ran like frightened deer, ducking below the bushes in the pitch-blackness. I brought up the rear, helping the twins make it safely down the track. The car continued up the lane, stopped at the end of the field, and turned in our direction.

They're following us!

I pumped my legs harder. William and the twins scrambled over a stone wall that separated the woods from the field. I'd nearly reached it when I tripped on an abandoned berry basket and went down. I fell face first onto the wet grass and my right knee skidded along the ground. Winded, it took me a moment to recover. The headlights grew brighter as the car rolled toward me. Moving like a snake, I slithered toward the stone wall and flattened against the base of the rocks in the tall grass. My flashlight dug into my side. I removed it and slid it into the other pocket, then forced myself to lie motionless on the ground as my lungs heaved, loud and raspy.

My heart thudded while a chorus of crickets sang in the background and the car's headlights played in the grass just beyond. A bead of sweat broke on my brow.

Two men emerged. They turned off the engine, but left the headlights on. Silhouetted in the light, they spoke. One pulled out a cigarette. The other lit it for him. They murmured in deep, gruff voices. I caught a word here and there, but froze when I heard them say, "Sharon."

I looked closer, parting the grass so I could see them. Shocked, I recognized the man who held the cigarette: Sharon's father. His face, dark and menacing, glowered in the harsh light of the headlamps. He ran a handkerchief over his face, as if he were sweating. The other man spoke sternly to him, chastising him for something. I heard the words "risky" and "liability." Mr. Adamski seemed to break under the pressure and collapsed on the hood. I wondered if the other man meant to harm him, and suddenly felt sorry for him.

Something crawled over my legs. Dozens of little feet danced over my body. I nearly shrieked in terror, but held my tongue and forced myself to lay motionless. A family of raccoons walked over my legs and onto the stone wall behind me. I froze, petrified I'd give myself away. Finally, the entourage of critters scuttled into the woods. My heart pounded in my ears, loud enough for the whole town to hear. I looked back at the men; they'd moved around to the back of the car, thankfully unaware of our presence. They opened the trunk and peered inside.

I squirmed a few feet closer, gaining visibility. They leaned inside and hefted something long and awkward out of the trunk. It thumped to the ground.

Twenty-four

I glanced toward the stone wall, wondering if my friends had seen the body. I wasn't sure if *it was* a body, but it looked like one. Elsbeth, Siegfried, and William remained tucked behind the wall, well hidden. I looked back at the men and slithered a few feet closer.

They closed the trunk lid after Mr. Adamski reached inside and grabbed a flashlight.

In the inordinate quiet of the black night, Elsbeth sneezed–a tiny hand-smothered sound. I held my breath and flattened against the wet grass.

Mr. Adamski switched on the flashlight and played it over the grass and trees beside me.

"Did you hear that?" he asked.

"Hear what?" The other man grunted as he leaned down to pick up one end of the long object on the ground.

He shone the light again, back and forth across the area where we hid. I prayed Elsbeth could control her allergies. She was probably laying in a patch of ragweed.

"Nothin', I guess," he replied after a long pause. "Guess it was an animal."

His partner sounded irritated.

"Come on. We have to get this to the cabin."

Each man took one end of the awkward bundle and carried it between them. When they headed onto a path not far from us, I risked raising up to get a better look. Adrenaline rushed through my veins. The object was wrapped in a blanket. It swayed between them much like a human body would do.

After they disappeared, I scrambled over the wall and nearly landed on top of Siegfried. He put his arm around my shoulder and whispered in my ear.

"*Mein Gott*, we thought you were going to be caught!"

Elsbeth reached over and took one of my hands, pressing it in hers, and William ruffled my hair. I felt better being huddled together with my friends, out of sight of the men.

I waited until I was sure they were out of earshot.

"Did you see what they were carrying?"

I could barely make out their faces; it was so dark. They whispered in unison. "No."

William asked, "What was it? Who were they?"

I looked back toward the trail they'd followed, watching for the bobbing light that would signal their return.

"It was Sharon's father and some other guy. They mentioned a cabin and took this… bundle out of the trunk and carried it away down that track. It looked like…" I hesitated a minute, not wanting to unduly alarm my friends.

"Like what?" Elsbeth asked quietly.

I took a deep breath and whispered,

"A body. It looked like they were carrying a body."

A series of gasps whispered through the darkness. Elsbeth moved closer to me, trembling.

William spoke up.

"We have to hide until they leave. Then we'll follow that trail to the cabin and see what they've done. Maybe they've buried it. We'll have to report it to the police."

"But we'll get in trouble!" squeaked Elsbeth. "They'll know we sneaked out here and stole berries."

I realized the risk of being found out was far greater for my younger friends. Their punishments were always more severe.

I patted Elsbeth's hand. "William? Couldn't we just say it was you and me? We could leave the twins out of it, right?"

I almost saw the vague outline of his head as he nodded.

"Sure. Sure we–"

I squeezed his arm. A light flickered on the path. The men returned and we huddled together, holding our breath. We heard them get back into the car and drive down to the field entrance where they replaced the barricade and continued down the road.

We let out a collective sigh of relief.

"That was close," muttered William. He stood up and turned to the twins.

"You two wait here while Gus and I check out the cabin."

Siegfried put his arm around Elsbeth.

"*Ja. Gut.* (Good.) We'll wait here for you." He sounded disappointed, but resigned to protect his sister.

"Okay. C'mon, Gus. Let's see what these fellas were up to."

I turned on my flashlight and laced my fingers over the lens to cut the light. We walked quickly to the area where the men entered the woods and were relieved to find a well-established path. William jogged forward. I loped behind him and the beam of the light jiggled up and down in rhythm with my gait. Before long, we reached a small shack. I shone my light on it, revealing old gray boards and holes in the roof. The door hung on one hinge. It must have been abandoned years ago.

I moved up close to William as he swung aside the creaking door.

"Give me the light, Gus," he whispered.

I handed him the flashlight with a trembling hand. Fear rippled down my spine. William played the light over the inside of the one-room building, illuminating an old table and two chairs next to a pot-bellied stove. A cot lay below shelves that lined the wall, emptied of their goods years ago.

"Where is it?" I asked with a shaky voice.

William flashed the light over the room again.

"I don't see anything, Gus. Maybe they buried it."

"Wait a minute," I said. "Shine the light on the floor over there."

We walked toward the far corner of the room and examined the floorboards. Something flashed. William knelt down and picked it up.

"It's just an old bottle cap," he said.

As the flashlight played over the dusty floor, I noticed a section of floorboards cut shorter than the others.

"What's this?" I moved over to the area, stomping my feet around.

William found a hole used to lift the panel of a small trap door. I froze, shocked that we actually found something. I imagined a body beneath the floor, and had the vision of Sharon's face staring up at me. I backed up quickly.

"You look. I can't do it."

William was equally adverse to the idea, but since he was the oldest, he was compelled to lift the panel and peer inside. He got down on his knees, inserted three fingers in the hole in the floor, and slowly lifted it. I slinked in the doorway while he leaned over and shone the flashlight into the hole in the ground.

"Well, that's weird," he said. He sat up.

I looked at him from the doorway, frozen.

"What is it? Is it Sharon?" I asked. My voice broke, filled with terror.

"Sharon?" He looked at me as he shook his head. "Heck, no. It's not a body. Come over here."

Relieved, I sprinted to William's side and leaned over the hole. Lying in the crawlspace beneath the floor were several long, heavy bolts of woolen fabric. A rusty toolbox sat beside them.

I looked at William in the beam of the dimming flashlight and scratched my head.

"What the heck?"

He motioned for me to back up and repositioned the panel.

"C'mon, Gus. It's time to go home."

Twenty-five

At ten o'clock the next morning we piled into our Oldsmobile station wagon and headed for Oakland. The woolen mill, first on the list, would be followed by lunch and a movie. I'd slept until the unbelievable hour of eight o'clock and nearly confessed all when my mother looked in horror at my blue lips and teeth. Mumbling something about a new kind of gum, I'd rushed to the bathroom to regain my composure and brush my teeth until all telltale traces of blueberry colorant had vanished.

We arrived at the mill in thirty minutes. According to my father, who lectured us about the history of the building, it was constructed in the late 1800s and had survived the decades well in spite of the limited attention received at the hands of its various owners. Stretching for three hundred feet along the banks of the river, it loomed tall and crooked against the landscape. I followed my parents up three flights of rickety wooden stairs to the sales floor. Inside, we were assaulted with the familiar scent of wool and dust. Worn gray floorboards spanned the aisles of shelves that housed hundreds of bolts of brightly colored wool. I sighed deeply and prepared to be bored.

My mother walked up and down each aisle as she fingered every bolt of material. I followed her for a while, tired from my less-than-usual ten hours of sleep.

"What do you think about this red plaid, Gus? Would you like a shirt made from this?"

I shrugged and looked at her indecisively.

"I guess so. It's nice."

A prodigious seamstress, each winter my mother made woolen shirts for my father and me. We wore them to the woodpile, on walks, and in the house on frigid mornings before the woodstove warmed the air.

She rolled her pale blue eyes in my direction.

"I don't know why I even ask you, Gustave."

I took the bolt of fabric from her hands.

"Sorry, Mum. It's a good color. Really. I like it."

She smiled indulgently and continued down the aisle.

After handing various selections to my father, who dutifully carried them to the counter at the end of the room, she finally attacked the remnants corner, examining assorted samples and asking my patient father for his opinion.

"Oh, look at this lovely pink. Maybe I'll make a new Easter suit for myself, André. What do you think?"

My father winked at me, then nodded his head sagely, answering her as if the fate of the world depended on his opinion.

"Hmmm... yes, Gloria. Yes. I think it would do just fine, dear. You'd be stunning, as usual."

She looked at him in surprise, blushed to match the fabric in her hands, and shooed away the notion by waving one hand in the air.

"Oh, André! You're such a flatterer!"

She worked systematically across the table. I found a spot on a ground level shelf and wedged myself between bolts of blue plaid and gray herringbone. I rested my elbows on my knees, chin on my hands, and sighed.

After two hours of pondering, stroking, and selecting, my industrious mother was done. She walked to the checkout counter and waved to me. I extricated myself from the shelf and plodded after her.

We waited patiently for a few minutes. The owner had disappeared into the office, with the door shut. I shifted from one foot to the other and leaned on the counter, thinking about Sharon Adamski again. It struck me as uncannily coincidental that today, of all days, we happened to visit the woolen mill. Just last night we'd found bolts of the stuff hidden deep in the woods under the floorboards of an old shack.

I glanced at my parents, feeling incredibly guilty. I'd never pulled a stunt like last night. I never lied to them about anything of importance. When I was five, I ran my finger through the frosting on a chocolate cake my mother made for company. She asked if I did it and I denied it. She knew I did it, and I knew that she knew. Eventually, I went to her in shame and told her the truth. We patched up the cake as best as possible just before the guests arrived.

My father was about to ring the bell on the counter, but stopped when two men's voices erupted behind the closed office door. The deeper, gruffer voice sounded extremely angry, and the milder respondent sounded repentant. I couldn't make out the words, but the conversation was heated.

Withdrawing his hand from the bell, my father exchanged puzzled glances with my mother. Her brow furrowed.

"André? Should we come back later?" she asked.

Before he could answer, the office door burst open. A tall man glowered in the doorway. I backed up, recognizing Sharon's father. He glared, then stormed past us and hurried to the exit, clumping rapidly down the steps. Tires squealed when he pulled out of the parking lot.

A short slim man emerged from the office, his face drained of color. My father looked quizzically at me, then smiled sympathetically at the man. I recognized him as the mill owner who waited on us last summer.

"Mr. Adamski," my father began. "You remember my wife, Gloria?"

My mother extended her hand and smiled.

"Nice to see you again."

Stunned, I looked at my father.

"This is my son, Gus."

I stood with my mouth half-open as he shook my hand. My father shot me a surprised glance and turned back to the man behind the counter.

"Any news about Sharon?" he asked gently.

The man shook his head slowly and looked down.

"No, not yet. Tomorrow they're going to drag the lake. Thanks for volunteering for the search party yesterday, Mr. LeGarde. Hilda and I really appreciated all the help we got from you folks."

I continued to stare as my father conversed with the man he kept calling Mr. Adamski. Finally, it hit me. I'd been wrong about the man who pursued Sharon in the woods.

He wasn't her father.

I tugged on my father's sleeve while Mr. Adamski unwound, measured, and cut wool from each bolt. He leaned down and I whispered in his ear.

"Can I talk to you for a minute, Dad?"

I led him down the aisle, turning a corner and stopping when we were out of view.

"What in the world is wrong with you, son?"

I looked at my feet.

"We got it all wrong, Dad. We were way off."

He put his hand on my shoulder and leaned closer to me.

"What *are* you talking about?"

I explained that the man who chased Sharon through the woods was the tall man who was arguing with Mr. Adamski in the office. I'd wrongly assumed that he was Sharon's father that night. He raised an eyebrow.

"Are you certain, son? Absolutely positive?"

I nodded. "There's no doubt about it, Dad. I'd know that guy anywhere."

My father looked out the grimy window.

"That explains a lot. The police said that Mr. Adamski was with a group of friends playing cards the whole time you kids were lost in that fog. They were confused by your statement. They'll certainly want this new piece of information."

I nodded, feeling awful that we'd almost implicated a man who was innocent. He had to be going out of his mind with worry.

"Wait here, Gus. I'm going to have a word with Mr. Adamski."

I lifted myself onto the dusty windowsill and waited. The window stretched eight feet toward the ceiling. I kicked my heels against the wall, feeling tired and confused. Finally, my parents came down the aisle with their arms full of packages. I took the large one from my mother's arms and walked beside them.

"Did you talk to him, Dad? Did you tell him I'm sorry?"

We started down the stairs.

"Yes, Gus. He understands. He's going to talk to the investigator tonight. They'll probably want to speak with you children about what you saw."

We made the first landing and turned the corner.

"Dad?"

"Yes, son?"

"Did you find out who that man is?"

He exchanged glances with my mother.

"He's Mr. Adamski's brother, Gus. His name is Frank. They have the cabin right next to Sharon's down on Black Bear Point."

I nodded. So it was Sharon's uncle who had been chasing her through the night, and not her father. I pocketed the information and decided to discuss it with the twins as soon as I saw them. This changed everything. We needed to find her, find her fast, and get her back to her family.

Twenty-six

After we left the mill, we drove into town and lunched across from the cinema. My father had been acting mysterious about the movie, and when we finally crossed the street to the theater I noticed the unfamiliar title: "To Kill a Mockingbird." I looked up at him, wondering if he was finally going to let me see an adult movie. Our previous excursions had always been to see the latest Disney films.

"This is supposed to be a fine film, son," he said as we waited in line for tickets.

I burped and excused myself, tasting the hamburger and malted shake I'd polished off at the diner. My mother forbade dessert, warning us that we'd be too full for popcorn or candy if we gave in to our whim for apple pie. She stood beside me, looking pretty in her pastel flowered sundress with matching kerchief tied around her ponytail.

"What's it about, Dad?" I asked, running my hands along the red velvet rope that hung between metal stands. Shabby elegance appointed the old lobby; worn red carpets covered the floor and heavy frayed curtains shrouded the wall-sized posters showcasing the new movies.

He paid for three tickets and ushered us into the inner lobby where we waited in the next line for candy and drinks.

"It's about two children and their father. It's set in the south, and deals with a very difficult subject. There's adventure, and incredible heroism… so I've heard."

I looked up at him with interest, wondering what the "difficult subject" would be. I waited for more clarification, but before he could elaborate we arrived at front of the line at the candy counter and I needed to deal with the important decision of choosing Jordan Almonds or chocolate-covered raisins.

My mother chose lemonade and a bag of popcorn. Dad picked a Mounds bar, and I finally decided on Jordan Almonds. We found three seats in the center section, halfway down. I sat between my parents, sticking and unsticking my sneakers to the floor where someone had spilled a drink.

"Gus. Stop," my father admonished.

After a few seconds, my mother wrinkled her nose and stood.

"There's gum on my chair."

We shuffled a few seats closer, resettling in more sanitary surroundings. After the usual prelude of dancing soda cups and candy boxes whirling across the screen, the film started.

Scout and Jem captivated me in the first scene. The children were such natural actors, I felt as if I stood beside their boastful little friend, Dill, and I shared in each of their adventures. I grew fond of Calpurnia, and frightened of Boo. Most of all, I connected with Gregory Peck in the role he played as Atticus Finch, the heroic lawyer who defended an innocent man from the horrendous charge of rape. I wasn't exactly sure what rape was, but it sounded awful. Atticus reminded me of my own father. Real tears threatened to spill down my cheeks as Brock Peters masterfully portrayed Tom Robinson, the innocent field hand wrongfully accused, convicted, and subsequently killed by the 1930's town of bigots.

My mother squeezed my hand during the sad parts and wiped her eyes frequently. My father sat still, totally absorbed by the film.

My heart hammered when Mr. Ewell chased Jem and Scout through the dark forest; reminiscent of my own experience when I recently panicked in the woods. Chills ran down my spine as the childlike Boo was revealed behind Jem's bedroom door. After the story came to its perfect resolution, I sat still in the seat between my parents with visions of Scout and Boo lingering, absorbing, consuming me. We remained in silence when the rest of the audience shuffled outside.

Finally, my father shifted in his seat. A sad smile flickered across his face when he rose and started down the aisle. We followed slowly behind him.

"Mum?" I asked.

"Yes, honey?" she said, sliding her arm around my shoulders.

"Can we see it again? Can we come back tomorrow?"

She looked at my father and back at me.

"Well, sweetie, movies cost money, you know. We can't be going to the movies every day, now, can we?"

I looked down at my feet and nodded.

"I know. It was just *so* good."

My father held the door for us and we walked out into the bright sun. I squinted, trying to get my bearings.

"Maybe we can bring you back next week," he offered. "I'd like to see it again, too."

I walked between them, feeling immensely secure. We headed for the ice cream parlor with picnic tables and colorful umbrellas in its grassy front yard. I recognized several people from the theater and although I'd eaten a number of the Jordan Almonds, I still had room for a small cone.

"Well, what'll it be today, son? Black raspberry or pistachio?" my mother asked

I chose pistachio; my mother had her usual frozen pudding, and my father had orange-pineapple.

We sat in the shade of an enormous elm tree. I licked the creamy confection and chewed on the pistachio nuts. Sunlight dappled the top of the table and danced across our clothes and a canopy of leaves above our heads rustled ever so slightly in the afternoon breeze. My fingers stuck together from the drips I hadn't caught in time.

"Dad?" I asked.

I bit a hole in the bottom of the cone and noisily sucked the melting ice cream out the bottom.

"Yes, son?"

He peered at me over his cone, systematically turning and licking so there were no drips. My mother nibbled at hers with tiny bites. She had eaten only half of the one-scoop cone.

"People aren't like that any more, are they?" I asked.

He stopped for a minute and met my gaze. A few drips plopped onto my hand. My mother handed me a napkin and I tossed the messy cone into the nearby trash where yellow jackets had begun to gather.

"You mean prejudiced, Gus? Against Negroes?"

I nodded. "Yeah."

He stopped eating his ice cream and looked into the distance for a second.

"I'm afraid there are still folks who don't see a person for what's inside his heart, Gus. Too many people still carry fear and bias against anyone who isn't of their nationality or skin color."

He held his strong arm across the table and turned it in the sunlight, examining his own skin.

"I think it would be perfectly wonderful to have nice, copper brown skin."

My mother warmed to the subject.

"You'd be quite handsome in any color, Mr. LeGarde. But, honey, no matter what you look like, there's nothing that could change that big mushy heart of yours."

She took his free hand in hers and looked into his eyes with an expression so full of tenderness I nearly blushed.

"You're just an old softy, André," she said, gripping his rough hand.

He flashed an embarrassed smile.

"Well, I don't know about that, Gloria. But to get back to our son's question about bigotry..." He turned and looked directly at me. "Doctor Martin Luther King is working very hard to eliminate prejudice. He's in favor of a colorblind America, son, and your grandparents, your mother, and I support him one hundred and ten percent. By fighting for his people, he's actually fighting for the soul of humanity, the good of the world. That's why he won the Man of the Year award. Because he's an incredibly gifted and spiritual person who's going to turn this world around."

My father had a picture of Dr. King on his desk at work, right beside the picture of President Kennedy. I sighed and was reminded of the awful dark days of November just after the president was assassinated. The country still hadn't recovered from the shock.

"Dad? Wasn't the President friends with Dr. King?"

His eyes misted over when he discussed Dr. King and his relationship with President Kennedy. As he expounded on the issues they both had supported, I remembered back to the day it had happened. I sat on the couch between my father and mother, watching little John-John in shorts waving his flag and kissing his father's coffin. A pang of sorrow washed over me. My father had squeezed my hand so hard when we sat in silence on the maroon Naugahyde couch. The solemn event cast a spell over our home for months.

"I'm glad we're from the North, then," I said.

"The problem is worse in the South, but there's still plenty to overcome up here."

I nodded as if I understood and sat quietly while my mother and father finished their cones, stood up, and dropped their napkins into the trash. We walked back to the ice cream window, asked for extra napkins, and ran them under the water bubbler on the side of the building. I gave my mother a horrified look when she spit on her napkin out of pure habit and started to wipe my face with it.

"Ma, *please*. I can do it."

I removed most of the stickiness from my hands and face and even dragged my comb out of my back pocket to please her. She pulled back a stray wisp of her long brown hair and tucked it behind her ear. Her ponytails usually fell out by dinnertime.

While we walked back to the car, I asked her the most difficult question, the one I'd been putting off since we left the theater.

"Mum?"

She smiled at me.

"Yes, honey?"

I pursed my lips, hesitated, and blurted it out.

"What does 'rape' mean?"

She widened her eyes and exchanged a worried glance with my father. I wondered if she'd palm it off on him, but was pleased when she handled it herself.

"Well, honey," she said. "It's an act of violence against someone. It has to do with... Well, do you remember the talk your dad had with you about the birds and the bees?"

I nodded, suddenly embarrassed.

"When someone forces another person to do what should be only done..." She paused for a minute, trying to find the right words as my father nodded and encouraged her. "What should only be done between loving adults in marriage, that's called rape, honey. It's not a very pleasant subject, I'm afraid."

I looked at my father for confirmation.

"Sometimes things happen that are beyond our comprehension, son... beyond our wildest imagination. I've never known anyone who was assaulted like that, but it has to be one of the most heinous crimes imaginable. Short of murder, of course," he added soberly.

I was quiet all the way home, thinking about poor Tom Robinson and his distraught family. I contemplated the acts of which some men were capable. As I pondered these deep and troubling concepts, one underlying question kept weaving through the tapestry of my consciousness.

What happened to Sharon Adamski and where in the world is she hiding?

I decided to tell my parents I'd seen something in the woods the other day, and that I planned to go back and take another look this afternoon. They doubted if what I'd seen had been human, saying the girl would surely have come forward to be rescued if she'd seen us. Although I admitted the possibility, I insisted that I needed to keep looking.

"You know the west end of the lake has been thoroughly searched by now, son. It's very unlikely she's hiding out there."

My father said it gently, trying not to upset me.

"I know, Dad," I said as we turned into the driveway to Loon Harbor. "But I *have* to try... just in case."

Twenty-seven

After changing into my bathing suit, tee shirt, and flip-flops, I raced around camp looking for the twins. I finally spotted them in the playground at the top of the hill near some toddlers in the sandbox. The children's mothers conversed nearby. Bursting with the news about Sharon's uncle, I couldn't wait to get the twins alone to tell them about the case of the mistaken identity.

Elsbeth polished something against the surface of the slide. The sunlight glinted off sheet metal and I squinted in the sharp glare.

"What are you doing?" I asked.

She turned to look at me, bit her lower lip in concentration, and continued rubbing hard.

"I'm polishing it with waxed paper," she said matter-of-factly.

She rubbed a crumpled piece of waxed paper hard in one direction, turned it, and rubbed again.

"Your grandfather said it would make it slippery." Siegfried shouted from the other side of the lot, in the process of dragging a heavy black hose toward the wading pool.

"Neat," I said. "Have you tried it yet, Elsbeth?"

"*Nein.*" She shook her curls so they tossed back and forth like a pup shaking off a rainstorm. "But it's almost ready."

I helped Siegfried drag the hose for the last ten feet over pine-needled ground. He stuck the nozzle in the pool and ran back to turn on the spigot. The hose exploded, spraying water wildly in all directions. Laughing, Siegfried ran back and grabbed it, setting it in the pool.

"How 'bout we take the boat out for a while and maybe do some more searching for Sharon?"

Siegfried nodded enthusiastically and looked at Elsbeth, who had just climbed up the slide to try it out. She whizzed down the metal surface with her hands held straight up, then eagerly beckoned to us. After several turns each, we declared it the slipperiest we'd ever seen. A young mother emerged from the long red cabin at the top of the hill and wandered over to the play area with her three children. After explaining about the new improvements, we handed her six-year-old the waxed paper so he could continue polishing. With excitement bubbling in my chest, I motioned to the twins and raced them toward the hill leading to the docks.

We sailed past the dining room and office, the shower building, five cabins, and finally pounded across the living room porch, taking a sharp right to run along the rooted pathway back toward Wee Castle. The late afternoon sun glinted from the water's surface, twinkling on choppy waves colliding in the afternoon breeze. The twins ran to their cabin to ask permission and get some towels. I stopped short at the second dock, where Grandpa's skiff bobbed on the breezy lake. I tossed three orange life vests into the boat, then opened the gas plug on the Evinrude to check the fuel level. It was half full.

The twins emerged in their suits and sandals, waving white towels above their heads as they raced toward me. Siegfried carried his waterproof pouch, which I assumed housed the compass and map. Elsbeth brought a bag of apples and bananas. I breathed a sigh of relief, glad she remembered food for Sharon.

As the twins leapt into the boat, I tossed them each a life vest and buckled myself into mine as a show of good sportsmanship. Although I hated wearing it, I wanted to keep my promise to my grandfather. I didn't want anything else, including such a major infraction, to keep us off the lake for the rest of the summer.

Siegfried untied the bowline while I lifted the loop from the rear post. I shoved against the dock, widening the gap between the boat and its berth. After three tries the Evinrude turned over, chugging and belching smoke, and the satisfactory aroma of gasoline wafted up from the engine. I twisted the throttle gently as the single propeller slowly turned in the water.

Once we cleared the dock, I warned the twins to hold on and twisted the throttle to full speed. We curved and headed for the west side of the lake. The boat thumped rhythmically over the waves, sending a spray of water across the bow that misted a shimmering rainbow. The mist moistened Elsbeth's dark hair, curling it tightly as it always did in a humid environment. She looked pretty in her pink swimsuit and laughed while clinging to her seat. Siegfried turned his bright blue eyes ahead, looking toward the woods with interest.

Three boats trolled in the distance, towing an apparatus behind them. As we drew closer, my heart sank. I recognized the official insignia of the state police and realized they must be dragging the lake for Sharon. I quickly directed the boat away from the search party, hoping to distract the twins so they wouldn't notice. Siegfried caught sight of them and exchanged worried glances with me. He pointed to a loon taking flight in the opposite direction, successfully diverting Elsbeth's attention. I knew she wouldn't appreciate being treated differently, but I couldn't control my desire to protect her whenever possible. There was something about the haunted look that invaded her eyes when she hurt that made me want to spare her the pain.

When we reached the deserted shore on the west side of the lake, I cut the engine and waited for the boat to float to shore. After a few seconds, I lifted the prop out of the water and slid into the cool waist-high water. Siegfried tossed the rope and I towed the skiff until I'd beached it. The twins hopped out and helped me pull it onto the sand. It would stay put until we returned from our hunt for Sharon.

Siegfried led the way to the boulder. As we hurried through the woods, I finally told the twins about the men at the woolen mill and the shock of meeting Sharon's real father. They stopped and looked at me with open mouths as I recounted the tale. We ran the rest of the way. Siegfried found the rock in record time, using the trail we'd made with the horses and his compass. When we arrived, we stopped and stood still, breathing in the sweet scent of balsam.

The sandwiches and Twinkies were gone. The blanket had vanished. We stared in disbelief for a few more minutes, and finally with a hollering whoop I jumped up onto the rock and began to yell in joy.

"She's alive!" I yelled to the trees around us. "Sharon's alive!"

The twins joined me on the rock. We burst with a medley of crazy shouts and joyous songs that reverberated through the forest as we danced in circles together. Finally spent, we dropped to the rock, laying side by side, looking up at the clouds.

"Do you think she got my message?" Elsbeth asked.

I jumped to my feet and prowled around for a sign of the piece of paper and pencil we'd left behind. The area was pristine.

"Maybe she found it in the dark, and couldn't see to write a response," Siegfried offered.

We warmed to the topic.

"Yeah. Maybe she just comes out at night when no one can see her."

"Like a ghost?" Elsbeth asked in a timid voice. Fear darted across her face.

"No, silly," I said. "Like a girl who's trying to stay hidden. We *have* to get to her, though. She *has* to know we'll keep her safe until they arrest that crazy uncle of hers, for whatever he did to her. They'll probably put him in jail, and have a trial, and everything," I said as I imagined the courtroom in "To Kill A Mockingbird."

"Do you really think so?" Elsbeth asked. Her expression blended relief with admiration.

I nodded my head wisely, feeling older than the twins.

"You can bet on it." I picked up a pinecone and started to peel away the layers.

Siegfried stood on the rock and called Sharon's name. Elsbeth and I joined him, shouting until we finally decided she must be too far away to hear us.

"How far is that old shack from here, Sig?" I asked. "Isn't it over that way?"

I lifted a finger sticky with pinesap and pointed roughly in the direction of the blueberry farm.

Siegfried unfolded his map and laid it on the boulder. He studied it for a few minutes.

"It's a couple of miles as the crow flies," he said, lifting his blond head. His hair was getting really long. Envy tapped me, calling attention to my short hair. I shrugged it off and looked into the thick woods. Shivering, I pictured the men who'd led us to the old cabin the night before.

"Maybe we should check it out sometime," I said half-heartedly.

Elsbeth laid the fruit on the rock and tucked the paper sack into her sweatshirt pocket.

"At least she'll have food tonight," she said solemnly.

I lifted my watch to my face and grimaced.

"Oh no… it's almost five thirty. Come on, I promised my folks I'd be washed up for dinner by six-fifteen."

We sprinted back to the shore, this time needing very little help from Siegfried. Hopping back into the boat, we buckled our lifejackets. I pushed the little motor hard and we arrived back at the dock by six-ten. When we secured it to the post, a scream echoed from the top of the hill.

William ran down the hill toward the lake with Betsy in his arms. She screeched and wailed, pummeling his chest as he bounded along the dock. When he reached the end of the pier, he tossed the fully clothed, flailing girl into the lake in the tradition of the customary Loon Harbor "waitress-dunking. " Each waitress suffered the humiliation at least once per summer. Betsy had known full well what was about to happen, and whooped and hollered extra loud to make a show for the guests who gathered at the bottom of the hill. Amidst good-natured laughter, she hoisted herself out of the water.

Her white nylon uniform was plastered to her skin. She walked toward William in her squishy white waitress shoes. He stood with his back to her, taking a bow to his shoreline audience. With one dripping foot placed strategically on his backside, she thrust the boy over the dock and into the water, laughing so hard she nearly toppled over the dock again and back into the drink. Elsbeth laughed the loudest when William popped out of the water with a most surprised expression on his face.

"Well, whaddya know," he shouted. "We've got a women's libber among us."

Betsy smoothed her hair and dramatically sniffed the air, sashaying up the dock, exaggerating the swing of her hips. A warm feeling of giddy pride crept over me when she winked at me.

"'Bout time someone put you cabin boys in your place," she laughed.

We ran along the path to our cabins, and I thought about Betsy and her theatrical response to William's prank. I had a feeling the tides would turn as a result of her performance, and that a brand new tradition had been established for Loon Harbor.

Twenty-eight

I snuggled into a green leather club chair in the living room, watching the guests as smoke swirled in the air over the lamps. I'd made it to dinner with five minute to spare, and after a quick washing up, had joined my parents and gobbled it down like a starving refugee. I still tasted garlic on my breath from the homemade spaghetti and meatballs. Toasted garlic bread was my favorite—I'd eaten five pieces.

I stroked a stuffed loon laying in my lap, marveling at the softness of the feathers and studying the red glass beads used to represent the eyes. They looked real. As I fingered the sharp black beak with my other hand, I lazily glanced around at the room full of family and guests. It didn't occur to me to be upset by the fact that I held a stuffed dead animal in my lap. It had been in the living room since I could remember, and I related it to good times and the simple pleasures of summering on the lake.

My grandmother sat beside me in a matching green chair. She held a thick library book on her lap and frequently cast her eyes over the top of the novel to watch my grandfather at the poker table. She'd changed into her cool-weather chino slacks and a thin blue plaid woolen shirt, but still wore the comfortable white shoes she'd grown to depend on when she had waited tables as a young girl at the camp. Grandpa called them her "nurse shoes," but she didn't care and lived in them all summer long.

She leaned over and poked the fire blazing on the open grate. Small sparks fluttered up the chimney. The flames transformed from yellow to blue to green and then back to yellow again. Shooting another furtive glance at my grandfather, she settled back to read a few more pages in her book.

Grandfather hunkered beside four other men from the camp. Cigar smoke spiraled from the poker table as they grunted and growled and laughed. Bottles of Narragansett Beer lay in a tub of chipped ice beside them. I'd filled it with chunks of ice earlier, having mastered the art of ice picking several summers ago. Occasionally, my grandfather would get a strange glint in his eye. He looked unusually excited when he played poker, tossing the grimy red, white, and blue chips around the table. During the ritual of the poker games, he'd switch from his pipe to a cigar. The soggy stump that hung from the corner of his lips was temporarily transported to the center of his mouth when he won a hand. He'd tip it up and down victoriously, grinning as he raked the chips toward him.

The twins lay on the scratchy woolen rug, playing a never-ending game of War with the greasy, curled cards we'd inherited from the poker players of past summers. Mr. and Mrs. Marggrander remained in their cabin, as usual. Elsbeth wore a new pair of yellow pedal pushers and a dark blue cardigan sweater. A yellow kerchief captured her hair in a ponytail. She lay on her stomach, feet kicking in the air. She hit my leg with one sneakered foot, looked up at me in apology, then flailed her feet some more. Their deck was larger than two normal decks combined. Siegfried occupied himself with calculations of chance, using a formula supposed to predict the outcome of the game. His brow creased slightly while he watched the game progress, shaking his head in frustration as his sister's pile of cards grew taller and his dwindled to a skimpy pack.

My parents sat on the faded brown couch beneath the porch windows, listening to the radio. Dad's thick black hair was slicked back from his forehead following his usual after dinner dip in the lake. He'd changed into gray slacks and a black and white short-sleeved knit shirt. My mother wore the sundress she had on earlier, but added a white ribbed sweater over her shoulders. She folded her hands neatly in her lap and leaned her head on my father's shoulder. Perry Como's silky voice filled the air, crooning a romantic tune. She flashed a smile at me and I smiled back.

Outside on the porch, William and the waitresses played ping-pong and drank Coca Cola. They'd turned their transistor radio to a respectful volume, but I could still hear snatches of *Yesterday's Gone* by Chad and Jeremy as the music drifted in and out of the open windows.

Earlier in the evening, Oscar had popped his head into the room to invite the occupants to a special slide show he planned to give Wednesday evening. The group all agreed it would be a nice change and arranged to convene at seven P.M. the day after next.

Grandpa spluttered when he lost a big hand. He ran his hands through his hair with agitation and muttered under his breath, tipping back in his chair. My grandmother watched him closely. Two dollars was the maximum bet allowed. By the way she watched him, I knew Grandpa had been in trouble before. I heard my parents whisper about the time he lost fifty dollars in a game. From that point on, my grandmother sat in her chair, watching. She never said a word. She didn't have to.

At the stroke of eight, the news program began. My father leaned over and turned up the volume. He followed world events religiously, always hungry for new tidbits of information about the country and its state of affairs.

"Nelson Mandela, advocator of non-violent resistance to apartheid, has been sentenced to life in prison in South Africa."

My father and mother bolted straight up and listened intently as the newscaster nonchalantly discussed the sentence and played several sound bytes from outraged world citizens.

"Communist China has detonated its first atomic bomb."

The poker game stopped. All five men at the table turned in their seats to listen to the cursory description of the frightening subject. After several minutes of discussion, the Boston newscaster finally turned to local news.

"WBZ just learned that St. Stephen's church in the North End has been ransacked and robbed. A number of valuable religious artifacts were stolen, along with the bell from the church tower cast by none other than Paul Revere. The stolen goods are valued at over two hundred and fifty thousand dollars. This is the second assault on church property in the last month. St. Patrick's cathedral in New York City continues to mourn the loss of its gold artifacts and a rare marble statue of the Virgin Mary."

A few quotes from shocked neighbors were broadcast, followed by the weather report for New England.

My parents shook their heads in dismay, sighed in unison, and rose from the couch, motioning for me to follow. The twins jumped up too, knowing their curfew paralleled mine. They raced ahead of us over the dark path, leaping over each memorized root like antelopes fleeing a predator. They rapidly dissolved into the dark night.

Light shone from the windows of Number Fifteen, silhouetting the shape of the Cheshire cat. The lady in mourning rocked on her darkened porch. Just as I walked under one of the overhead path lights, I turned to her and waved. She lifted a hand and waved back with little enthusiasm.

I walked behind my parents, trying to digest the events of the day. The atomic bomb scared me. I remembered the drills in school when we crouched beneath our desks and wondered where we'd hide if it hit tonight. Under the kitchen table? In a doorway? Glancing up at the starry night sky, I imagined the horror of a missile flying overhead, heading for Boston or New York. My thoughts of destruction were interrupted when my parents suddenly stopped and sat on the Wee Castle porch steps. My mother slid sideways and patted the space between them.

"Honey? Sit down right here. We have something to tell you."

I looked from my mother to my father and back again as my mind reeled in a thousand directions. I couldn't see their expressions in the dark, and wondered why they were taking so long to tell me whatever it was. Fear of the dreaded word "divorce" raced along my spine, but I quickly suppressed it, praying that the thought was ridiculous.

"We'd planned to make the announcement in the living room, but after that newscast it just didn't seem appropriate," my father said.

Why is he being so mysterious?

"Announce what?" I asked. A sick feeling invaded my stomach.

My mother leaned over and grabbed my hands in hers.

"You're going to be a big brother. We're going to have a baby."

I slumped on the step in stunned silence.

"Son? Aren't you happy for us?" my father asked after several uncomfortable moments.

I shook myself from a state of shock and forced myself to answer.

Good Grief.

A baby.

"Um... yeah. That's great. Um... congratulations. Will it be a boy or a girl?"

My father answered.

"Well, we won't know until he or she is born, son. But it'll be kind of a Christmas present. The baby's due December 20th."

They both leaned over and hugged me, and I hugged them back, trying to act normal in spite of the enormously disturbing fact staring me in the face.

My parents had done *that* together. It was too disgusting to contemplate, so I shoved the thought way back into my subconscious and jumped up to let Shadow out the screen door. He trotted toward the woods and lifted his leg against a fern, then galloped back and followed us indoors as we prepared for bed.

Twenty-nine

The police investigator showed up at camp early the next morning. I'd eaten breakfast and just finished refilling the water bucket for the bathroom when my grandfather arrived with Officer Lawson. As my grandfather headed back to the kitchen to cook for the masses, Dad took over and ushered the policeman to the Marggranders' cabin so Officer Lawson could interview us together.

Elsbeth was painting in a coloring book on the porch. It was one of the newer types that called for a paintbrush and plain water. When moistened, the paper miraculously turned to a pre-selected color. She was halfway through a picture of a woodland fairy hovering over a toadstool. My father introduced Officer Lawson to Mrs. Marggrander and the twins, and Mrs. Marggrander offered her cabin for the interview. Dad sat in the far corner, to allow the officer time with us, but stayed near in case I needed him.

Elsbeth, Siegfried and I sat on the couch. The officer chose an armchair facing us. Mrs. Marggrander smiled and offered coffee to the men, who both accepted. She busied herself in the kitchen when the interview began.

"So, children... I heard you had quite an adventure the other night when your boat went down."

We nodded. I was thrilled someone was *finally* talking to us, and imagined myself in an episode of Perry Mason.

Officer Lawson settled more comfortably in the chair and flipped open a notebook. He took a pencil from his jacket pocket and began to take notes.

"Can you remember what time you saw the girl?"

I spoke up, surprised at the squeaky tone of my voice.

"It was Friday night, sir. We hit Big Blue around six, and were lost in the water for a good three hours. It was dark by the time we finally made it to shore."

Siegfried cleared his throat.

"*Ja*. We saw the girl and the man who chased her, then ran about ten minutes to the campground store. We got there at nine-thirty."

Elsbeth nodded vigorously, agreeing to his observations. Officer Lawson made some more notes, saying,

"So… it was about nine-fifteen or nine-twenty when you saw them?"

We nodded as one. He wrote for a moment, then studied us, one by one.

"Can you tell me what she was doing? How about you, Elsbeth? What did you see?"

Elsbeth shuddered and looked at her brother for support.

"Well, she was running away from the man. She was scared. Her face was messed up. You know, bleeding."

I nodded in agreement and offered my own observations.

"It was her mouth. It looked like she'd been hit in the mouth and blood was running down from her lip."

My voice cracked as I remembered the awful sight. Sharon's face had played in my dreams and subconscious since we nearly collided in the foggy woods.

"I'd like you to carefully describe the man you saw, kids. Starting with you, please."

He nodded to Elsbeth. Her eyes widened. She sat up straighter at the table and swallowed before she spoke.

"Well… he was scary. His face and his voice were very angry. He had messy hair…" She thought for a few more seconds, then added, "…and a ripped shirt."

The officer nodded politely, thanking her. He turned to me next.

"Gus? Can you add to that? How about height, weight, coloring?"

I closed my eyes and pictured the man I'd seen chasing Sharon, unloading bolts of wool from the trunk of the car, and storming out of the office at the mill.

"He was tall," I began as I looked at my father, "taller than Dad by at least two inches. He was heavy, too. His middle stuck out over his belt, it was sort of a beer belly."

I closed my eyes for a minute and summoned up the face, then added, "His eyes were kinda squinty. Looked like he needed glasses or something. And he smelled really bad… like… rotten fish and whisky."

My father nodded to me from his chair in the corner, pleased with my description. I'd clearly eliminated Sharon's father as the suspect.

Officer Lawson turned to Siegfried.

"Can you add anything to this, young man?"

Siegfried focused on the officer with analytical clear blue eyes.

"Yes, sir. The man had a cruel mouth and a deep voice. It was lower than most men's by at least an octave. He ran awkwardly, as if he could barely keep his balance. I believe he was inebriated."

Officer Lawson raised his eyebrows and glanced at Mrs. Marggrander, surprised at Siegfried's succinct description. Siegfried's genius was commonplace in our lives, so we barely noticed. Lawson collected himself and scribbled in the book again.

"Okay, then. Gus? Your father said you saw the same man again at the mill, is that correct? Are you sure it was the same one, son?"

I looked at my father, who encouraged me with a slight nod of his head.

"Yes, sir. It was the same man. My father said it was Frank Adamski, Sharon's uncle. He was yelling at Mr. Adamski in the office. I'm positive it was the same guy."

Officer Lawson crossed one leg over the other and leaned forward slightly, looking at me.

"Your dad tells me you think you've seen Sharon in the woods, Gus. Would you be willing to show me where you saw her? Could you find the place again?"

I nodded quickly, relieved that someone was finally listening.

"Yes, sir. We've marked the spot. We've left food several times, and it's been gone by the next morning."

He nodded and looked hard at me.

"Have you actually *seen* her, Gus? I mean, really seen her close up, since that first night?"

I hesitated, and looked at Siegfried and Elsbeth. I'd been the only one to see something flash white in the forest. It seemed to be running away from me and I hadn't actually seen a person, just a glimpse. I explained it to the officer.

After several more turns each, Officer Lawson closed his notebook and stood up. He finished the coffee and thanked Mrs. Marggrander for her hospitality.

Before he left, he asked one more question.

"You're quite sure Sharon was running *away from Frank Adamski*? There's no doubt about it?"

Siegfried answered for us.

"Sir, the girl was frightened for her life, and the man looked as if he'd kill her if he caught her."

The import of his words created a hush. A mayfly landed on the screen door and rubbed his wings together, making a soft fluttering sound. I shifted on the plaid fabric of the couch cushions, uncomfortable with the image thrust into my head. My father set his coffee cup down on the side table with a clunk and rose from the armchair.

Officer Lawson followed suit, tucking his notebook into his shirt pocket. He ran his hand through thinning blond hair and put his cap back on.

"Thank you. You've been very helpful. We'll come back later today to take a look at the boulder, okay? I've got some work I need to finish first, then we'd like to head out to the woods with you. How's four o'clock?"

I nodded seriously; still troubled by the visions that Siegfried's observation had brought to mind. My father came to my side and put his arm around my shoulders.

"Four o'clock will be just fine, Officer. We'll be ready."

Thirty

My father walked Officer Lawson to the door and accompanied him up the hill to his car. Mrs. Marggrander turned to us and clapped her hands.

"Well. Enough of this awful topic. I have something wonderful to share with you."

Elsbeth and Siegfried watched her in surprise as she walked to the small desk in the corner and opened one of the side drawers. She withdrew a brown paper package wrapped in twine, covered in multicolored stamps and unfamiliar markings. Settling into the same chair Officer Lawson used, she cut the string with a small pair of scissors. After removing the wrapping, she opened the box and pulled out the crumpled newspapers. Finally, she took a letter from the top of the box, and handed it to Siegfried.

"Would you like to translate for us, *mein Sohn?* (my son?)"

Elsbeth sat up in interest.

"Is it from Germany, Mama? From Aunt Frieda?"

"Yes. It's from Aunt Frieda. Go ahead and read it, Siegfried. *Langsame, bitte* (slowly, please), so that we can enjoy every word."

Frieda Hirsch discussed life in the small village of Denkendorf, West Germany. The cramped spidery writing covered four pages of pale blue airmail stationery. We learned about Frieda's flower gardens, church activities, and her son Eberhardt's progress in the academy.

As Siegfried continued to read, Mrs. Marggrander opened the box and withdrew several bars of chocolate. Laughing, she unwrapped one of the lavender wrappers and broke off pieces, doling them out to us. The word, "Milka" sprawled in large white letters on the label beside a lavender and white cow. The chocolate was unlike any I'd ever tasted. It melted into a creamy confection that transported me to Heaven and back. As we listened to the letter, I longed to taste one more square.

As if reading my mind, Mrs. Marggrander broke off another piece for each of us while Siegfried flipped over the last page of the letter. The newsy tone darkened as Frieda discussed the passing of a woman named Audhilde Mauritz.

Mrs. Marggrander dropped a half-eaten piece of chocolate and grew silent. Her eyes filled with tears that puddled and overflowed. Siegfried stood, rested his hands on her shoulders, and murmured comforting words in German. Finally, she spluttered in German to the twins and buried her head in her hands. I sat mute, wondering what the connection was between Mrs. Marggrander and Audhilde Mauritz.

Mr. Marggrander stomped up the porch steps carrying two brown paper bags full of groceries. He dropped them on the couch and rushed to his wife's side, pushing past Siegfried, who moved back to the couch beside me.

"What's going on, Sig? Who was she?" I whispered.

Mr. Marggrander helped his wife stand and walked her toward the bedroom. She began to sob in earnest when he closed the door behind them.

Siegfried and Elsbeth froze. I looked from one to the other, hoping for an explanation.

Elsbeth looked at me first, then at her parents' bedroom door. She lowered her voice.

"She was my mother's best friend in the camps. They both lost their families in Buchenwald and became like sisters. She died from an accident last week, and left three children behind."

I looked toward the door and listened to the mournful sobs coming from the bedroom, wishing I could help, but knowing there was nothing I could do.

Although she'd been released from the camps over nineteen years ago, the memories often tortured Brigit Marggrander. On good days, she would talk endlessly about her family and life in the concentration camp, trying to assure that no one would ever forget those lost and the enormity of the atrocities. Although I realized later that she watered down the description of the violence for the sake of our tender souls, I never forgot her face when she described the horrors and I constantly wondered how such an event could have taken place in our modern world.

Thirty-one

Shadow's frenetic baying roused us. Elsbeth and I exchanged a surprised look and ran outside to see what had driven the beagle to such a state. We stood on the porch, shading our eyes against the strong mid-morning sun. Shadow flashed past us, racing along the shore. He howled and dashed after a water-skier being towed past the docks.

"Come on," I said. I hastened after him, beckoning the twins to follow.

The dog was going bonkers. When the boat turned at the end of the cove and pulled the skier back toward camp, Shadow appeared again, racing back along the shore. He yipped and ran as fast as his short legs would carry him. He didn't stop, but ran past us, oblivious to our shouts.

"Shadow!" I hollered. He continued with the frenzied chase. His tail whipped back and forth, his legs blurred in motion, and he zoomed out of sight.

Shrugging, I beckoned the twins toward the living room porch. We settled on the glider and watched the action for a half hour. Finally, the boat slowed and the woman sank into the lake, releasing her skis and handing them over the side of the boat to her husband. I recognized the couple as the newlyweds who rented the cabin the Murphys had vacated. Shadow trotted toward me, tongue lolling and foam flecked along his jaw. His eyes shone with pure joy as he snuffled against my ankles and stood still for what he probably thought were congratulatory pats. After circling around a few times, he fell into a deep, exhausted sleep at my feet.

William rounded the corner. We squeezed together to make room. He flopped heavily onto the glider, stretched out his long legs, and released a long sigh.

"I'm sick and tired of being bossed around," he said. His eyes narrowed atop a petulant expression.

I exchanged worried glances with the twins.

"What's wrong?" Elsbeth asked in her little girl voice.

He snorted, jumped up, and stomped to the red and silver Coca Cola machine. Digging in his pocket, he found a nickel, pushed it into the slot, and stabbed at the button.

"Oh, nothin' really. They've just been workin' me like a dog all morning. I've been hauling suitcases, moving kitchen supplies, chopping firewood, and washing pots and pans. I'm pooped."

He positioned the bottle under the cap remover. With a practiced flick of the wrist, the metal cap flew off and he lifted the soda to his lips, draining half of it in seconds.

We watched him enviously. Our eyes followed his hand as he finished it. He tipped it up to get the last few drops, then placed it in the rack of empties beside the machine.

"You kids thirsty?" he asked matter-of-factly.

We nodded eagerly and he pulled out three more nickels.

"It's on me today, kids. And by the way, I have something for you to try."

We gathered around, holding out our hands. I let Elsbeth and Siegfried go first, standing behind them while I listened to the wonderful clink-clink of the coins tumbling down the chute and the resounding thunk of the bottles when they dropped into the bottom of the machine.

After we'd opened our drinks, we settled back on the glider, thirstily lifting the thick green glass to our lips. I felt the worn, recycled glass against my tongue, savoring the taste of the beverage as it bubbled down my throat.

William reached into his other pocket and took out a small yellow tin of Bayer aspirin. He looked around furtively, then squatted in front of us, lowering his voice to a conspiratorial level.

"You kids wanna get high?"

We looked at him blankly. He tried again.

"You know, wanna feel kinda wild? Wanna fly to the moon?"

It sounded interesting, but I was completely confused.

"What do you mean?" Siegfried asked.

William popped open the tin of aspirin and moved closer to us.

"Add some aspirin to your coke and you'll go on a trip," he whispered, fingering an aspirin. "Who's up for it?"

Siegfried shook his head.

"No thanks," he said. He turned away and took a sip.

Elsbeth looked at her twin and did the same, shaking her head. "No way. Not me."

"What about you, big guy?" William said, leaning closer. "It's the latest rage. It won't hurt you, it'll just make you feel kinda silly."

I remained silent, evaluating my options. If I said yes, I'd betray the twins. If I said no, I'd look timorous in front of William.

"What's the matter, ya scared?" he taunted.

That pushed me over the edge.

"No," I said firmly. "I'm not scared. Go ahead. Do it."

I held out my bottle. He dropped the aspirin into it. It fizzed for a few moments as it dissolved. My grandmother came around the corner seconds after William snapped shut the container and slid it back into his pocket.

"There you are, William. I've been looking all over for you. We have a new arrival."

William straightened and looked at my grandmother with a guilty smile. "Okay. Coming."

"Come on, son. Chop, chop. It's a big family and they need help with their bags."

He nodded and sprinted toward the steps. With a long-legged leap, he flew into the air and landed in the sandy dirt. Barely breaking stride, he churned in a full gallop up the hill. She dusted her hands together as if having finished a satisfying chore, smiled at us, and followed William up the hill to the office.

I studied the contents of my Coke bottle. It didn't look different. I lifted it in the air and swirled it around.

"Are you gonna drink it?" Elsbeth asked.

Her brown eyes opened wide in concern as she turned toward me, pushing a wayward lock of curls back over her ear. I noticed her dark lower lashes fluttering upon the creamy skin of her cheeks. She was actually very pretty and I shocked myself by noticing. She cocked her head and pursed her ribbon-curved lips, pushing them out in a fluid motion.

"Gus? Aren't you scared?" She tapped the back of my hand.

Siegfried sat still, studying me. I wondered if he were calculating the odds of my decision. Chances of boy choosing reckless danger over safety. His vivid blue eyes bored into mine.

I lifted the bottle to my face and sniffed. It smelled like Coke.

I tilted the bottle and took a sip.

I didn't feel a thing. Disappointed, I took another drink, longer this time. Nothing. Shrugging, I chugged it. Besides a slightly gritty taste at the end of the bottle, it tasted normal.

The twins watched me carefully as I downed the last few drops. I tried to imagine what I was supposed to feel, and came up with nothing. Would I see swirling colors, feel dizzy? Would my vision become distorted? I sat for several minutes, waiting for it to happen. I stood up and felt a little lightheaded, then grabbed Siegfried's arm when I lost my balance.

"Gus!" whispered Siegfried fiercely. "Are you okay?"

I shook my head to clear it.

Probably my imagination.

Although I never took anything but the orange chewable aspirin, I'd seen my mother swallow two aspirin tablets with a glass of water off and on for years. They made her headaches go away, that was all.

I straightened and felt perfectly normal.

"Heck, it's probably just a joke. I'm just fine," I said to the twins as I dropped my empty in the rack and walked steadily toward the sundeck. "Come on. Let's do some sweeping."

Thirty-two

I swept the pine needles from the sun porch deck and thought about the news my parents delivered the night before.

I'm gonna have a little sister or brother.

Siegfried and Elsbeth moved in next door when I was five, and that was just about the best thing that could have happened to me in lieu of a natural brother or sister. I adopted them as my own siblings, and we'd been the Three Musketeers of Sullivan Hill ever since.

Four ladies sunbathed on the deck with their eyes closed. Some wore shorts and tops, others bathing suits. Mrs. Herring had been holding a reflector under her chin, but she fell asleep and it lay useless on her midriff. Magazines tumbled from the loosened grips of two ladies who'd also fallen asleep.

Is it the Maine air that zonked them out? Are they really asleep?

They seemed to be completely unaware of my presence. I picked up a slippery bottle of Coppertone suntan lotion and set it on the railing. Trying not to stir up dust clouds, I made an effort to sweep quietly while they dozed on the yellow webbed lounge chairs.

I worked methodically and began to think about the baby again. Would a little brother or sister affect my relationship with Siegfried and Elsbeth? Would I have to babysit instead of boating or swimming all summer? The child would be almost twelve years younger than me. When I was in college, he or she would be in first grade. I stopped and thought about how strange it would be to have a baby in our house. Would he move in with me, or would he get the spare room? I imagined my mother would redecorate the spare room with goofy baby stuff, and shook my head as I fervently wished it had never happened. I didn't *want* to share my parents with another child.

The twins lounged in deck chairs in the far corner. I'd indulged their sudden desire to rest and had taken the broom from Elsbeth's limp fingers. The Maine air seemed to be affecting them as well.

The sun burned the back of my neck as I pushed the broom over the floorboards, wiping the sweat from my brow with a shirtsleeve. When I finished, I approached the twins and propped the broom in the corner. I blocked Siegfried's sun, trying to will him to look at me. He lay shirtless in the sun with his cutoff jean shorts and sandals. His long brown legs stretched straight out, nearly touching the end of the lounge chair. A multitude of fine gold hairs glistened on his calves. I looked down and compared them to my own tan legs, examining the fawn colored soft hairs creeping up to my thighs and wondering when I'd start to get black hairs all over, like William.

After several seconds, he opened his eyes.

"Ready for a swim?" I asked.

He nodded and closed his eyes again. Elsbeth unfurled from her comfortable position and stretched her arms toward the sky.

"Can I have the first turn on the rope swing?"

She looked drowsy and innocent when she asked. I felt a pang of affection for her and decided to be magnanimous.

"Okay, squirt. You can go first. But it's 'May I', not 'Can I'. Haven't I taught you proper English?"

I sounded like my father and almost laughed out loud at my ludicrous tone of voice. To minimize the impact, I leaned over and held out my hand. She took it and pulled herself to her feet, smiling.

"Okay, okay. But one of these days I'm going to teach you proper German."

Siegfried sat up, rubbing his eyes with his fists. He began to speak in his native language, but quickly corrected himself and switched back to English.

"I dreamt about Candy Land. It felt *so* real. Lollypop trees and licorice growing out of the ground. Rock candy as big as that boulder," he said as he motioned toward the large granite rock under the trees. "We climbed on it and it sparkled like a diamond."

He sat up and drew his knees to his chin. Running a hand through his shaggy locks, his eyes sparkled.

"Keen," Elsbeth said.

"Neat," I said, imagining the slippery feel of a giant crystal boulder that tasted like sugar.

After a few minutes, both twins stood up and we headed toward our cabins. By the time we passed the living room, we were pounding along the porch boards in an easy sprint.

I ran in the lead and leapt from the top of the porch to the ground. Although I'd done it a hundred times already that summer, my foot slipped and I fell hard. My knee scraped along a pine root, splitting the skin on my kneecap. Excruciating pain shot through my leg.

I sat on the ground and examined the wound.

"Atch. Oh, man. Atch." I said through gritted teeth.

The slang "atch" had replaced "Ow" several years ago, becoming the cooler, more mature way to express pain. I leaned over and blew on my scraped knee. The blood pooled up along the split in my skin.

Elsbeth looked in horror at the laceration, covering her mouth with her hand. Siegfried leaned over to help me up. I placed my arms over his shoulders and he helped me hop back to the cabin. The guest in Number Fifteen drew back the curtains in the window and watched as I hobbled along. I waved to her to assure her I was all right. She waved back, this time with more animation.

Once inside, I realized both of my parents were gone. Dad had left to help my grandfather prepare for the lunch crowd, and my mother was doing some of our laundry in the icehouse. Elsbeth took a handful of Vanity Fair paper napkins from the cabinet and wet them under the faucet. She handed them to me while I stood beside the kitchen chair with my knee up and my foot on the seat. I dabbed the knee gently, wiping away some of the dirt and blood.

Something about the incident sparked a memory in my subconscious. It had been in a movie. Something about blood brothers... It was a ritual that bound friends together for life.

I looked back and forth at the twins.

"We should become blood brothers," I said.

Elsbeth looked at me dubiously. Siegfried's eyes lit up.

"*Ja.* Blood brothers," he said, warming to the topic.

Elsbeth suddenly understood. She lifted her right arm, examining a scabbed-over mosquito bite. She began to pick at it until a little prick of blood bubbled to the surface.

Siegfried found a scrape on his own forearm and followed her example.

"Easy now," I cautioned as they pressed their small wounds gently against my sore knee.

"Now spit on it and rub it around to mix the blood," I said.

To complete the triad, they touched their own blood together in spite of the fact that they were already genetically bound. We held hands and bowed our heads.

Siegfried began to chant.

"This ceremony binds us as blood brothers for life. We will be lifelong friends until the day we die."

Elsbeth added, "Until the day we die. Amen."

We lowered our hands and nodded solemnly to each other. I finally sat down on the chair, and dabbed at the cut again with the wet wad of napkins.

"It's stopping now," I said, relieved I wouldn't need a Band-Aid. It would just fall off when we went swimming, anyway.

We agreed to meet at the rope swing in five minutes.

Thirty-three

After changing into my swimsuit, I bolted back to the living room just in time to see Elsbeth wrap her petite hands around the rope and swing out over the water. She dropped into the lake with a splash, was submerged for several seconds, then popped to the surface. She swam back to the ladder on the side of the dock.

I dropped from the side of the porch onto the boulder next to Siegfried, who caught the rope on its return swing and generously handed it to me.

"Go ahead, Gus. Take a turn."

I grinned.

"Thanks, pal."

I stood on the sun-warmed boulder in bare feet and looked over the lake as the wind freshened, causing waves to ripple on the surface. The rope was thick and the hemp fibers bristled between my fingers. I gripped it above a large knot and pushed off, flying through the air, shouting, "Geronimo!" The sensation was stomach-twistingly delicious.

I pinched my nose shut and let go of the rope, dropping into the lake with a huge splash. It had taken me several tries last summer to perfect the move.

The water rushed around me, roaring in my ears and shooting hundreds of bubbles up in a rising flurry of yellow and green froth. My feet touched the soft sand and I pushed back up to the surface, exhilarated.

Siegfried shouted, "Watch out below!"

I stroked quickly away from his imminent touchdown.

He landed three feet from me. The waves bobbled and I floated beside a boiling circle of water that marked his entry. Within seconds, his head appeared and he grinned at me.

"How many points if I had landed on you, Gus?"

I skimmed water toward his face and laughed when he returned the favor. We both decided to swim back to the boulder on shore, instead of climbing up the ladder. I arrived first and stepped onto a submerged rock to access to the hill. I shot my hand out to balance on the smooth bark of white birches swaying over the lake. A taller pine supported the rope swing. Elsbeth sailed over my head. I quickly climbed the staircase of warm boulders, then reached up and grabbed the rope on its return swing, ready for my second turn.

We jumped and swam until lunchtime, then scattered to our cabins to rejoin our families. I imagined Siegfried and Elsbeth had a more trying time than I did, although I suffered through discussions of baby names until I thought I'd throw up.

Nicole, Anna, Pamela, Loretta, Sylvia.

John, Raymond, Maxwell, Wayne, Richard.

I chewed miserably through my tuna sandwich until my mother rose and returned from the kitchen with a hot pan filled with chocolate pudding.

"I made this 'specially for you, honey," she said, spooning the pudding into three glass dishes.

I looked at her in surprise. Dessert at lunch was a rare treat.

"Why?" I asked.

She smiled at me and took her place at the table, blowing across a steaming spoonful of pudding.

"Well, I just want you to know that you'll always be special to me. Having this new baby won't change that one little bit."

I glanced at her, hoping she hadn't sensed my small-minded thoughts of jealously. The guilt slid down my throat along with the hot pudding. It landed in my stomach and pooled as I mentally kicked myself for thinking bad tempered thoughts about the baby-to-be. I smiled weakly at my parents and almost lifted the dish to lick it, then thought better of it and carried my dishes to the kitchen.

To salve my guilt-ridden soul, I began to wash the dishes. Both parents followed me into the kitchen, bringing their dishes to the sink. They exchanged surprised glances.

My father frowned. "Gus? Is everything okay?"

I swirled some soap in my glass and finally looked up at him.

"Yeah, Dad. I just thought I should get used to helping out around here, what with the new baby coming and all."

My mother remained shocked. She returned the milk to the Frigidaire and gently closed the door.

"That's very nice of you, honey."

I smiled and relaxed, feeling much better about my villainous thoughts. Maybe it wouldn't be so bad, after all.

Thirty-four

Officer Lawson returned at four o'clock as promised. The twins and I had just finished digging a large pail full of worms from the dirt pile behind the icehouse. After covering it with moss, we stowed it beneath the sundeck to keep it cool for the evening fishermen, then joined Officer Lawson in Grandfather's boat and headed for the west shore of the lake.

My father and I sat in the back. He handled the boat as easily as he drove a car or cast a line. It was second nature, since he'd grown up on the lake. Elsbeth and Siegfried perched side-by-side in the middle seat, and Lawson took the bow. The boat wallowed low in the water from the additional weight of two grown men. I reached my hand over the side to trail my fingers in the tepid water as the boat skimmed across the lake.

When we beached, we pulled the skiff onto the shore and followed Siegfried and Elsbeth toward Sharon's rock. Officer Lawson trailed after the twins, my father followed next, and I took the rear. A prickly sense of excitement tripped down my spine as I marched behind them. Something monumental was about to happen, and I guessed it would be the rescue of Sharon Adamski. I was certain we'd find her today.

When we reached the boulder, Elsbeth shrieked. "The fruit is gone! She was here again."

She grabbed Officer Lawson's hand and pulled him toward it, gesturing toward the rock.

"I left apples and bananas right here, Officer Lawson. See? They're gone."

Lawson looked left and right and then held out his hand to stop us as we congregated around the rock.

"Hold on one minute now, we might be able to get some footprints to find out who's been taking this food."

We stopped short and backed up. I studied the pine needles covering the ground, wondering if he'd be able to learn anything. I assumed our own footprints from the past several days were everywhere, since we'd traipsed around while we hollered for Sharon and ate our lunch.

Officer Lawson bent down and examined the ground, the boulder, and the trees and bushes in the surrounding area. My father walked beside him, pointing out several tracks he recognized as black bear cub footprints.

The twins sat on a clump of moss while Elsbeth hummed "Can't Buy Me Love" and Siegfried carefully observed the investigation. His bright blue eyes flicked back and forth as he analyzed each move. After five minutes, I became bored and decided to climb a towering oak near the boulder. The truth dawned when I realized I might be able to spot Sharon from the top of the tree. My father and Officer Lawson stooped over a set of animal tracks as I began my swift ascent to the top. Hand over hand, I moved toward the sky. I leaned back against the bark as I looped my right arm around a particularly good limb. I wasn't above the tallest treetops, but I could see for quite a distance. The lake glimmered on the horizon. Twittering came from a red tailed hawk's nest in the next tree over. The mother hawk rose up in her nest and flapped her enormous wings several times, peering at me with sharp eyes.

"It's okay, girl. I won't hurt your babies."

I glanced around the forest, looking for some sign of Sharon.

A flash of white whisked through the trees in the distance. It moved across the forest floor, flickering beneath the dense branches. I couldn't make out the shape, but it moved as a human would move. Galvanized into action, I clambered down the tree, yelling to my father and Officer Lawson. I fell from the last branch onto a clump of ferns.

"Dad! I saw her. She's over there," I screamed. I began to run toward Sharon.

Officer Lawson grabbed me by the shoulders and peered into my face.

"What did you see?" he asked firmly.

"I climbed that tree and saw something white again, it was running in that direction. It wasn't too far from us. Hurry! We might lose her," I cried.

"You kids stay here," my father said. He and Officer Lawson loped into the woods. The twins leapt to their feet and looked at me in wonder.

"Did you see her? Was it really Sharon?"

My heart thumped hard. I nodded, watching the men melt into the woods. I hoped that they wouldn't frighten her into bolting further from us.

"I think so. It was just like before. Someone in white… running… I caught glimpses from up there."

I pointed to the tree. Suddenly both of the twins raced toward the oak and climbed like monkeys to the top. Elsbeth followed Siegfried. I remained on the ground below, peering into the woods, hoping for a sign of Sharon.

Siegfried shouted from the top of the tree, his voice infused with excitement.

"Over there, Gus. I see something. Over there! It's running that way," he cried.

I peered through the blinding sunlight and could barely see his skinny arm gesturing in the air. It was about thirty degrees off from the direction in which I'd sent my father and Officer Lawson. She must have darted sideways in her attempt to avoid them. I wished that I could tell her we weren't here to hurt her.

I set my sight on a particularly tall pine that lined up with Siegfried's flailing arm and ran toward it at full speed.

The twins yelled from the treetop, telling me to veer to the right. I turned right and leapt over a thick bush, plunging through the woods at breakneck speed.

After racing for a few minutes, I began to tire. The sound of the twins' voices dimmed as I forged ahead, hoping I'd maintained a true direction. Just as I rounded a clump of decaying birch trees, a flash of white filled my vision and something reached out from behind a thick tree trunk to grab me around the middle.

A hand clamped hard over my mouth. I struggled against my attacker, kicking and yelling. I beat him with my fists and squirmed to get out of his iron grip. My feet were lifted off the ground. I nearly blacked out as the creature wrapped a large hand around my neck. A rough burlap bag was pulled over my head. I continued to struggle and writhe against the strong arms that squeezed my throat and chest. I screamed, calling my father as I sucked air through the bristly burlap. The monster's hand went back over my mouth again, pressing the awful burlap into my lips and teeth.

"Shaddup," he hissed. "Shaddup or you're dead."

The voice was low and gravelly. I smelled the whisky on his breath.

Frank Adamski.

I heard his belt being unbuckled and felt a chill as he whipped the belt out of his pants.

Is he going to flog me?

My breath quickened. He drew my hands together roughly and tightened the belt.

"Bringin' the cops around. Just great. You kids were bad enough, now I have to deal with that idiot Lawson," he grumbled, towing me through the woods.

I stumbled as he half-carried/half-dragged me behind him. Smothered with rough fabric, I struggled to breathe. I tried to go limp to encourage him to loosen his grip. Quieting my thrashing arms and legs, I submitted as he held me against his barrel chest.

Wild thoughts assaulted me. *If I could just slip from his arms and get the bag off my head, I might have a chance.*

Instead of loosening his hold, the monster suddenly lifted me across his shoulders and carried me like a ten-pound sack of potatoes. Humiliated, my fear foamed into anger while I fumed in the awkward position. The man's left arm was locked across the back of my knees. He started to run. I bounced up and down on his shoulder, jostled around until nausea threatened. I twisted my hands, trying to loosen them from the belt. It didn't help. Raising my hands to my face, I tried to push the bag up so that I could see. I was only partially successful, and caught a glimpse of the back of the man's legs and shoes as he ran along through the woods. Except for the sounds of his crashing feet, it was absolutely silent, and the much hoped-for sound of my father's voice was not to be heard.

Thirty-five

Frank Adamski dumped me on the floor of the old shack, slammed the door shut, and threw the bolt. I lay in a heap. My shoulder smarted where I'd taken the brunt of the fall and I could just see out the bottom of the hood. I lay still, watching him as he paced around the cabin. He fastened long dark curtains across the open window frames. They were wool, cut from the bolts that William and I had seen hidden beneath the floorboards on Sunday evening. Adamski pressed them onto nails hammered above the windowsills. The room darkened. I shivered on the hard, musty floor and pondered my fate.

Will he kill me?

I shuddered again.

Had he done the same to Sharon?

I shifted onto my left side and watched him beneath the hem of the grain sack until he disappeared while rummaging along one of the wall shelves.

The smell of sulfur filled the air. Adamski walked around to my field of vision again and lit an oil lamp on the dusty table. Several empty bottles of whisky shone in the eerie glow. Next to the empty bottles was a bunch of bananas and four small apples.

I froze. My breath caught in my throat. Staring at the produce on the table, I recognized the bag and the small, penciled note laying crumpled beside it. Blood roared through my ears and I nearly shouted when I realized that Frank Adamski had taken our offerings for Sharon since the first day I chased "her" through the forest.

I shivered and thought back to the day I'd seen the flash of white.

Had it been Sharon? Was she still alive?

Or had this drunken ogre been following us all along, waiting for the right moment to pounce on us?

Had he seen us that night? Did he know we witnessed the chase?

Perhaps he heard from the police reports that we were involved. After all, the police were in constant contact with Sharon's father after her disappearance. A feeling of cold dread slid into the pit of my stomach, spitting like grease on a grill.

Frank reached across the table to a fresh bottle, ripped the seal from the neck, and unscrewed the cap. He muttered as he walked around, swearing and tilting the bottle to his lips.

"Can't leave a witness," he rasped. "Gotta get rid of these stinkin' kids."

He continued to drink until his eyes gleamed with a dull black luster. He ran his fingers over the stubble on his chin and leaned down, leering into my face. He expelled a cloud of noxious odors and barked a chilling laugh.

"Watchin' me, huh, kid?" he laughed, sliding the bag off of my head. "Go ahead and take one last look around you, you meddling little crap shooter."

Cold sweat trickled along my brow. My stomach bucked.

"I think I'm gonna throw up," I said in a shaky voice.

My response startled him. He stopped dead and strode purposefully to me.

"No time for that, kid."

He jerked my tethered arms and dragged me across the rough floorboards toward an old metal cot in the corner. In one swift motion, he flung the thin mattress off the bed. A musty aroma filled the air as it flew across the cabin. He reached down and unbuckled the belt from my wrists. Before I could pull back and try for the door, he clamped one huge hand around my arms and re-buckled the belt through the bed frame.

While I struggled, he spun and walked to the secret panel in the floor. He lifted the loose floorboard and drew out his toolbox and a bolt of the fabric. Slowly, he unraveled the dark material, tossing it aside in an untidy heap. A long thin cavity had been carved into the centerboard.

Reaching under his white tee shirt, Adamski pulled hard on one end of a strip of adhesive tape. He gasped when a clump of black hair ripped from his chest. A foot-long scepter sparkled in the light. He placed it in the cavity and began to rewind the wool on the cardboard center.

"Where did you get that?" I asked.

He tilted his head. "Nice, huh? It'll fetch me a pretty penny in Europe. Those fools up at St. Martin's won't even miss it 'til next Sunday."

He hefted the woolen bolt under one arm, picked up the toolbox, and glowered at me.

"You shoulda minded your own business, you little weasel."

I watched as he drew back the dead bolt and opened the door.

Is he going to leave me here?

I became hopeful, realizing that in time I would be discovered by a search party or would be able to worm my way out of the belt holding me captive.

He sneered at me and twisted his face into an ugly grin.

"Oh no, you're not going to have time to get loose. You'll be burned up by then."

I watched in horror as he strode forward and purposefully tipped the oil lamp onto the mattress he'd doubled up against the side of the table. The flames licked hungrily at the dry cotton batting.

"See ya in Hell, little buddy."

He backed out the door, snickering.

I panicked. Twisting and writhing, I began to work at the belt locking me to the bed frame. My heart thumped hard against my ribs. I pushed and pulled, struggling frantically. The lashing was tight and held fast in spite of my gyrations. The fire had traveled up the table leg, and flickered onto one of the woolen curtains. Smoke filled the room, gagging me and making me cough.

Re-examining my bonds, I leaned over and began to work on the belt buckle with my teeth. I pushed hard against the thick leather end, trying to make it bulge up in the buckle. If I could move it slightly, then I could pull it with my teeth and yank on the loose end to release the metal prong from the hole.

It didn't budge. I tasted the thick leather on my tongue and fought against a feeling of desperation. My eyes watered from the smoke. I worked for several minutes with no success. The angle was wrong and I couldn't get a good grip.

The flames flew along the cabin wall in a sudden eruption as a bottle of kerosene exploded on the shelf. The fire traveled across the floorboards, moving toward the bed frame against which I writhed.

Realizing that my current tactics were useless, I began to drag the cot with me toward the window on the far side of the cabin. I pulled hard and found it could be dragged fairly easily. I reached the window and with my teeth and tethered hands, I pulled at the wool curtain. It came down in a heap around my feet. Smoke billowed out the opening. The fresh oxygen fanned the flames and revitalized the fire. It roared across the room toward me. I kicked the fabric away, trying to minimize the fuel for the hungry fire that worked its way toward me at a frightening speed.

I stuck my head out the window and screamed.

"Help! Help! Dad! Siegfried! I'm in here!"

I lifted the end of the rusty cot from the floorboards and tried to gauge its width. Could I drag it behind me out the window? I yelled again, and then began to panic in earnest as I felt the heat of the fire on my bare arms and face. It had traveled along the roof now, and would momentarily work its way down the wall. I lifted one leg to the windowless sill and straddled it. Moving quickly now, I threw my other leg over the sill. Both feet barely touched the ground and my upper body was still held fast to the end of the cot. I dragged it closer to the window and began to lift it, using every ounce of my remaining strength as hot tears spilled down my face. I pulled it nearly to the frame and was straining to twist the end so it would fit lengthwise in the opening, when the fire flared above me and began to burn the roof and the upper end of the windowsill.

Hysterical now, I screamed and pulled hard. The end of the cot stuck in the window frame and held fast. I looked up in horror. The flames licked the side of the cabin. I could barely breathe through the thick smoke and heat when I felt strong hands closing over my arms and loosening the belt buckle. I was dragged away from the inferno when the entire cabin became engulfed in flames. The roar of the fire filled the forest.

I looked up into the horrified face of my father, quickly surrounded by Officer Lawson and the twins. My father crushed me to his chest.

"My boy. My son."

I melted into the safety of my father's embrace, sobbing with relief. He patted my head and enfolded me in his strong arms.

In the distance, Officer Lawson barked into his radio, ordering airborne fire fighters and an ambulance. Just before I blacked out, I heard Siegfried telling him that the blueberry field was just up the trail, and that it would make an excellent spot for a rendezvous.

Thirty-six

On Wednesday morning, the day after the fire, I rubbed the spot on my arm punctured by the IV. A cloth Band-Aid anchored a cotton pad over the wound. It itched and pulled at my skin. We'd been in the emergency room all night and had finally been allowed to go home when the pediatrician arrived at seven A.M.

"Leave it alone, Gus," my mother cautioned as we wound our way over the bumpy dirt road to camp. "The nurse said to leave it on until tonight, remember, honey?"

I stopped picking at the edge of the Band-Aid and nodded, leaning back against the seat. I'd slept very little in the hospital. The oxygen mask I was forced to wear was uncomfortable, and the cries of the feverish infant in the bed beside me woke me throughout the night. My parents had taken turns sitting in the single chair beside my bed, never leaving my side.

I thought back to the day before, remembering the ride to the hospital. I woke up in the ambulance briefly. My father had crouched beside the cot, his hand gripping mine. His worried tone of voice and furrowed brow had distressed me. I wondered if I'd sustained life-threatening injuries as we sped along the back roads of Maine with the siren blasting.

Officer Lawson had come to ask questions after I was admitted, and scribbled furiously in his book while I recalled the awful adventure. I told him about Frank Adamski, about the fruit and the note, and about the golden scepter from St. Martin's he hid in the bolt of wool. Officer Lawson's eyes widened when I told him about the stolen item, and I wondered if it was reported missing yet. He told my father there was an intensive search in progress for the depraved man. By morning, we'd received no word of his capture, but passed a number of state troopers along the way to camp. The search was still in full force by the time we arrived at Loon Harbor.

My grandparents met us in the parking area and scrunched into the backseat to welcome me home.

"Well look who's here. It's our little hero," Grandpa said gently.

I got out feeling shaky, and stood under the tall pines, breathing in the fresh clean air and feeling very much *unlike* a hero. I still tasted soot on my tongue, and the acrid smell of smoke clung to my hair and skin.

My grandmother reached over and ruffled my hair.

"Are you okay, honey?" she asked.

I nodded, sensing the real threat of hot tears as my calamitous adventure roared back from my memory. I swallowed hard and looked down at the lake; the sun glistened and sparkled on the early morning surface.

"Yeah. I'm okay, Grandma," I said.

My voice sounded raspy. I cleared my throat and asked, "Where are the twins?"

Grandpa lifted his hand to his chin and squinted down toward their cabin.

"Guess they're still asleep, Gus. They were up pretty late waiting for news about you. They finally went to bed around midnight, I'd say. Wouldn't stop pestering us until we gave them the whole scoop."

A smile flitted across my face. Good old Siegfried and Elsbeth. What great friends. Comfort washed over me as I pictured them safe in their cabin, sleeping heavily.

"Everyone was concerned about you, honey. The Marggranders and the Stones spent the evening with us as we stayed by the phone. Even our guest in Number Fifteen came out to inquire about you. She wants to see you when you feel up to it."

I looked up in surprise.

"Honest?" I asked.

My grandmother smiled at me and smoothed her gray curls. Her green eyes sparkled when she exchanged glances with my mother.

"Honest. When you feel better, you can go over to say hello."

I felt honored. Being invited to trespass onto the previously forbidden territory appealed to me immensely. I'd been so curious about the woman and her Cheshire cat that my mood brightened.

My grandmother gave me an unusually long hug, smiled tremulously at my father, then slowly walked with my grandfather toward the dining room.

"I feel pretty good now, Mum. When can I visit her?"

My parents flanked me as we walked down the hill toward Wee Castle. I looked up at my mother expectantly. There were dark smudges beneath her eyes. She probably hadn't slept all night.

My father spoke up. "You need some sleep, first, Gus. We all do. Let's go down and get some rest, and then we'll see how you're feeling. Okay, sport?"

I glanced up into his tired eyes and nodded. He seemed worn out and his skin looked gray and drawn. A pang of guilt shot through me as I glanced back and forth between their tired faces.

"I'm sorry about all this. I really am."

A pair of mourning doves flew past and landed beneath the pines siding the trail. Their lavender-gray feathers looked invitingly soft. I had the sudden urge to stroke them. They strutted around, pecking at the ground, and then finally flew up to a branch overhead, sitting side by side. Their soft cooing wafted through the pines. My father slipped his arm through mine and squeezed my hand.

"It's not your fault, son. You did what you thought was right. But next time, wait for me before you go chasing someone in the woods, okay?"

I gazed at my heroic father. He saved my life. He plucked me from the horrible fate of being burned alive. My throat constricted, dry as a discarded snakeskin and I remembered the feeling of his hands grabbing me and pulling me from the burning building. I squeezed back and smiled at him. My mouth trembled.

"Okay, Dad. I will."

Thirty-seven

"He looks awful."

The whisper teased at my brain. I lay semi-conscious in my comfortable bed, with Shadow's warm body snuggled beside my feet. I nearly drifted back to sleep, but another whisper filtered through the fog.

"What's he doing? Move over. Let me take a look."

I coasted closer to consciousness, certain the second whisper was Siegfried's. My eyelids felt amazingly heavy, but I pried them open to slits. Elsbeth's pixie face pressed against the screen on the porch window. Her nose and lips compressed against the mesh. Siegfried squeezed in beside his sister, staring at me with concern.

"Ought-oh. I think we woke him up," Elsbeth said in a small voice.

My eyes fluttered open and I smiled at them, beckoning them inside. Elsbeth squealed and they raced around to the screen door. A short conversation took place between my father and my friends. Finally, the door opened and he announced the visitors.

"Someone to see you, son."

I sat up against my pillow and twisted my wrist around to glance at my Mickey Mouse watch. One-thirty. I couldn't believe I'd slept five hours.

They both climbed up on the bed. Elsbeth was the first to throw her arms around my neck. I thought she was going to cry and hoped fervently that she wouldn't. She gulped a few times and laid her head on my shoulder, then kissed my cheek with her soft lips.

"I'm glad you're okay. We were so worried," she said.

I blushed and lowered my eyes, feeling unusually awkward with one of my best friends. She backed up a little, surprised at her own actions. Siegfried circled my neck and pulled me forward, rubbing his knuckles against my scalp. I laughed and pulled away from his gentle grip.

"Noogies for the nerd," he said, repeating one of our favorite mantras.

I snorted a laugh, relieved to be back on familiar territory.

"You snorted!" Elsbeth giggled. Once again, the rhythm and tone of her laugh was identical to the song of the loons, the tremolo.

"You sound like a loon!" I teased, laughing even louder.

I snorted again and the guffawing began. It built to a crescendo. We gasped for breath as tears spilled down our cheeks. My stomach and sides began to ache and I lost total control. I couldn't stop chortling and doubled over, gulping and shrieking with my friends. My throat felt tight and the glands beneath my jaw began to ache. Each time we tried to stop, we'd look at each other and start up again. I foolishly mimicked Elsbeth's loon laugh, followed it up with a loud snort, and started them up all over again.

"Stop!" Elsbeth begged between shrieks. She rolled on the bed, holding her stomach. "I can't take any more!"

Shadow looked back and forth between us while we convulsed in laughter. He cocked his head to the side, trotted up to my pillow, and licked my cheek. His tail wagged furiously.

Finally the tumult died down. Elsbeth lay on her side at the foot of the bed, her head pillowed in her arms. Her sides still heaved and a grin blossomed across her face. Siegfried sprawled on the side of the bed catching his breath, his back to me. Finally he rolled over and scooted up toward the headboard. It grew quiet in the room. He picked at a scab on his thumb.

"Gus?" His brow furrowed.

I sat up against my pillow.

"Yeah?"

"Did you ever actually *see* Sharon out there?"

Elsbeth sat up cross-legged on the foot of the bed, listening intently. I looked at her expectant face, then back at her brother. Siegfried avoided my eyes.

"Ummm... no. It wasn't her," I said slowly.

Elsbeth looked at me. Her eyes widened in surprise.

"Was it Frank Adamski the whole time?"

I hesitated. Siegfried continued to avoid my glance. I wondered what he had deduced.

"I don't know, Elsbeth. I just don't know," I answered honestly.

She stared at me for a long moment. Without warning, her face crumpled.

"She may still be out there," I hurried to add. "There's a good possibility that she's still hiding. We just ran across the wrong person this time."

I tried to convince myself. I didn't tell them that Frank Adamski had collected our offerings at the rock. Although Sharon wasn't the one we were feeding, there was absolutely no evidence of foul play. She could certainly be hiding in another area of the woods. Or she might've found shelter with someone. Anyone. She was afraid to go home, I was certain of that. Her uncle had some sort of power over her father. She might not be protected if she returned.

I reviewed the possibilities with the twins, and we agreed not to give up hope. We'd start searching again as soon as Frank Adamski was caught.

At the mention of his name, the twins grew quiet again. Siegfried was the one to ask this time.

"What happened, Gus? What did he do to you?"

I hesitated again, wanting to vent the feelings of horror, but reluctant to frighten my friends. I decided to hold it in, glossed over the story, and ended with the fact that he'd revealed his association with the church burglaries.

Elsbeth's eyes sparkled and Siegfried raised one eyebrow in surprise.

"You saw the loot?" Elsbeth asked, using the word she'd heard in the movies to describe the scepter.

A faint blush of excitement crept onto her cheeks. She began to breath faster and moved closer to me.

"Yeah," I said, conjuring up the memory, "It was gold. It flashed in the light. There were stones set in it… red stones, I think."

"Rubies?" Siegfried asked. "Wow. It must have been worth a million dollars."

"At least," I agreed. "Maybe more."

"Wowee," Elsbeth whispered, her eyes dancing in pleasure. "Rubies."

The bedroom door opened.

"Anybody hungry in here?"

My mother entered, bearing a tray with a bowl of steaming tomato soup. Three grilled cheese sandwiches lay on a plate beside a huge glass of milk. Siegfried jumped up and cleared a spot on the bedside table. She laid the tray down and leaned over to brush my hair from my brow.

I pulled back before she could kiss me in front of my friends. She smiled and stroked my cheek instead.

"How are you feeling, sweetheart? Ready to eat?"

I nodded. The empty cavern in my stomach growled in agreement.

"I'm starving," I said, reaching for the first sandwich.

"Are you twins hungry?" she asked. "I can make more in a jiffy."

They both shook their heads.

"No thank you, Mrs. LeGarde. We've just eaten."

I was surprised that she intended all three sandwiches for me.

"Okay, then. Let me know if you need anything else, honey."

"I will," I mumbled through grilled cheese. "Thanks, Mum."

As I wolfed down my food, the twins explained what happened after I was dragged away by Adamski. It was Siegfried who climbed up the tree and saw the smoke. He was the one who summoned my father and Officer Lawson to the rescue. He had a feeling, he said, a strange feeling that I needed help.

I looked into his startlingly blue eyes and smiled.

"You knew I was in trouble?" A sense of amazement filled my heart.

He nodded and smiled, embarrassed.

Elsbeth breathed in sharply. Bolting upright, she looked at us with shining eyes.

"I know what it was!" she said.

A mysterious undertone laced her voice. Her eyes danced and her face lit up. She held up her arm and pointed to a scab.

"It's the bond. We're blood brothers, remember? That's why Siegfried knew you needed help. He sensed it."

Siegfried stared at her as if struck by a bolt of truth.

I pushed down the covers and lifted my pajama leg, fingering the scab on my knee.

"Wow. You're right, Elsbeth. That *has* to be it."

We held hands, forming a circle and chanting in unison.

"Blood brothers, forever."

After a moment of silence, Elsbeth whispered two words.

"Forever. Amen."

Thirty-eight

I ran a wet comb through my hair, leaning toward the mirror over the bathroom sink. My mother handed me a freshly pressed shirt. It smelled like spray starch and felt stiff in my hands. I pulled it on over my clean undershirt and fastened the buttons.

"Now, Gus. This is a very cultured woman. You need to be on your best behavior. Remember to use your napkin if she offers you anything. Don't fidget. Sit up straight. Answer with 'Yes Ma'am' or 'No Ma'am'."

I rolled my eyes and smiled indulgently.

"Mum. I know how to act. I'll be polite. Really. I will."

She spilled a nervous laugh.

"Okay, honey. I know you will."

She watched me as I hopped off the porch steps and walked to Number Fifteen. The man in the dark suit and sunglasses across the way waved to me. I was expected.

As I approached the front porch of the cabin my heartbeat quickened. When I reached the front door and was about to knock, it swung open. A kindly woman in a black dress greeted me.

"Please come in, young man."

I smiled and obliged. She stood before me, with her right hand extended. For a moment I thought I was supposed to kiss it and kneel before her. She reached for my hand and shook it gently.

"I'm pleased to meet you, Gustave."

I shook back and looked into her tired eyes. They seemed infused with deep sadness.

"You may call me Mrs. Jones, young man. I'm afraid it's not my real name, but my protectors assure me my privacy would be compromised were my true identity revealed."

I tried to digest her formal words.

"Um... Pleased to meet you, too, Mrs. Jones."

She gestured toward the small sofa in the living room.

"Won't you please take a seat?"

I nodded and walked to the sofa, careful not to knock into anything or trip on the thick rug. My mother's warnings rang in my head. *Be on your best behavior.*

"Thank you, Ma'am."

She sat beside me in an overstuffed chair. Through frequent visits with Millie Stone, I recognized the slow descent of an arthritis sufferer. I fidgeted with my collar and smiled awkwardly, suddenly tongue-tied.

A collection of silver-framed photos stood on the coffee table, on the side tables, and on the shelves above the small dining nook.

"Are you quite recovered from your adventure last night, young man? We were all worried about you."

She spoke with a strong Boston accent. I looked up at her and smiled. It was an easy question to answer.

"Oh, I'm fine now, thank you very much, Ma'am."

I folded my hands on my lap, remembering to sit up straight, and examined the closest photographs. The first was a picture of a young man and woman surrounded by a large group of children. I assumed it was her family. I looked to the next photo, and found the same faces arranged in different poses. The remaining photos were similar. Beach gatherings, birthday parties, boating shots... they stood on the table in a packed cluster, offering memories from the past in neat black and white capsules.

"Is this your family, Mrs. Jones?" I finally asked.

She nodded and answered.

"Yes it is, dear. Of course these photographs were taken a long time ago. All of my children are grown now."

I nodded. She reached for a brown paper bag.

"These are Bing cherries, Gustave. Would you care for some?"

My eyes widened. I loved cherries. I nodded eagerly and shoved my hand in the bag to grab a handful. Instantly, I heard my mother's voice in my head. I opened my hand, released the bunch, and removed three cherries.

"Thank you, Ma'am."

She reached into the bag and withdrew a small handful for herself, chewing slowly as she enjoyed the flavor.

"These are some of the sweetest cherries I've ever tasted," she said.

I popped the first burgundy cherry into my mouth. Large and meaty, it burst with flavor. I worked my way down to the pit, then stopped and immediately panicked, wondering how to dispose of it. I rolled it around in my mouth for a while longer, then just sucked on it. Finally, Mrs. Jones reached over for a small blue and white bowl, deposited her pit inside, and placed it between us on the coffee table.

"Here you go, just put them right in there."

I smiled with relief, spit the pit into my hand, and dropped it in the bowl.

"These are delicious, Mrs. Jones," I said, starting on my second one.

The curtain in the window fluttered. A large cream-colored Persian cat jumped to the floor. He tripped across the floorboards and leapt into my host's lap. His large, copper eyes glowed atop a small, pug nose. He pushed his head against her sleeve, and began to purr.

"It's the Cheshire cat!" I said, spitting my second pit into the bowl and reaching over to pat him. He pushed his head against my hand and then jumped beside me.

"His name is Ivanhoe," she said. "He's quite good company for an old woman."

I looked up at her. "You're not old."

As soon as I said it, I wondered if I'd goofed. *Was I being too familiar? Would my mother have frowned?*

She smiled and offered me more cherries. I took a handful this time and began to work on them in earnest.

"You're sweet to say that, dear. But I'm afraid I sometimes feel as if I've lived a hundred years."

She wiped her hands on a blue paper napkin and offered me one, too. I put it on my lap and nibbled more cherries.

"My parents said you needed peace and quiet, Mrs. Jones. They said not to bother you."

She cocked her head to the side as if surprised.

"Oh? Well, that was very thoughtful of them. I wondered why you hadn't stopped by to pay a visit yet."

I glanced around the room, examining more photos. While I munched on the cherries, my eyes landed on a grouping of photos on the sideboard. A picture of the President in the oval office stood in the front. I looked closer, noticing a number of shots of him. They weren't familiar poses; none had been featured in Life Magazine. In several shots, Mrs. Jones stood proudly beside him. His arm was around her in two of the photos.

My pulse quickened.

"Did you *know* the President?" I asked in awe.

She smiled sadly at me and looked down at her hands.

"Yes, Gus. I knew him very well."

Suddenly, it hit me. She was dressed in black. She was in mourning. She had a large family. The men in suits were protecting her. I leaned over and looked again at the photo of the young children before me and recognized the face of John Fitzgerald Kennedy as a young teenager. My mouth dropped open in a clear breech of etiquette as I stared at her.

"Yes. He was my boy. But now he's gone."

My throat constricted with emotion.

"I'm so sorry for your loss," I choked. "We all are."

I thought I'd said the right thing, but wasn't sure as it took her a few moments to compose herself. Finally, she took a deep breath and looked directly at me.

"Well, thank you, young man. I appreciate your sentiments. I really do."

She stood and looked out the window. Ivanhoe followed her and wrapped himself around her legs.

"Perhaps it's time for you to rejoin your friends, Gustave. It looks like they're waiting for you on your porch."

I rose and put my napkin in the blue and white bowl.

"Thank you so much for the cherries, Mrs. Jones," I said, making my way toward the door.

"You're quite welcome. It's been a pleasure meeting you, young man."

Her voice still trembled. I sensed she was near tears and hoped my questions hadn't saddened her.

"Gus?"

"Yes, Mrs. Jones?"

Her eyes searched mine.

"Can we keep my identity a secret? Just between us? The men who are hired to protect me tell me it's the best way to ensure my safety."

I smiled up at her.

"Of course. I won't tell a soul, I promise."

She smiled through moist eyes, squeezed my hand, and reached down to peck my cheek.

"Come see me again. It will do me good."

I nodded and smiled back at her.

"Okay. I will. Thank you."

I raced back to Wee Castle with the news bursting inside my chest. I had to try to keep the secret, and not tell my friends, in spite of being blood brothers with the twins. I shouted that I'd be back in a jiffy and ran inside to change into more comfortable clothes.

Thirty-nine

I choked down a dinner of chipped beef on toast and mixed vegetables. Almost gagging, I hurried to the bathroom to brush my teeth to get rid of the taste. After the dishes were done, we prepared to join Oscar and his guests in the living room for the long promised slide show. Although I sometimes found the ritual boring, this time I was actually looking forward to the event since it featured a family of abandoned kittens who adopted the Stones last year. I'd grown fond of the litter and was saddened when they all found homes.

"Take your sleeping bag, son," my father suggested.

I ran into the bedroom to get it and stuffed it under my arm.

"Better bring a jacket," my mother yelled. "It will get cold later."

I scooped my blue hooded sweatshirt from the back of the chair and met my folks on the porch. The twins and their parents were already walking toward the gathering. I was surprised that Mrs. Marggrander was accompanying them, but delighted for the sake of the twins. No excuses would be necessary tonight for her absence, and they could stand tall with both parents in attendance.

The peepers started their evening chorus. A bat swooped over the lake in search of juicy mosquitoes. I chuckled as I remembered our adventure and the image of my father in his red and white polka dot shorts, chasing the bat with my butterfly net. My mother carried the cheese twists and chips, and my father toted a case of root beer. The bottles clanged against the metal separators in the wooden box. It looked very heavy.

"Want some help, Dad?" I offered, wondering if I could lighten his load.

He grunted and repositioned it, answering through gritted teeth.

"Nope, I've got it, son. Thanks."

My mother wore a pale pink sundress. I noticed the fabric was pulled tight across her middle and realized she was already showing signs of the pregnancy. She caught me looking, pulled her white sweater around in front with her free hand, and grimaced.

"I've got to buy some maternity clothes this week, André. I don't believe I can make do much longer!"

My father shifted the case of soda to his left side and nodded in quiet assent just as we reached the living room. I held the door for them, then ran over to join the twins who had already spread their sleeping bags on the floor five feet back from the projector screen.

The room was filling up quickly. My grandfather had set up several rows of folding chairs in advance for the anticipated audience. Millie Stone and William sat on the couch. William fiddled with the small phonograph he brought down from my grandparent's cabin. Several thirty-three rpm records lay on the side table. I assumed he was in charge of the background music.

Oscar turned on the slide projector. Five boxes of slides towered on the table. I realized it was going to be a long night, and was grateful I'd brought my sleeping bag.

"C'mon, Gus. Put your bag right over here."

Elsbeth scooted to the left and made a space between Siegfried's bag and her own, patting the ground between them. I unrolled the bag and flattened it out. Kneeling down, I unzipped it halfway and pulled over the flap to reveal the pale green flannel decorated with flying ducks.

By the time the room filled with all of the guests and camp staff, the roar of lively conversation became deafening. Betsy, Annabel, and June sat cross-legged behind us, and William had abandoned the records to sit beside Betsy. I frowned and turned back to the twins.

"Anybody want some chips?"

Both nodded eagerly. I jumped up and trotted to the food table—simply a tablecloth thrown over the pool table. My mother and grandmother busily arranged the snacks and utensils. Everyone brought something, from packaged cookies and chips to a plate of homemade brownies. I realized my grandfather probably made them in the huge black oven, then looked around to find him. He came in and took a seat beside Mr. and Mrs. Marggrander. They were chatting amiably in the back corner while he puffed on his pipe.

I turned back to the food table and noticed a large bowl of chipped ice covered with Bing cherries. I turned and scanned the crowded room. Ensconced in one of the leather club chairs in the back corner was "Mrs. Jones." She wore the usual black dress and a small dark hat and veil. I waved to her. She raised one hand and wiggled her fingers. One of her protectors sat in the second club chair, still as a stone. His impassive face didn't move, but his eyes inspected the room and windows on a regular basis. I looked out on the porch and located two more men dressed in dark suits. They stood erect and at attention, their heads swiveling slowly back and forth across both the lake shore and the woods.

I separated a paper plate from the stack, then loaded it up with chips, cheese twists, and cherries.

"Save some for the other guests, honey," my mother warned.

I looked at her sheepishly.

"I will, Mum. There's plenty here."

I surreptitiously added a Twinkie to the plate and wove my way through the approaching guests who descended on the food table. I'd been the catalyst, and I hoped my mother and grandmother were ready for the onslaught.

Laying the plate on my sleeping bag, I invited the twins to help themselves. I selected a cherry and began to savor it, glancing back at Oscar Stone.

His pale silky hair was brushed straight back and his brilliant blue eyes sparkled with animation. A sheaf of papers lay beside the projector. I figured it was a packet of narratives to accompany each slide. He'd published a book last year entitled, *Autumn in Upstate*

New York. Each glossy photograph was captioned with poetic imagery. Our copy sat proudly on the coffee table at home. I flipped through the gorgeous pictures many times, enjoying the close-ups of the animals the most.

After several more noisy moments of food gathering and fussing about, the lights flicked off and the show began. William abandoned Betsy's side and returned to his job as music director. He set the needle down on a scratchy recording of Beethoven's Pastoral Symphony. The music was turned to a low setting, so Oscar's voice could be heard.

"I've entitled this presentation, *Through the Year with the Magnolia Tree*," Oscar began.

His normally faded British accent sharpened for the occasion. I looked at him curiously and wondered if it was consciously affected or if it just happened when he spoke in public. He flipped on the projector light. An image of his white farmhouse filled the screen. Standing nestled between fields and woods at the base of the Genesee Valley in our mutual hometown of East Goodland, New York, the little house welcomed visitors. The photo was taken in the early morning mist, with sunrays casting light across the yard. Vivid spring grass glowed in shimmering veins of sunlight, while heavy dew cast a bluish hue over the rest of the land. The bare branches of the Stones' magnolia tree were visible in the distance.

"In the early springtime, our upstate lawns doff their dull brown winter garb and change to one of delicate green."

Oscar began to speak in a lilting voice. He clicked the projector controls and a new slide filled the screen.

"Each year we are spellbound by the lovely blossoms of the magnolia tree."

Clusters of dewy-soft cream and raspberry petals filled the screen. The details of the shot highlighted the drops of moisture on the petals, freezing them for eternity in a striking composition.

"All too soon, with the whipping May breezes…"

Oscar clicked to the next photo. A full shot of the tree in its glory filled the screen. The photograph instantly froze the action, revealing a crisp shot of the heavily laden branches being blown sideways in a strong gale. "...the colorful petals fall, creating a thick blanket on the grass."

I turned to Elsbeth and Siegfried. They seemed captivated. Elsbeth leaned over and placed her lips against my ear.

"Is it over already?" she whispered.

I wondered if the cycle of blooming and falling leaves could possibly mean the end of a ridiculously short show, but quickly realized that Oscar often went on for hours in these situations. I shook my head and motioned back up to the screen, where a new shot filled the screen.

"Until the tree seems to become just another shade tree," Oscar continued.

The slide carousel inched forward and a new slide dropped into the slot. The screen was filled with a winter scene, featuring the same tree.

"The frosts arrive and winter casts a soft cloak of snow on its branches. Although the tree is usually ignored until its next flowering period, we may—if we look closely—observe the detailed preparation that nature provides for the coming season's welcome event."

Oscar was using the technique he called a "flashback." He started at the end, showed the fully flowered tree, and was now going back to the previous winter to chronicle the tree's complete cycle. I slid my legs into the sleeping bag, settled on my stomach, and wiggled around until I was comfortable. Reaching for another cherry, I popped it in my mouth, and settled in to enjoy the show.

"During the white cloaked rest period for all flowering trees and bushes, we find other events of passing interest in the vicinity."

The screen filled with the face of a gray and white kitten. Snow sprinkled his whiskers and he looked directly into the camera lens. I smiled, happy the interesting shots were so close to the beginning of the show.

"Mittens waits for her playmate, Fluffy, to join her in an early morning romp."

The next shot showed a fairly longhaired tiger kitten creeping around the corner of the dilapidated garage that stood beside Oscar's house.

I elbowed Siegfried.

"Remember that one? She was the friendliest."

Siegfried nodded and smiled. He reached for some chips. His eyes remained glued to the screen while he stuffed them in his mouth. The aroma of salty chips filled the air between us when he leaned over and whispered, "Look!"

The next shot featured Mittens and Fluffy tumbling in the snow, playing in the early morning light. The rosy gray hours before Millie awoke—Oscar's on free time in the day—were moments of solitude and freedom, and many of his famous photos were known for their characteristically soft, pre-dawn shots. He flipped through several photographs of the kittens in various modes of play.

"Our fingers are so cold that we go indoors for a moment. On the storm windowpane, a delicate tracing is forming. It seems to resemble a landscape with oddly shaped trees on a hillside."

The close-up of the fragile frost formations on the window was breathtaking. It *did* look like a hillside. Fascinated, I gazed at the trees he described in the randomly etched pattern on the window.

"The warm air, as we raise the inner sash, begins to dissolve the picture."

I plucked the Twinkie off the paper plate, offering it up in turn to both Elsbeth and Siegfried. Each knew my passion and refused it. I smiled, ripped off the cellophane, and stuffed half of it into my mouth. I looked back toward the audience in the front row. Mrs. Marggrander rested her head on her husband's shoulder. They held hands and she actually smiled.

"Outdoors, the sun is rising and a neighbor's dog has left his tracks in the snow."

The simple photo of the deep footprints in the snow was glorious. Rosy-saffron shafts of light colored the frozen ground as the sun rose behind the crest of the ridge. My family's home was on that ridge on the west side of the valley. In an uncharacteristically deep moment, I wondered if I'd seen the sun rise before Oscar that morning. I often saw its rays creep over the east ridge of the Conesus Lake trough from my vantage point that separated the Genesee Valley and the western most Finger Lake.

I gobbled the remaining half of the Twinkie and turned back to scan the crowd once more. Grandpa had already started to nod off. My grandmother elbowed him. Stifling a laugh, I returned to the screen.

"We hear a soft but insistent call from across the street. Could it be this little one from the neighbor's pasture?"

The face of a white lamb filled the screen. I recognized the Johnsons' barn in the background.

Oscar turned to look over his shoulder when the music stopped, and nodded to William who had resumed his duties as operator of the phonograph. William returned the Beethoven album to its cover, and reached for the next selection. He smiled at his father and gently dropped the needle into the first groove. Oscar cleared his throat and announced the title.

"The next musical selection is from one of my favorite operas, 'Die Fledermaus.' We've had some recent interest in bats around here. I thought it an appropriate choice."

As the overture began, Oscar first smiled at me, then turned to my father, looking most mischievous. With his mouth twisted into a prim smile, he winked at both of us and then continued to move through a myriad of slides, each chronicling the infinitesimal signs of spring. My father guffawed loudly from the couch amidst curious stares from the uninitiated guests. My mother giggled and tried to shush him. I grinned broadly at both parents and then turned back to the screen.

Oscar had captured the crocus, forsythia, daffodils, and of course the magnolia tree in excruciating detail. Each stage of development was beautifully shot, and poetically narrated. My head began to nod. I decided to rest it on my forearms as I nestled down deeper into the sleeping bag.

"With the arrival of April showers come the buds—soon to be followed by the blossoms of dewy freshness and nearly transparent beauty. In the stencil-like shade of the magnolia tree…"

My eyelids grew heavy. I shook my head a few times, trying to fight it. Elsbeth had already dropped her head onto her sleeping bag and lay motionless beside me. Her breath fluttered against a dark curly lock of hair as she slept. Her lips parted and a partially eaten cheese twist lay in her limp hand. A single orange crumb clung to her cheek.

She looked so angelic that a twinge of affection washed over me. I gently brushed the morsel from her face and removed the cheese twist from her fingers, putting it back on the plate. Oscar's voice continued in the background as the slide projector clicked onward.

"The white pine also sparkles with moisture as the starlings prepare rather noisily to nest in its upper branches. Close by, the maple tree responds to the urgency of spring with its buds and intricately detailed blossoms."

The images of dew-covered tree branches and sleek black birds began to swim before my eyes. I lowered my head to the sleeping bag and decided to close them just for a minute. As Oscar's voice continued, the overwhelming, molasses-like pre-sleep urges finally dragged me into their soothing depths.

೫೦೦೩

I woke with a start in the dark room. Oscar droned on about the magnolias.

How long had I slept?

Raising my head, I looked around the room. Siegfried smiled and tipped a bottle of root beer to his lips. I smiled back, embarrassed I'd fallen asleep.

"It's almost over," he whispered.

I nodded and pulled myself up, sitting cross-legged on the sleeping bag. My mouth felt dry and my eyes gritty. I looked at my watch in the soft light of the projector, surprised to find I'd been asleep for almost an hour.

The slide featured a close up of two blue jays feasting on seeds from the moist ground beneath the magnolia tree. I vaguely heard Oscar describing the seedpods cracking open to reveal tidbits that would be greedily devoured. The next shot featured the pair of birds on a branch overhead. Finally, Oscar showed a photo of a much younger William sitting beneath the tree, looking into the overhead branches with a startled expression on his face.

Oscar joked about being wary of unwelcome droppings from above, and the crowd roared. From the expression on William's face, it was clear that he must have warned the boy of the potential dangers just before he snapped the shot. The slide show ended with a shot of the glorious tree in full bloom.

Oscar finished his final narrative and extinguished the projector light to a round of applause. Chatter filled the room and the lights came up. I stretched my arms to the ceiling, trying to wake up enough to stand and rejoin my parents. Siegfried leaned over and gently shook his sister's shoulder. Her dark eyes fluttered open, filled with confusion. He smiled at her and whispered a few comforting words in German. She sat up and rubbed her eyes.

The crowd dispersed slowly, each guest stopping to say a few words to Oscar. Pleased with their reactions, he smiled and graciously nodded while accepting each compliment.

I rose and rolled my sleeping bag, waving to the twins as they disappeared out the door. "Mrs. Jones" had slipped out first with her protectors close at hand. My mother and father sat still on the couch, whispering and smiling at each other. William helped his father with the equipment, and we all walked back through the cool moist air to our cabins. I was too tired to wonder if the elusive Frank Adamski stood waiting in the dark shadows, and when I finally reached my bed, I tumbled into it fully clothed.

Forty

I woke late the next morning to the sound of voices in the kitchen. The smell of coffee and toast filled the air.

"They broke in while we were at the slide show. It's as if they knew we'd all be occupied last night."

I sat bolt upright in bed listening to my grandfather's voice.

"She's pretty upset. They took some of her family photos and a silver candy dish that belonged to Odette. She's most upset about the cat. Apparently he escaped and hasn't returned."

I swung my legs over the side of the bed and felt around for my sneakers.

My mother asked, "How do you think they discovered Rose's identity, Jean-Paul?"

I could hear the tension in her voice. There was silence as I tied my sneakers and then raced into the kitchen. Grandpa looked directly at me with a sad and questioning look in his eyes. My heart dropped to the soles of my feet.

He thinks I told someone.

"It wasn't me, Grandpa. I haven't breathed a word. I'll swear on the Holy Bible. I haven't even told the twins," I panted, circling around to my mother's side.

I was startled to see Officer Lawson beside my father. A collective sigh of relief filled the room.

"Well, then, it must've been one of the staff," Grandpa continued. "If none of us spilled the beans, it can only have been one of our girls or one of her own people. The FBI is going to interview everyone here to figure out if…" he hesitated for a moment, "…if Mrs. Jones is in danger. If it was a local person and they haven't told anyone else, she might be safe. If word has spread, her safety could be compromised. There were two attempts on her life in the last six months."

I walked over to the window and looked anxiously toward Number Fifteen. My mother leaned over my shoulder. Her eyes danced with concern. The place swarmed with officials. Just as I was about to turn away, the curtain in the living room was pulled aside and I saw her. She beckoned to me urgently.

"Mum?" I asked as I turned to go.

"Go ahead, honey. She seems to have taken a shine to you. Just don't get in the way, all right?"

I spun around and raced across the kitchen, flying over the floorboards, out the screen door and across the porch. I churned up the pathway and was abruptly stopped short by two strong arms. The man had come out of nowhere.

"But…" I sputtered.

Mrs. Jones came onto the porch to call me.

"It's okay, Barney. He's my friend."

He released me immediately. Straightening my clothes, I ran up to Mrs. Jones.

"We'd better talk inside, Gustave. These men get so nervous about my safety."

ರಂಚ

After my conversation with Mrs. Jones, I ran to the twins' cabin. I'd been commissioned with the very important task of searching for Ivanhoe and needed reinforcements. Mrs. Jones' protectors threatened to remove her from the area and she feared she might have to leave her beloved pet behind.

The men were busily analyzing the risks involved. They arranged to interview everyone on the premises by noon. After promising the Marggranders not to leave the grounds, we circled the cabin. Frank Adamski was still at large, and although the police believed he'd probably left the area shortly after he tried and failed to incinerate me, there was still the possibility that he was hiding somewhere in the woods.

"Here, kitty, kitty, kitty," Elsbeth's small voice rang through the pines.

I copied her tone, and repeated the call.

"Kitty, kitty... here, Ivanhoe."

After several minutes, Siegfried raised one finger to his lips.

"Shhh. We need to stop and listen between calls. He might be meowing and we'll never hear him."

We stopped, listened, and heard nothing but the sounds of camp. The birds screeched overhead and a motorboat droned on the lake. Our footsteps whispered against the pine needles as we walked. We started to call again.

"Here kitty, kitty, kitty."

A breeze blew up from the lake, filled with the fresh scent of balsam. We continued for another hour, circling wider until we reached the perimeter of the camp. Finally, we stopped beneath the sign for Loon Harbor and looked at each other.

"What now?" Elsbeth asked.

She stood beside her brother in lime green shorts and an orange shirt. Twin pigtails bobbed about her flushed face. She looked about five-years-old.

"Good question," I said.

I plopped down on the ground beside the wooden signpost. The painted image of a pair of loons swung gently in the breeze. The twins copied me. Looking down the road in the direction of the blueberry farm, I contemplated widening the search area and was sorely tempted. After a few moments of careful deliberation, I realized I could jeopardize the twins' safety if I decided, once again, to disobey my parents. I sighed and looked at Siegfried.

He plucked a long piece of grass from the base of the sign and chewed on it. Elsbeth unraveled one of her pigtails and began to refasten it. Sig stretched out one long brown leg and closed his eyes. I sighed again.

"We should double back and recheck. We might have missed him."

Elsbeth nodded and Siegfried opened his eyes, scanning the woods around us. The image of Frank Adamski lurking out there proved a most formidable deterrent to each of us.

Siegfried suddenly rose.

"Wait a minute, we didn't try behind the icehouse. Maybe he wandered over there."

We scrambled to our feet.

"Let's go," I shouted. We ran down the hill and passed the children's playground, rounding the corner to the red cabin. We skirted along the front of the dining room and kitchen building and finally reached the icehouse.

"Here kitty, kitty, kitty."

We called for several minutes. Finally we stopped and looked at each other, discouraged. I walked to the table where the fishermen cleaned their catch and scuffed my sneakers against the ground, turning over a pile of iridescent fish scales.

"Shoot," I whispered. "I really wanted to find him."

The twins exchanged glances. Siegfried moved closer and put his arm around my shoulders.

"We did too, Gus. *Es tut mir leid.* (I'm sorry.) We can look again after lunch, *Ja?*" He spoke in his most mature voice.

Nodding, I walked to the icehouse steps and slumped down.

"You're right. You go ahead and get lunch and I'll meet you down at the living room at one o'clock."

They disappeared in a wink. They had missed breakfast, too. Siegfried's stomach had been growling for the last half hour.

I reached down to pick a cluster of sour grass and chewed on it. The tart lemon flavor spread across my tongue, making my lips pucker. I picked another bunch, repeating the delightful process as I thought hard about Ivanhoe, Mrs. Jones, and Frank Adamski.

Another theft of religious artifacts was reported on the news yesterday. It happened in Augusta at a large catholic church. The same types of precious relics were stolen, but this time the sanctuary was desecrated. Tables were overturned, statues were smashed, and a stained glass window was broken. According to Officer Lawson, the police thought either Frank Adamski or his accomplices were still responsible.

I shook my head and wondered if Frank or his crowd had a grudge against churches in general. Why attack only churches? Was it because they were more loosely protected and housed items that could easily be fenced? I supposed it was easier than home robberies. The risk of surprising someone in church at night was low. I wondered what had happened to the robbers to make them so angry.

I sat on the rough wooden steps, chewing on the sour grass and listening to the whir of the freezer compressor. It ran for a while and then stopped. Temporarily satisfied with the internal temperature of the walk-in freezer, it paused between cycles. I closed my eyes and listened hard, then pressed my fingers to my temples, rubbing them in slow circles. Straining, I listened hard against the soft noises of the forest. A pinecone dropped to the ground behind me. The wind whistled gently through the pine needles above.

My sneakers squeaked against the steps and I repositioned myself, listening harder. A flock of crows landed in the branches of the tall oaks beneath the icehouse. They chattered raucously. I looked up in annoyance, wondering what caused them to screech so loud. I waited patiently for them to stop. Seven birds gathered together to complain and squawk in the swaying oak tree overhead. I sighed and got up. I'd never hear Ivanhoe if they continued with the incessant din.

Walking around to the back of the building, I squinted up toward the noise.

"Cut it out! You're disturbing the peace."

Their cries sounded almost human as they cackled. Reminiscent of the ladies in *The Music Man* who sang, "Pick a Little, Talk a Little," they gabbled in dissonant tones. I reached down for a pinecone and chucked it up in the general direction of the noise.

"Shoo," I shouted. "Go away."

A flurry of black feathers emerged from the tree as they lifted in flight, ducking and sliding around each other while they searched for a more hospitable perch. The top of one of the younger trees continued to sway after they vanished. I shielded my eyes and focused on the treetop.

There, perched precariously in the top of the swaying tree, was Ivanhoe. He clung to the thin trunk in terror, mewing.

"Ivanhoe! Here, kitty, kitty."

The cat had climbed thirty feet straight up the spindly tree. Various sturdier trees grew beside it, but Ivanhoe had chosen the weakest and wobbliest of the bunch. I looked around for reinforcements and saw none. Ivanhoe's sapling was far too slim to climb, but a plan formulated in my fevered brain as I called up to him and then dashed into the icehouse. Rummaging around on the workbench, I found a length of nylon rope and tied it around my waist. At the last minute, I grabbed an old oilcan and tied it to the end of the rope. Scurrying out of the icehouse, I jumped from the top step and scrambled over to the tree that held the terrified feline.

"It's okay, boy. I'm coming for you. Don't be afraid."

The answering mew spurred me on and I began to climb the closest tree to the sapling. It was not an old tree, but the trunk was ten inches in diameter and it sported many two-inch branches that held my weight well. I scrambled up quickly. Within moments, I was ten feet below the cat. The thin tree continued to sway above me, enhanced by his heavy weight. Ivanhoe mewed at me, his eyes large with fear.

I imagined that the only time he'd been higher than ground level before would have been as a passenger in his cat carrier on Air Force One.

I whispered softly, trying to calm him and steeling my own nerves.

"Don't worry, Ivanhoe. I'm coming to get you."

I reached one arm around the trunk of my tree, hooking my elbow over a solid branch. With my free hand, I untied and slid the rope from my waist. The oilcan remained attached to one end of the rope. I swung the rope toward the sapling. After several unsuccessful tries, it finally caught. The weight of the oilcan spun the rope around the trunk. I'd snared it.

I repositioned my grip on the tree and pulled gently. The sapling moved toward the larger tree, bending easily. I looked up and watched the cat, careful to stop just as the smaller tree trunk came close to the sturdy tree that held me. Satisfied, I looped the free end of the rope around a branch and tied it off.

I'd planned to climb higher and reach over for Ivanhoe, but to my surprise he jumped from the sapling to my tree and began to howl. It was louder now, more strident.

Afraid he'd fall, I scurried up the trunk and made my way to him. His claws dug into the bark. Securing myself by looping one leg over a limb, I held the cat with one hand and pried his claws loose with the other. Finally, he let go and allowed me to lift him up and hug him to me. He purred, pushing his head against my chin. I worked my way slowly down the tree with my precious cargo clutched to my chest.

Forty-one

When my feet touched dirt I breathed a long sigh of relief. Ivanhoe clung to me, shaking. He nuzzled his face into my neck and reached one paw to my shoulder. I disengaged his claws from my skin and sat down on the ground to rub my fingers under his chin, pulling several dried leaves and one burdock from his fluffy underbelly. After a few minutes, he relaxed and began to purr.

Rising, I held him in my arms and stroked his head with one hand, supporting his plump body with the other. When I rounded the corner of the icehouse, the sound of sobbing coming from the kitchen startled me.

I crept to the screen door with the cat in my arms. The crying grew louder, wailing like wind through the pines, soul-searing and frightening.

I pressed my face against the screen and peered inside.

June sat in a small chair beside the enamel table. She held her head in her hands and wailed, rocking back and forth. Betsy stood beside her in her white uniform, stroking her hair and consoling her.

"I knew it wouldn't work," June sobbed.

My grandfather sat near her. His shoulders slumped forward, lending him a defeated look. Disappointment lurked in his eyes.

June broke down and confessed her crimes. She pulled gobs of tissues from the dispenser Betsy offered. Mascara ran down her cheeks. Saddened and horrified, I watched in silence.

"I'm so sorry," she cried between hiccupping sobs, "my mother loved the president. She wanted a few mementos. Just a few pictures, that's all."

"Did anyone help you, June?" my grandfather asked gently.

She raised her tear-stained face to his. Her thin blond hair ponytail lay limp on her back. She hesitated, then shook her head and buried her face in her hands once more as her shoulders shook.

Her voice was muffled. "No. I slipped out during the slide show and ran over to the cabin. No one else was involved."

An expression of disbelief crossed Betsy's face. She exchanged glances with my grandfather and leaned over to whisper to June.

"You'd better tell the truth, sweetie. They'll find out eventually."

June shot a searing look at Betsy, appalled she'd betrayed her. She sobbed even louder and pressed a wad of wet tissues against her face.

Oddly enough, the smell of fresh donuts wafted onto the stoop, producing rumbles in my stomach. Grandfather fried the donut holes especially for me. I felt simultaneously disturbed and ravenous, but I ached for June, who wailed pitilessly while my stomach rolled with a complete lack of empathy.

Betsy pushed her smooth bangs back from her forehead. She stretched and rubbed the small of her back as if it were sore, then noticed me lurking on the porch. My legs wobbled when she swished toward me.

"Good Golly, Miss Molly. Look, Mr. LeGarde. Gus found Ivanhoe!"

She pulled open the screen door and drew me inside, urging me toward my grandfather. While she chattered, she leaned over to pat the cat and her breath warmed my face.

"What a hero," she whispered.

I flushed when she dropped a swift kiss on my cheek and draped her arm around my shoulders. Mesmerized by her angelic presence, my strength waned and I melted beneath her praise.

Grandpa came over and Betsy returned to June's side. Her sobbing subsided and was replaced by intermittent whimpers and snivels.

"Well, well, well. Where'd you find him?"

I explained the morning's events, careful to include the twins in the story. After all, it was Siegfried who sensed Ivanhoe's location.

He summoned his extraordinary sense of intuition once again and directed our attention to the area near the icehouse.

A look of amazement crossed my grandfather's face, playing there briefly as his eyes danced. He glanced back at June and put his hands on my shoulders.

"I've got some serious business to attend to now, sport. So I can't go with you right away. But I wanted you to know…" He stopped for a moment as his face worked with emotion. He took a deep breath. "I'm sorry I doubted your integrity this morning. I should have known you'd never betray a confidence. You're a good boy, Gus, a very special boy."

Flushing with pride, I smiled thanks and headed toward Number Fifteen. As I was about to turn the corner past the office, Betsy hailed me.

"Gus! Wait a minute."

She trotted down the path, her ponytail bouncing in the sun. She smiled broadly and carried a paper bag.

"Your grandfather forgot to give you these."

She handed me the grease-stained bag and tried to catch her breath. Her soft pink lips stretched into a broad smile. I stammered and my heart fluttered. She stood with one hand on her left hip, poised to turn back. Her uniform pulled snug around her slim waist. I remembered tying the apron strings for her and the feeling of the white silky fabric against my shaking fingers. My legs trembled dangerously. I longed to blurt out my feelings, but was betrayed by my clumsy mouth.

"Th… thanks," I mumbled, shifting the cat to one shoulder and accepting the bag stuffed full with donut holes.

Her fingers brushed mine. She tilted her head as she slowly tucked a stray lock of hair behind her ear.

"No problem, honey."

Light flashed in her eyes. My face muscles sagged in adoration. She turned and hurried back to the dining room.

She called me honey, I thought.

I floated along the path to the lake. The water shimmered and blinked in the distance under the hot afternoon sun. I shifted Ivanhoe around and managed to reach into the bag and grab one crusty donut. I popped it in my mouth and speculated about my feelings for Betsy, then dug for another donut. Ivanhoe snuggled against me, sniffing my breath. I turned and watched Betsy flounce around the corner of the building. My heartstrings pulled with sweet agony and I wondered if this torture was what they called *true love*.

Forty-two

The screen door closed behind me and I bid Mrs. Jones goodbye. A smile played across my face as I plucked long, fuzzy hairs from my shirt and headed down to Wee Castle. She'd been so relieved at the recovery of her precious cat, she'd wept for joy. She hugged and blessed me, pushing a ten-dollar bill into my hands against my vehement protests. Finally, I promised to share it with the twins and skipped down her porch steps, waving to Barney. He tossed me a barely perceptible nod, standing tall and vigilant in the shadows beneath the pines.

Shadow met me at the cabin steps, sniffing my hands and shirt. I squatted down beside him so he could thoroughly inhale the cat-smell, then surreptitiously fed him a donut hole. He wolfed it down and looked at me for another. His tail wagged in anticipation.

"Okay, just one more," I said, reaching into the bag.

"Gus?" My mother's voice resonated with restrained urgency. "Gus? Are you out there?"

Something's wrong.

"Mum?" I called. I raced up the steps and charged into the living room.

"In here. I'm in the bedroom," she said. "Don't come in. I need you to go get Dad or Grandpa. Tell them I need to go to the hospital."

The color drained from my face. I stood rooted to the spot.

"Gus? Did you hear me?"

I tossed the donuts on the kitchen table and ran to her door, pressing my lips against the crack. "Yes! I'll be right back with help."

I spun and bolted from the house. My legs churned faster than I'd ever pushed them. I leapt over the roots, up and down the steps of the boardwalk, around the living room, up the hill past the shower building, and across the office porch into the empty dining room. Bursting into the kitchen, I found my father and grandfather sitting at the table with two security guards and June. She was crying again, sobbing loudly.

My lungs ached. I doubled over and reached deep inside, summoning my voice.

"Dad!"

He rose and hurried to me. "What is it, son? What's wrong?"

"Mum's sick! She needs a doctor."

"What?" he asked. Disbelief flared in his eyes.

I motioned for him to follow.

"What's wrong with her, Gus?"

I trotted beside his rapid, long-legged stride.

"I don't know. She wouldn't let me in the bedroom," I choked, nearly losing control.

His lips compressed in a tight line. In a flash, he ran down the hill. I followed, sprinting behind him. We reached the cabin in less than a minute.

When he reached the bedroom, he said, "Wait here, son. I'll let you know what's happening in just a minute."

I stopped dead and waited. Fear quivered in my gut. I swayed and breathed hard. A drop of sweat slid down my neck and moistened the collar of my shirt. Within seconds, Dad called me.

"Gus? Get my keys from the kitchen."

He exploded from the bedroom with my mother in his arms, wrapped in a quilt. Her face was ashen and her eyes closed. I grabbed the car keys from the shelf in the kitchen and ran to him, pushing them into his pocket.

"Thank you, son. Listen, run up to the office and tell your grandparents I'm driving your mother to the hospital. You'll have to help them with the dinner shift. Do you think you can handle that, son?"

I nodded and followed him to the porch, my eyes riveted to my mother's slack body. He took the path leading to the parking area on the far side of camp, where our wagon was parked. I stood for a moment on the porch, watching his broad shoulders as he carried her effortlessly to the car. After he disappeared around the bend, I took a deep breath and ran back up the hill.

୧୦୧୫

I nearly collided with my grandparents as they hurried toward me.

"What's wrong, Gus?" my grandfather asked. "You and your father took off like bats out of—"

My grandmother shot him a warning glance.

"Heck," he finished contritely.

Tears welled in my eyes. I swallowed hard and forced myself to remain calm. My grandmother put her arm around my shoulders and squeezed.

"It's my mother," I choked. "She's sick. Dad's bringing her to the hospital."

"What's wrong with her?" my grandmother asked in a tight voice.

"I don't know. But Dad had to carry her up the hill."

They exchanged worried glances.

"Now, don't you worry, sport," he said with forced cheerfulness. "She'll be in good hands. They took great care of me when I had my heart attack two years ago. They'll fix her right up. You'll see."

I nodded and bit my lip.

My grandmother turned me to face her and looked into my eyes. "I'm sure your father will call as soon as he knows something. Try not to worry. If we don't hear from him by suppertime, I'll call the hospital, all right?"

I nodded again. The threat of tears puddled and surged behind my eyes. My throat constricted.

"Why don't you play with the twins? We'll call you when we hear something," my grandfather said. "Look. There they are."

I turned to see Siegfried and Elsbeth emerge from their cabin. They waved vigorously and ran toward me.

Forty-three

We sat on the Wee Castle porch steps and finished off the rest of the donut holes. The twins were elated I'd found Ivanhoe, but their mood quickly dampened when they discovered my mother was on her way to the hospital. Siegfried draped his arm around my shoulders.

"I'm sure she'll be all right, Gus. Try not to worry."

"I'll try."

Elsbeth took my hand and pressed it.

"We're here for you, Gus. Blood brothers. *Forever.*"

My mind repeated the phrase again and again.

Blood brothers. Blood brothers. Blood brothers. Strange how we didn't care about the gender of the term. Elsbeth was really a blood sister, I thought, trying to push away the vision of my mother's pale and listless form.

Elsbeth smiled and brushed a donut crumb from her wrinkled green shorts. A thought flitted across my fevered brain.

My mother would insist on ironing them if Elsbeth was her daughter.

I squeezed Elsbeth's hand, released it, and stood up.

"I'd feel better if I did something. Anything." I looked toward the screen door. "Maybe I should straighten up the place? You know, make it nice for her when she comes back."

The twins jumped to their feet and nodded in unison.

"Good idea," Elsbeth said. "Let's sweep, dust, and change the linens. We'll have the place shining in no time."

"*Ja. Auf Geht's.* (Let's go.)" Siegfried said.

I ran into the kitchen, yanking open the utility closet door. Elsbeth grabbed the dustpan and broom and handed the mop to Siegfried.

"I'll make up the beds," I said, grabbing a pile of fresh sheets from the top shelf. I lifted them to my face and inhaled the cathartic clothesline outdoorsy smell.

Walking briskly into my parents' bedroom, I laid the linens on the chair beside the door. When I turned toward the bed, I froze, staring at a blood-covered floor and bedspread.

My knees wobbled.

It's everywhere.

A black splotch encircled my vision. My stomach rolled. I backed up slowly, bumping into the ladderback chair in the corner. I sat, then put my head down and forced myself to breathe deeply.

After several fuzzy moments, my head cleared. I looked around the room in horror. The window yawned wide open and the yellow curtains blew in the breeze, attracting my attention.

Had Frank Adamski attacked my mother in her bedroom?

I raced to the window and forced myself to look outside, fearful I'd find him standing with knife in hand against the building. The woods remained quiet. Slowly, I breathed in a deep lungful of fresh air, then returned to face the blood. My stomach churned again as I stared at it.

What happened? Did she accidentally cut herself?

It seemed improbable that so much blood could have resulted from such an event. Feeling queasy again, I backed toward the door and collided with Elsbeth who was about to enter the room.

I spun toward her to shoo her away, but her eyes widened, riveted to the red bedspread and pools of blood on the floorboards.

She screamed: a shrill, ear-piercing shriek. I tried to calm her but she flailed in the air, batting me away. I patted her hand and attempted to guide her out of the room. She backed to the wall, her eyes still huge and her mouth working noiselessly. Siegfried raced into the room.

"*Was ist los?* (What's wrong?)" he asked, staring at his sister.

She began to sob, pointing to the blood. Loud and hysterical, her cries were punctuated by frequent gulps. Siegfried's glance followed hers and his faced drained of color. The panic was almost catching. His mouth dropped open and he looked around in fear.

"What happened? Was she attacked?"

"I don't know," I answered. Hysteria crept up my throat.

A face appeared in the bedroom window and another surge of adrenalin raced to my heart. I quickly realized it wasn't Frank Adamski, but my grandfather. He leaned in the windowsill. "What in tarnation is going on in here? Are you kids okay?"

Elsbeth pointed to the bed with a shaking hand. My grandfather paled. He looked at me with concern, then beckoned to me.

"Why don't you come up to the dining room now. Let's bring the twins back to their cabin and then we'll try calling the hospital from the office."

I nodded, shepherded the shaking twins out the door, and walked them to their cabin while my grandfather spoke with Mr. Marggrander. The twins were whisked inside and we headed back up the hill.

"What do you think happened to her?" I asked.

He put his arm over my shoulders as we walked, shaking his head. "I'm not sure. But we'll get to the bottom of this. Try not to worry." It would've been easier if he'd told me not to breathe.

Forty-four

We finally got through to the hospital at four-thirty. The woman at the desk explained that a doctor was examining my mother, and that she'd ask my father to give us a call when he could. My grandfather was unable to wrest any more details from her, even after explaining that their son was anxiously waiting for news. He shook his head in disgust and called her an "old battle-axe" after hanging up and heading back inside to serve the evening meal.

After dinner was served, I sat on the office steps with Shadow curled at my side, nodding good evening to each guest as they emerged. The sky darkened and a spirited wind wailed through the pines. I'd been hoping to hear the phone ring for the past hour and was starting to wonder if my father would *ever* call.

Mr. Peterson strode across the porch, leaned over me, and stubbed out his cigarette in the tall receptacle with a sand ashtray. The acrid smell of smoke stung my eyes. I pulled back involuntarily and nodded goodnight to him. He slung an arm around his plump wife and they hurried to their cabin.

Shadow raised his snout and sniffed twice. The sky over the lake had turned a disturbing blackish-purple and billowing clouds raced across the water. Fat drops of rain began to fall as tree branches swayed overhead. Slowly at first, the drops splatted against the dusty ground—it puffed in response. As the rain quickened, the gentle plopping of the drops created a rhythm reminiscent of a melody in counterpoint. I moved under the porch roof, then took a few steps back as the storm increased in fury. Shadow followed and whined beside me.

"You'd better come in, honey. Looks like it's gonna blow real hard."

My grandmother stood behind the screen door, beckoning. Her short gray curls hung damp with perspiration. Faint smudges puddled beneath her eyes. June had been fired earlier, after a lengthy interview with Mrs. Jones' guards. My grandmother had donned an apron and cap and waited tables with Betsy and Annabel in the packed dining room.

"Can we please call again, Gram?" I asked. "It's been hours since we tried."

"Of course, honey. " She rushed across the porch to the office. I took a seat on the hard oak chair on the far side of her desk and Shadow settled at my feet. She untied her apron and laid it neatly on the desk, then sat down and picked up the black telephone handset and a pad of paper. She used the eraser end of an old yellow pencil to dial.

When the hospital answered, she nodded in my direction and straightened.

"Hello. This is Odette LeGarde, from the Loon Harbor Resort. I'm calling to inquire about my daughter-in-law. She was brought into the emergency room this afternoon."

Her no-nonsense, patrician tones usually evoked immediate respect. She uttered the words anticipating cooperation, oozing with confidence and businesswoman finesse. She stressed the word "resort," although Loon Harbor was more of a homey fishing camp than a fancy resort.

"Yes, that's right. Her name is Gloria LeGarde. My son André brought her in earlier. I'd like to speak with him, please."

She spoke firmly and smiled at me over the desk. I relaxed a bit and smiled back at her as the wind howled. Without warning, the lights in the office dimmed. A loud crack sounded outside as a bolt of lightning struck nearby. My grandmother leaned forward and spoke louder into the phone.

"André? Is that you? I can hardly hear you!"

I sat forward. Goosebumps prickled on my skin.

"What's that? The doctor said what? What did you say?"

She frowned into the mouthpiece and pulled the receiver away from her ear.

"I don't *believe* it. It's dead."

As she spoke, the lights flickered and finally blinked out. Although it was only six-thirty, the sky dripped black. Thunder crashed and the moist air smelled of ozone. I shifted nervously in my chair.

"I guess this isn't going to work, honey. I'm sorry, Gus. I really am."

She gave the phone a final, disgusted look and then replaced the receiver cautiously, as if expecting the lightning to reach up and strike her.

The generator kicked in, assuring safety for the frozen food in the icehouse.

When the squall increased its fury, I helped my grandparents close the shutters in the dining room, trying to forget about my mother's plight and the unheard words whisked away from my grandmother's ear.

What had my father said? Was my mother okay?

I buckled down and ran through the pelting rain to my grandparent's cabin, preparing for the worst.

Forty-five

A half hour later, my grandfather leaned forward in the car, gripping the steering wheel.

"Can't see a dang blasted thing."

I wiped his red bandana across the foggy glass.

"Any better?"

Rain splashed against the glass and the windshield wipers struggled to keep up.

"A little bit. Thanks."

I settled back in the Chevy's comfortable seat, straining to see the road. The trees nearly bent over sideways in the gale. A large branch flew through the air and smashed against the driver's side window.

"Wow. It's really bad out, Grandpa. How much farther to the hospital?"

He leaned forward another inch and squinted.

"Hard to tell. I don't even know where we are right now, sport. Wait a minute. Can you make out that sign over there?"

He slowed to a crawl and nodded at a suspended sign swinging heavily in the wind.

"Wait a minute," I said, peering out the window. "It says 'Seventh Heaven'. Isn't that the Olsens' camp?"

"Ayah. Right you are. We're almost to Route 11 now. At this rate we'll get there in about forty-five minutes."

I glanced at my Mickey Mouse watch: seven-fifteen. I sat up straight and peered through the window, watching for landmarks. Through the rain, the windswept trees bowed and thrashed along the roadside. I rubbed a patch clear on my window with my shirtsleeve and pressed my face against the moist glass, wondering what had happened to my mother.

Is she okay? Will she greet me with a smile? Will she be awake? In surgery? Alive?

I tried to ignore the racing morbid thoughts and shoved them deep into my brain.

Grandpa's brow furrowed as he concentrated on the impossible drive. When we rounded a sharp corner, a large figure loomed in the road. Grandpa slammed on the brakes. I braced myself against the dashboard and the car fishtailed in the mud.

Finally, it stopped. Breathing hard, I turned to face a young moose, whose nostrils were level with my eyes. The car had slid sideways, placing it perpendicular to the direction of travel and my window within inches of his muzzle. A rivulet of rain drizzled down his snout and dripped in a constant stream from his fuzzy lips. He lowered his head, stared with confusion into the car, then swung his big head away from us and lumbered into the woods.

After several tries, Grandpa straightened the car and continued onward, more slowly now. By the time we reached Waterville, beads of sweat rolled down his face. He'd been silent since the moose incident, forcing himself to concentrate.

We stopped at a red light. Several people were out on the road, running beneath folded newspapers or hunkering under their rain gear. A man in a dark green hooded slicker jabbed at the walk button on the pole. A hood shielded his face from our view. Aggravated, he began to cross the street just as the light turned green. Grandpa hadn't seen him and accelerated.

"Watch out!" I shouted.

The car jerked as my grandfather slammed on the brakes, swearing under his breath. The man in the raincoat slammed his hands onto the hood of the Chevy, glaring into the car as he backed onto the sidewalk. The car eased forward again, and as we passed him I exchanged a look of surprise with Frank Adamski.

My mouth dropped open in stunned silence. The car moved forward. I turned to be sure, and found him grinning cruelly, drawing his forefinger across his throat in an unspoken threat. An electric shock ran through me. Memories of the cabin, the fire, the smell of him… I took a deep breath and looked back. He'd disappeared in the rain.

"Damned lunatic!" spat Grandpa, turning down the road to the hospital.

I sat back in my seat, shaking. Clasping both hands to keep them still, I remained mute, digesting the fact that my intended killer was still in the neighborhood. I glanced at the troubled face of my grandfather and decided to tell him later.

Forty-six

A hundred cars jammed the hospital parking lot. As we approached, a parking attendant in an orange slicker held up his hands to stop us. My grandfather rolled down his window and the wind and rain snatched the words out of the attendant's mouth.

" ... pileup up on Route 95 ...twenty-one people hurt. You'll have to park up the road a ways."

I looked at the long line of parked cars spanning the roadway, wondering how far we'd have to walk. An ambulance careened past us, red lights flashing as it screamed up the highway to pick up the next victim.

"Can the boy get out here?" my grandfather shouted, pointing to me.

The attendant grimaced, then capitulated, pointing to a small blacktopped area near the doorway. Grandpa backed around and pulled the Chevy up to the door. I looked at him nervously.

"Go ahead, sport. Don't be afraid. I'll meet you in the Emergency Room as soon as I park the car."

I hesitated, then braced myself and pushed into the wet night, darting across the sidewalk to the glass doors leading to the Emergency Room. Although I remembered very little from my episode after the fire, I'd been in the ER last summer when my father slipped on a wet tree root and twisted his ankle, and was familiar with the layout. I knew how to get to the waiting area, the rest rooms, and the vending machines. I had gobbled two Almond Joy candy bars and downed several bottles of Coke that day as we waited hours for the orthopedic surgeon to examine my father's X-rays.

The admitting area was mobbed. I froze and searched the bloodied faces. Fear welled in my throat. My stomach flipped in surprise at the number of injured people who stood in line or sat on chairs, holding towels or bandages to their wounds. A child ran past, screaming for his mother. I felt a connection with the little boy and had to control an insane urge to scream out for my own mother as he darted in and out of the crowd.

I collapsed against a wall and tried to get my bearings. Suddenly, a hand touched my arm. I looked into the shocked face of my father.

"Gus? What are you doing here?"

He pulled me out of the chaotic room and into the far end of the waiting room. When we'd reached a quiet spot, he drew me to him and held me for a long time.

"Dad?" I mumbled into his shirt, aching for news of my mother.

He led me to a row of hard plastic seats and we sat down, facing each other. He continued to hold my hands in his, looking at me with an expression of doleful sadness. His eyes were red-rimmed, his face gray and gaunt. Fear rumbled in my stomach.

Why isn't he talking? What's he hiding?

Finally, he swallowed hard and began to speak in a halting soft voice.

"Son? I'm afraid I have bad news."

I stared at him, mouth working in anticipation of the terrible news he was about to reveal.

"We lost..."

His voice tightened and faltered. He turned his head away, rubbing at tears that trickled down his cheeks.

My world turned upside down as I mentally finished his sentence.

He's trying to tell me we lost my mother. My mother's dead.

I shuddered and went cold.

My mother's gone.

My face twisted. "Mum? We lost Mum?"

He looked at me in shock. His dark eyes widened. I began to sob, my shoulders shaking as the tears poured down my cheeks.

"No! No. Your mother is fine. We lost the baby."

I stopped and stared at him in disbelief. My chest heaved.

"What? Mum's okay?" I suddenly laughed hysterically as my emotions switched instantly from despair to relief. The tears continued to flood my cheeks and my shoulders shook under the weight of the tumult. I was sick with relief, but saddened by the loss. My father's expression troubled me further when I realized how deeply it affected him.

"Yes, son. She'll be fine. I guess the baby just wasn't meant to be."

His voice caught in his throat. Feeling confused by the raging flood of emotions, I threw my arms around his neck.

"I'm sorry, Dad. I'm really sorry."

Forty-seven

I woke at six o'clock Friday morning in my grandparents' cabin, where it had been decided I'd sleep temporarily. Stretching, I stared bleary-eyed at Shadow, a warm lump on my feet, and at the unfamiliar patterns on the knotty pine walls.

It all flooded back to me.

My mother. The hospital. The baby brother or sister who was "not meant to be."

"Not meant to be?" Why would God give a baby like that and then take it away?

I felt confused and saddened. Guilt slid in my stomach due to my uncharitable thoughts of sibling resentment. It bubbled up and floored me. I dressed quickly and ran down the porch steps to the dining room and into the kitchen.

For the past few days, my grandparents had spoken with a comforting sense of normalcy, grounding me with everyday topics and giving me chores to keep busy. My grandfather was already at the stove, stirring oatmeal in a big pot, preparing it ahead for the guests who would arrive soon for breakfast. My grandmother was folding napkins at the table. She motioned for me to sit, then walked to the stove to get a covered plate from the oven.

"Here you go, honey. I made 'em special for you. Eat up. You'll need your strength today. You want to get your cabin ship shape for your mother, don't you?"

"You bet. Thanks, Gram."

My smile faltered, but I managed not to gag. Poached eggs weren't my favorite. I hated the gooey parts, but got through it by dunking my toast in the sloppy yolk and trying not to look before I took a bite. Orange juice worked well to wash it down.

I dawdled for a while, finally finished, then was excused from the morning chores so I could prepare for my mother's homecoming.

"Watch for us sometime around noon," my father had said. "She should be released as soon as the doctor examines her. But there is paperwork, so I can't be sure when we'll actually get home."

He'd been at her side since the day she was admitted. My grandparents had ferried clothes and personal items back and forth to the hospital for several days.

I ran down the hill and got to work, sweeping the Wee Castle deck from seven to seven-thirty. Not one pine needle remained. I viewed it proudly while Shadow snoozed on the top step, but was discouraged when I realized how much time I had to kill. After putting away the dishes, I took another tour around the cabin, adjusting a crooked lampshade and straightening the rug in the living room. By eight o'clock the tension of waiting was unbearable.

Four hours to go. At least.

The bathroom occupied my time for the next hour. With my mother's big rubber gloves, I scoured the toilet and sink and even washed the steel drain pipe beneath the sink so that it shone. I swept the floor, mopped it, and brought the stepladder to reach the cobwebs that had started to form in the ceiling corners. A few daddy long legs escaped my broom and scurried away through invisible cracks between the wall and ceiling.

When I finished, I poured myself a tall glass of cherry Kool Aid and sat at the kitchen table, feeling lonely. I moved to the porch and sat next to Shadow. He woke, lapped my hand, then returned to his doggy dreams. The lake was glassy and calm. I stared for a while, watching fisherman troll past the docks.

A mockingbird settled into the balsam tree beside the porch and delivered the most amazing song repertoire. I recognized most of his calls—the black-capped chickadee, red-winged blackbird, mourning dove, cardinal, goldfinch, killdeer, and meadowlark. There were a few more that sounded familiar, but I couldn't place them.

Scenes from "To Kill A Mockingbird" flashed before me: Scout, Jem, and Dill racing through the garden at night, Jem's pants getting caught on the fence, Calpurnia chastising Scout when she was rude to her young guest after he poured maple syrup all over his dinner, and the look on Tom Robinson's face when Mayella Ewell accused him of accosting her. I thought about the evil spreading through that little town, the mob of men who wanted to lynch poor Tom Robinson, and the bravery Atticus Finch showed in the face of their evil. He reminded me of my father. Quiet. Principled. Full of wisdom and integrity. I hoped that someday I would be a good man, like him.

I watched the bird sing his heart out and wondered if he had a song of his own.

Who in his right mind would want to kill a mockingbird, anyway?

He entertained me for another ten minutes before flying away. Finally, I drained the glass of Kool Aid and went back inside.

My parents' bedroom had been scoured by two of the cabin girls. It now smelled of fresh linen and faintly of ammonia. The white curtains billowed in the window, lying to me, telling me that none of this had happened.

My mother didn't lose the baby. There had been no blood on this bed, this floor.

I shook myself, then smoothed out the wrinkles on the bedspread one more time and looked around the room. The clock on the nightstand ticked. The curtains fluttered, playing in the sunlight. The loons' tremolo wafted on the breeze into the house. I looked at my watch. Still only eight-thirty.

A brainstorm hit.

Flowers! She loves flowers.

Racing around the camp, I found clumps of orange tiger lilies, white daisies, Queen Anne's lace, buttercups, and ferns. Unsure what to house them in, I finally chose the chipped white enamel pitcher and filled it halfway with water.

I spent a long time trying to arrange the stems like my mother did. Whenever she was done, her wildflowers looked like a painting—neat, tidy, artistically arranged. Mine looked like a two-year-old had stuffed them in the container.

I sighed and looked at the clock again.

Not even eleven.

Resigned to make time fly, I opened up the utility closet and took out the broom again. It couldn't hurt to sweep the cabin one more time.

The rest of the day was torture. Lunch came and went. The twins were conspicuously absent. I suspected their father insisted they stay away, knowing my mother was due home soon.

Mrs. Jones rocked on her porch and waved to me a few times. She seemed sadder today. It was something to do with the way she rocked and stopped, rocked and stopped. My heart went out to her. Although I was tempted to visit her, I didn't want to impose without an invitation and wanted to stick close to Wee Castle.

When they hadn't showed by two o'clock, I gave Shadow a much-needed bath in a tin tub behind the cabin. He smelled like he'd rolled in something rotten, so I soaped him up and rinsed him clean. Afterwards, I groomed him with a soft brush and put some of my father's hair tonic on him. It seemed to do the trick.

Finally, when I could think of no more jobs, I picked up my comic books and read them. Superman. Little Lotta. Richie Rich. Five times each. I tried to read my father's mystery, but the words were too hard and I gave up after a few chapters. Frustrated, I cleaned off the refrigerator one more time, swiping the white metal surface with a moistened dishrag.

By four-thirty in the afternoon I was about to accept the fact that my mother would *never* come home when the Oldsmobile rumbled into the parking lot at the top of the hill. I raced to meet them.

With some difficulty, my mother emerged from the back seat and leaned on my father until she got her balance. She saw me, beckoned, and hugged me tightly until my father broke it up and insisted she go inside to rest. I shadowed her until she dropped into bed at just after six.

৩০০৩

Early the next morning, I leaned over to pluck another flower from the patch growing next to the steps. The wildflowers had begun to wilt, and I wanted to freshen up the bouquet before my mother woke.

Tall, fuzzy stems rose three feet, exploding in sunny yellow flowers that bloomed all summer. My grandmother called them *Helianthus*, or false sunflowers. I'd thought of them as the helicopter flowers for years. I gathered the flowers and brought them into the kitchen, pulled out the wilted flowers from the old bunch, and added the Helianthus. Afterwards, I went over to listen at my parents' door again. A soft stirring came from within.

She's up.

The door opened slowly. She had brushed her hair and put on one of my father's flannel shirts. Lumberjack snoring came from behind the bedroom door, signaling he was still asleep.

"How's my boy today?" she whispered, leaning down to give me a hug.

"I'm okay," I said. "How are you?"

She smoothed my hair and looked into my eyes. Her color had improved.

"I'll be good as new in a few days, honey. Oh my goodness. You really need a haircut."

She tugged at my hair, then looked in surprise at the table.

"Gustave. Did you pick those?"

I smiled. "Uh-huh. "

She hadn't noticed yesterday, she'd been in a fog. My father said it was due to the medicine. She'd slept for almost twelve hours.

"They're just beautiful, honey. Thank you."

She hugged me again, then walked over to the stove, reaching for a fry pan.

"What'll it be, son? Pancakes or eggs?"

I looked up in surprise.

"Really? Are you up to it, Mum?"

She walked to the Frigidaire and opened the door, looking inside.

"Yes, honey. I'm up to it, now don't you worry about me any more, okay?"

I walked over to the cabinet and reached for the flour.

"Okay, pancakes, then. Can I help?"

She looked at me as if she didn't recognize me for a moment, then answered.

"Sure you can, sweetheart. Why don't you get the milk out of the fridge for me?"

I basked in the presence of my mother. I'd almost lost her, and had faced the horrible fact of her mortality. The nagging thoughts creeping around in my brain tortured me. If I could lose her, I could lose Dad, too. My insides constricted as I remembered the horrible pain of that one moment when I misunderstood my father's statement. "We've lost…"

I stirred the batter harder and swallowed, wanting so badly to tell her everything.

She sprinkled a few drops of water into the cast iron skillet. They sizzled and popped. It was ready. She walked toward me and cupped my chin in her hand, lifting my face to hers.

"Are you okay, honey?"

Tears welled in the corners of my eyes. She knew me so well, even better than Siegfried and Elsbeth. I choked out the words.

"Yeah, Mum. I'm okay. I'm just so glad you're home."

I threw my arms around her waist and hugged her, pouring out my deepest feelings as she soothed my fears. I felt five years old again, but didn't care. Finally, the smoking skillet drew us back into the here and now. I wiped my eyes and we resumed the comforting task of making breakfast together.

Forty-eight

Four pleasant days passed. The twins and I caught crayfish, dug worms, swept the decks, and helped William with chores. We watched as he completed his model, coating it with lustrous metallic green paint. I ached with envy when he displayed it on his shelf in the bunkroom.

I visited Mrs. Jones and Ivanhoe several times, enjoying the attention and delighting in stories about the President's childhood antics. Although I knew she was really Mrs. Kennedy, I found it easy to think of her as Mrs. Jones. I enjoyed the clandestine nature of our relationship. Her guards relaxed a little, or seemed to. They even joked with me as I came and went.

I confided in my parents about seeing Frank Adamski in the rainstorm, and after that they kept me under a watchful eye. The police reinitiated a search for Adamski in Waterville and Oakland. It seemed to me that they'd nearly given up in the long and futile search for Sharon.

We rode the horses, but were instructed to stick to the Andersons' pasture. Each time we rode, my father read John D. MacDonald novels under the shade of the oak tree while we cantered around the pasture.

On Wednesday, we constructed jumps from galvanized buckets, tree stumps, and smooth logs we gathered from the edge the forest. Starting low, we leapt the horses over the jumps and worked up to a height of two feet by Friday. One of us was assigned to the jumps, raising the bars with various articles we found around the barn, or replacing the knocked-down logs. The other two rode until they tired, then we switched places and started all over again.

Sir loved to jump and rocketed toward the rickety contraptions spread around the pasture. I grabbed a handful of his mane when he surged toward the jumps, then leaned forward and gripped hard.

As we cantered around the field, I found myself wondering about Sharon Adamski.

Did she find another family? Did they adopt her? Maybe she pretended to have amnesia to conceal her identity...

I dismissed the last idea, assuming any potential rescuers would have heard about the girl with the long blond hair who'd been missing for weeks.

After several hours of riding, my father waved to us and we headed home for an afternoon of swimming. We'd just arrived back at camp when Oscar Stone hailed us from the pathway. He smiled primly, walking with a confident easy stride in our direction as he smoothed his long silky hair. After a few exchanges of pleasantries, he asked, "Would you children care to accompany us to the Waterville fair? William and I are heading out just after dinner. He assures me it's a ..." he looked at my father and winked, "...a 'blast,' which I assume means a great deal of fun."

I glanced at my father and sensed his hesitation as he considered the safety of the situation. His eyes narrowed and he stroked his chin.

"Please, Dad? Please?" I begged, tugging on his arm.

"Pretty please with sugar on top?" echoed Elsbeth.

"I'll keep a real close eye on them, André," said Oscar.

My father smiled indulgently.

"All right. But you'll have to stick with William or Oscar, son. You need to promise."

I wheeled around and grabbed the twins' hands.

"Oh, I will. I promise, Dad. Come on, guys, let's go ask your folks."

We raced down the hill together, bubbling with excitement.

Forty-nine

"You sit on the inside," I shouted to Elsbeth. We scrambled into the Tilt-A-Whirl dish and snapped the bar over our laps.

Siegfried sat in the middle and I took the outer position that would bear the weight of both twins. The remaining saucers quickly filled with chattering kids.

"Here we go," Elsbeth said. Her voice rang with excitement.

Our pod swung in slow circles, building momentum as the giant platform sped faster. I gripped the metal bar and Siegfried and Elsbeth slid against me, squashing me to the end of the pod.

My hands felt sticky from the pink cotton candy I wolfed down ten minutes earlier. A giddy sensation spiraled in my stomach and the background of the park blurred in dizzying colors. We swung in circles, spinning and tilting until our insides were deliciously rattled.

Tears of laughter streamed from our eyes. Our bodies slammed against the metal bar when the car plunged and dipped. Several times, I thought I might fly out of the car and my laughter nearly turned to shouts of fear. But as hard as the centrifugal force pushed me, I remained securely inside the pod while it swooped across the platform for the last slow twirl.

Elsbeth's face had turned green. I wondered if it was due to the corn dog and candy apple she demolished, or the popcorn we all shared before that. I offered my hand to help her out.

"*Danke*, Gus."

We balanced on the swaying deck and followed Siegfried to the ground where Oscar Stone sat on a bench, rewinding his Leica camera.

"Are you okay, Elsbeth?" I asked.

"*Ja*. I'm okay. Just a little sick in my stomach, that's all," she said, pushing her wild hair back from her face.

Her mother had pulled it up in a ponytail with a red ribbon, but she'd removed it as soon as we arrived at the fair. The thick dark curls created a soft halo around her heart-shaped face.

"Are you gonna throw up?" I asked.

She laughed.

"I hope not. Come on. Let's go on the Ferris wheel next."

Oscar led the way.

When we reached the line, he said, "I think I can handle this one, children. I'll be behind you in the next car. Wait right here for me when you get off."

We promised to wait for him when we got off, and moved up in line. Finally, after several groups of people were loaded, it was our turn. We scrambled into the green car swaying on the loading platform, were safely latched inside, and then watched below as Oscar was directed into a red car. He began to take pictures of us as soon as he was airborne and while the other cars were loaded, flashing multiple shots and leaning out at crazy angles with his camera. Finally, all of the cars were filled and the huge wheel began to turn.

Night had arrived. Festive lights blinked in reds, pinks, and greens from every pavilion. When we reached the top, the black velvet view stretched for miles. I recognized the glimmer of a nearby lake and enjoyed the unusual vantage point while circling the wheel.

Elsbeth sat between us. Her face grew flushed with excitement and she swung her legs back and forth. She chattered happily about everything. Apparently, her nausea had passed. Oscar's flash continued to go off as we frolicked above him, leaning down and making silly faces in his direction.

When we finished, we walked between rows of gaming tables, stopping occasionally to try our luck. Elsbeth won a stuffed pink poodle after tossing a penny into a glass jar. Oscar excused himself and sat down under a tent to recuperate when William and Betsy met up with us and took over what William called "babysitting."

We sashayed along the long line of vendors, following the two teens. I was surprised earlier in the day when Betsy agreed to come with us, and was envious of William's position as her escort. I watched as he tried to hold her hand. She pulled it away and laughed as if nothing happened, skipping forward toward the next attraction.

The hawkers screeched, their microphones squawking as they competed for customers against the rumbling of the generators. We moved down the long line of vendors and the crowd changed from young families with cranky children to an older crowd of teens and adults. People teemed between stalls and the crowd trampled over asphalt sticky with cotton candy and gum. The smell of popcorn filled the air. I looked longingly at the popcorn counter, but regretfully realized I had already filled my stomach to its maximum capacity.

Betsy tripped over a bundle of thick black wires and landed in William's arms. He mooned at her, held her far too long, and finally released her. She seemed uncomfortable, so I pushed forward and moved between them.

"Betsy! Can we go see the sideshows? Please?"

Betsy looked at the tent that advertised a bearded lady. She tilted her head thoughtfully for a moment, then capitulated.

"Okay. I don't think it would do any harm."

Excited to enter the realm of the unbelievable, we each paid five cents for our tickets and began to walk through the maze of pitiful creatures sitting alone in their tents.

The bearded woman was tiny. Obviously suffering from some glandular condition, her dark black beard hung six inches from her chin. She wore a blue and white polka dot dress and white pumps. I stared, looked away, and stared some more. Feeling ashamed, I pushed toward the next exhibit.

Elsbeth stuck to me like glue and held my hand as we were whisked past people with terrible deformities. Betsy realized her mistake by the time we saw the man with three arms and tried to hurry us through the rest of the exhibit. When we finally erupted from the tent, we walked in silence for a while toward the darker end of the fair. I breathed in the fresh air, feeling rotten inside.

Why did I want to see those unfortunate people?

Both Elsbeth and Siegfried looked disturbed and I felt responsible.

We walked along under the stars in silence. The tents turned into adult gatherings where cards were the game of the evening. Smoky air swirled around the tables and the atmosphere suddenly darkened to that of a back alley in the city.

Betsy pulled her sweater closed and shivered. "I think we ought to turn back," she said.

"Let's just walk to the end of the line and then turn around," William said as he swung his arms and drew away from us.

We hurried behind him, feeling increasingly uneasy. Motor homes and house trailers were parked at the end of the line, each facing diagonally toward the walkway. Several had electric lights inside and awnings sprung from their side doors, creating small verandas over tables and chairs. Although many trailers were unoccupied because their owners were running the fair games, several were home to a bunch of rough-looking characters. I shivered as we passed the last of the trailers and pulled on William's sleeve.

"C'mon, Will. We've gotta go back."

"Yeah, okay. Guess there's not much else to see."

When we pivoted around, my skin crawled. I stopped for a moment and listened, imagining footsteps behind me. I looked back and saw nothing but dark shadows and house trailers. Exasperated with myself, I shrugged and moved quickly behind my friends, hurrying to catch up to them.

A group of four men loomed from an opening, laughing and grinning as they blocked the way. The men were the age of my parents, or older. The leader had a shaved head and small mustache. He leered at Betsy, his liquor-laced breath poisoning the air between us.

"Look at thees one, *mes amis*. She's a pretty *jeune fille, n'est-ce pas?*"

Betsy twirled away from his hand when he tried to lift her chin to his face. He smiled wickedly, revealing a row of uneven brown teeth.

"How about a leetle kiss, *mon amour?* Just one leetle kiss to pass through?"

William stood stock-still, his face drained of color. I looked up at him and prodded him with my elbow.

"Do something!" I hissed.

Finally jolted out of his state, he moved forward and stood tall before the offensive man.

"Let us pass. My father is right over there and will call the cops if you give us any trouble."

"Yeah!" I said, moving up beside him. "Let us through, or there'll be trouble!"

I pushed Betsy behind me, shocked at my own bravado. I'd been aching for a chance to show Betsy how grown up I was and found myself staring the man in the face. I didn't flinch.

He looked down at me, growled, then laughed, turning to his friends.

"Ah, hell, they're just leetle *enfants*. No fun here. Leetle babies."

We hurried past them, breaking into a run. Just as we were about to pass the final trailer and re-enter the hawker's aisle, someone grabbed me from behind and pulled me around the corner. A large hand clamped over my mouth. I tried to scream, but could only manage a muffled "Phlop," as I was dragged further into the dark recesses of the carnival campgrounds.

"Why are you following me, you little weasel?" he snarled, "Haven't you had enough?"

The pressure on my mouth released slightly. I recognized the stench of Frank Adamski, the smell of stale sweat and alcohol. I struggled in his grasp until he pushed a sharp knife tip into my neck.

"Yell and you've had it, you little piece of crap. I'll run this knife right through your neck."

I nodded and he removed his hand.

"I'm not following you," I gasped. "You're following me!"

He slapped my face hard, then pressed the knife tighter against my skin, dragging me backwards.

"Your testimony could put me away for life. You've seen too much, you little creep. Way too much. It's over. See you in hell..."

William and Siegfried came at Adamski with the force of bulls while Elsbeth shrieked for help at the top of her lungs. The strength of the attack knocked him down and the knife clattered to the ground. Carnies streamed toward us from their trailers. I put my hand to my neck, feeling a warm trickle run down my skin. Shocked into action, Adamski mumbled nervously at the approaching crowd, then heaved to his feet and bolted into the darkness.

Fifty

Three days later, I lay on my stomach on the floor of my grandparents' cabin with the twins nestled beside me. Grandpa leaned over and took a swig from his Narragansett beer. He wiped froth from his mouth with the back of his sleeve, set the green bottle back on the T.V. tray, then attacked the twin lobsters on his plate. The aroma of the seafood tantalized me. I'd eaten hotdogs earlier, but eyed the red crustaceans while my stomach growled.

"Didn't you have your dinner?" my grandmother asked as she splintered a claw in half with a pair of silver nutcrackers.

She plucked a chunk of white meat from the claw, dipped it in clarified butter, and raised it to her lips. An expression of delight crossed her face while she chewed the tender morsel. I licked my lips, imagining the flavor.

"Yup. I had supper. But it was at four-thirty. I'm getting hungry again, Grandma."

The twins and I had been playing Tiddlywinks on the scratchy wool carpet for the last half hour. The low pile rug afforded a decent surface for snapping the plastic pieces. Siegfried plunked a blue chip in my direction, expressing a satisfied, "Ahh" when it sailed far in the air. I pressed the green plastic disk onto the yellow one, and made it pop across the carpet toward Elsbeth.

My grandfather pulled three skinny legs from the body of the first lobster and leaned over to hand one to each of us. Elsbeth wrinkled her nose in disgust, but Siegfried and I reached for them eagerly and began to extract the tender meat from the tiny leg. I sucked on it for a while, then finally cracked the shell and worked on that. There wasn't much meat inside, but I enjoyed the slim morsels that I dug out and looked up at my grandfather for more.

"Okay, okay. Here's another one," he said, feigning irritation. "I suppose you would eat the whole thing if I let you."

Lobster and Tiddlywinks were a Saturday night tradition. By the end of the meal, I'd usually finished eight legs. Eagerly, I reached for the second one as Siegfried accepted a leg from my grandmother's lobster.

"Thanks, Grandpa. It's good," I mumbled, attacking the second piece.

I scratched the side of my neck with greasy fingers. The superficial cut I'd sustained at the hands of Frank Adamski itched as it healed. I tried to push the dreadful memory away, but had been plagued by nightmares for the past two evenings as Adamski repeatedly attacked me in a variety of scenarios. I never knew if it would be fire or knives, but either method pushed me wide awake, frequently crying out for my parents. I felt embarrassed, but my father told me it was to be expected after all I'd been through.

Siegfried promised to sleep over this evening. I hoped that his company would drive away the demons for one night.

After being interviewed by the police for an hour at the Waterville station Wednesday night, we'd spent a tense couple of days confined to the more populated areas of the camp.

My grandfather cleared his throat and wiped his chin with a red and white checked cloth napkin.

"Did you ever think about trying to recover the hardware from my boat?" he asked, he taking another sip of beer. "You know, the oarlocks or the anchor?"

I looked up at him and shook my head.

"Uhnt-uh, I thought it was too deep out there, Grandpa."

He shook his head.

"It's not. The water near Big Blue is only eight or ten feet deep."

Siegfried looked up with interest.

"That could be fun," he said, looking back and forth between Elsbeth and me. "We haven't been out on the boat for days."

My grandmother shot a scowl toward Grandpa.

"Jean-Paul LeGarde. It could be dangerous, you old fool. You shouldn't suggest such things. Diving in deep water? They might drown, for goodness sakes."

She set her beer bottle on the side table with a thump and glared at him, eyes burning. While she glowered at him, her lower lip began to tremble. "I'm sorry, but don't you think we've had enough heartbreak around here? What with that maniac running around loose after our grandson, and the troubles poor Gloria had just a few days ago? We've really had more than our share, Jean-Paul."

He smiled apologetically and reached for her hand. She pulled it away and covered her face, trying to compose herself.

"I'm sorry, Odette. Of course you're right. It was a foolish notion. Don't you kids even think about it, y'hear?"

I nodded, surprised to see such emotion from my normally stoic grandmother. I couldn't remember ever seeing her cry, and felt an awful sensation in the pit of my stomach while I sat helplessly on the floor.

Elsbeth jumped to her feet and walked to my grandmother's side. She stroked her sleeve and whispered in a sweet voice.

"Don't worry, Mrs. LeGarde. We won't go out there. We'll keep Gus safe, I promise."

Elsbeth looked at my grandmother and smiled. Grandma straightened, collected herself, and leaned over to give Elsbeth a hug.

"Aren't you the cunnin' little one. Well, I worry about you twins, too. You all need to stick together and stay by the grownups, okay, honey?"

We agreed to be careful and turned back to our lobster legs and the cutthroat game of Tiddlywinks.

Fifty-one

On Sunday morning, I turned off the spigots in the shower building and reached for my towel. The wooden slats that served as a floor were wet and slippery. I walked carefully to the rack holding my clothes, inhaling the scent of Ivory soap that permeated the moist air. Although I'd protested that I didn't need a shower, since I swam so often, my mother insisted. As usual, she was right and in spite of my protests, the warm soapy water felt good on my skin.

I'd been thinking of Big Blue and the sunken rowboat all morning. Last night, Siegfried and I discussed it for a long time while the lake lapped against the boulders under our floor. We'd envisioned other treasures, too. Perhaps other boats had crashed on the rock over the years and sank to the golden bottom, leaving valuable items to corrode on the lakebed. It was an exciting fantasy. The only impediment was a young girl with curly dark hair who promised my grandmother we wouldn't venture near the sunken rowboat.

I stepped into my swimming trunks and reached for my clean shirt. The idea rooted and grew in my imagination.

If only we could find a way to ditch Elsbeth.

Immediately, I felt guilty. Although my parents hadn't forbidden me to use the boat, Big Blue was far out, unprotected by adults. Sliding into my flip-flops, I bundled my dirty clothes in the damp towel and reached for the plastic soap case. I'd have to give the idea some more thought.

I pushed out of the men's side of the shower and nearly collided with Betsy.

"Whoops!" she laughed, stepping aside.

"Sorry, Betsy," I said.

She started up the stairs to the women's side, then hesitated and turned with her head cocked.

"I've been meaning to speak to you, Gus. About the other night."

She backed down one step and rested her arm on the railing, looking at the ground as she spoke.

"I wanted to thank you for standing up for me the other night. That man was just horrible, and you were so brave."

I swayed in place, drinking in her words. She smiled. It was a little girl smile, free from the trappings of the usual teen attitude. She extended one hand to me. I responded, taking hers as she gently shook it.

"Anyway, I just wanted you to know how grateful I am. You're an amazing young man, Gus LeGarde."

She released me and walked into the shower.

Immobile, with my wet towel in hand, I melted beneath her praise.

I love you.

I mouthed the words, but nothing came out.

Slowly, in a trance-like state, I headed down to the lake. Suddenly, Siegfried and Elsbeth hailed me from the top of the hill.

"Gus! Up here!"

I shook myself out of the dream-like state and trotted up the sandy path toward them. Elsbeth sat on the ground behind the long gray bench that flanked the office. Her brother stood on the opposite side, arranging various rocks on the painted surface.

"Wanna buy some rocks, Gus?"

Smooth round stones, quartz, sparkling mica, and various other shapes and sizes marched in neat rows.

"Nice collection, twins. How much are you asking for this one?"

I pointed to a piece of rose-colored quartz. Siegfried smiled; relieved I hadn't made fun of them.

"It's Elsbeth's store, Gus. You'll have to ask her."

"Well, Elsbeth, what do you say? How about one stick of gum?"

She pursed her lips and pretended to agonize over the decision. Finally, she nodded, wrapped the stone in a large leaf, and handed it to me.

"You drive a hard bargain, Mister."

I pulled a pack of Teaberry gum out of my pocket and slid out a stick, holding it out for her. She drew it out of the pack and laid it on the bench.

Siegfried looked at me, his eyes filled with suppressed excitement.

"So, you're all set up now, Elsbeth. Need any more help? Gus and I were gonna do some sweeping down at the sundeck."

"*Nein, danke.* The store's all ready to go. I'll be pretty busy up here. You go ahead."

I looked at Siegfried, unwilling to believe our good fortune.

"Well, good luck, Elsbeth. Hope you sell a ton of them."

She carefully arranged several rocks to fill the spot the white quartz had vacated. Preoccupied with her store, she thanked me, but didn't look up from her wares.

Siegfried and I exchanged glances, turned on our heels, and ran down the hill.

"You sweep real quick while I dump these clothes and get the masks. I'll meet you at the dock in five minutes, okay?"

Siegfried grabbed the broom from the living room porch, vaulting down the stairs and up the sundeck. He'd already begun to sweep by the time I rounded the corner of the porch and pounded down the boardwalk fronting the lakeside units.

Shadow greeted me at the Wee Castle porch, wagging his tail slowly. I stopped for a moment to pat him. When he seemed satisfied, I ran past my parents who were drinking coffee at the kitchen table, dropped the damp towel bundle in the wicker hamper in the bathroom and raced into my bedroom to grab both sets of masks and fins Siegfried and I had stowed there last evening.

"Going swimming, son?" my father asked from the doorway.

I froze, smiled sheepishly, and nodded.

"Yup. We're gonna take the boat out a little ways, Dad. Maybe do a little swimming or fishing. Just Sig and me. Is that okay?"

He studied me for a moment, thinking.

"All right, but don't go too far, son. And come back in time for dinner. Remember to wear your life vests in the boat. And if you do any swimming out there, be extra careful. We've had our share of—adventures—this summer, don't you agree?"

I nodded woodenly, knowing full well he wouldn't approve of my plans. I scurried out of the house and grabbed two towels from the porch railing, shouting as I went.

"Okay. See ya later."

Fifty-two

I cut the motor. The skiff glided along the flat water toward the sullen shape of Big Blue glimmering beneath the surface. A flutter of nerves danced in my stomach as I exchanged excited glances with Siegfried.

"There it is... Big Blue."

Siegfried tossed the anchor overboard, letting the rope run through his fingers until he felt it hit bottom. It took only seconds, confirming my grandfather's knowledge about the depth of the water. We'd stopped about five hundred feet from the sparsely populated west end of the lake. I shivered involuntarily, remembering that night in the fog: floating in the dark lake, running along the misty shoreline, and seeing the bloodied face of Sharon Adamski.

Siegfried knotted the rope at the bow to prevent us from drifting too far off target.

"Okay. We're secure," he said, leaning over to look into the water.

I joined him while the boat circled slowly around its tether, rocking in the hot sun. I peered over the side, trying to locate the sunken rowboat. I discerned a shape or two—a large boulder that reached up from the bottom, a tall stretch of weeds floating under the surface—but it was difficult to see clearly because of the reflection.

"I can't see very well," I said.

The sun beat down on my back. Rays bounced off the surface of the water and back up to our faces, heightening the effect of the overwhelming heat. Stripping off my shirt, I wiped a bead of sweat from my brow.

"*Nur einen moment,* (just a minute,)" Siegfried said, picking up his facemask with a flourish.

He pushed it against his face and leaned over the side of the boat into the water. After a while, he raised his head and gesticulated.

"It's over there. I see it!"

"Come on," I shouted, putting on my black rubber fins and adjusting the straps.

We grabbed our facemasks and lowered ourselves over the side of the Starcraft. Treading water, we rinsed the masks and then put them on. I breathed in through my nose, sucking the mask closer to my face to make a tight seal. Siegfried began to swim on the surface with his face down in the water. He stopped and looked at me. His blue eyes shone through the mask lens.

"It's right under us, Gus. *Auf geht's!* (Let's go!)"

We took three deep breaths and then somersaulted into the clear water. The fins gave our kicks extra power, and we reached the boat in seconds. It lay upside-down at an angle against Big Blue, its splintered hull facing us. Shafts of sunlight filtered onto the skiff, causing iridescent ripples to play over its surface. Siegfried spied the anchor first, and motioned that he'd get it. The gold sand puffed beneath his feet as he swam to it and took out his pocketknife, sawing at the rope. I moved closer to the boat and tried to reach under it to locate the oar locks. A large bass surprised me as it flitted out from the boat and swam past my mask, its scales glittering. The pressure built in my chest and I was forced to release a stream of bubbles into the water; I'd have to resurface soon. I pulled back and turned to see Siegfried's fins flipping toward the surface. Pushing off from the sandy bottom, I followed him and broke through into the light, breathing deeply in the brilliant sunshine.

"Did you get it?" I asked.

He pushed his mask onto his blond hair and smiled, holding the side of the boat with one hand.

"*Ja.*"

He raised his free hand in the water and showed me the end of a frayed rope.

"Neat," I said, helping him drag the anchor up and over the side of the boat.

"We'll have to flip the boat to get at the oarlocks, Sig."

He rinsed his mask in fresh water and nodded.

"*Ja.* Let's go."

I did the same and dove down to the wreck with him. We pulled on the starboard side and flipped the boat over. Clouds of sand billowed, temporarily obscuring our vision. Finally, the water cleared and we began to work on freeing the oarlocks. After several tries, we finally squeezed hard enough on the cotter pins at the base of the locks. They pulled free. We swam to the surface, located the boat where it had moved around on its tether, and dropped them into the boat. I breathed through my mouth, still wearing the mask.

"Any chance we could tow the old boat back? Do you think it's worth it?"

He thought for a minute and shook his head.

"*Nein.* I don't think so. Unless you could float it again, it would be too heavy to drag and would probably catch on rocks."

"Yeah," I agreed, disappointed. "I suppose you're right."

He moved closer to me so that our masks nearly touched. "But how about searching for other wrecks? Remember?"

His eyes flashed with excitement, sending a shiver of anticipation down my spine.

"Yeah. Come on," I said. I took several deep breaths and disappeared beneath the surface.

Fifty-three

We swam slowly along the bottom, searching for salvage among rocks and weeds. After several minutes of disappointment, we surfaced.

"Let's try on the other side of Big Blue," I suggested.

Siegfried nodded and we swam hand over hand toward the submerged boulder. He pulled himself onto the rock. I knocked my right knee against the slimy surface when I followed him, breaking open the scab I'd earned from my previous fall over the roots. I winced, then stood beside him knee deep in water. He pushed his mask on his face and shaded his eyes, peering into the water. I looked down at the blood seeping from my knee into the lake. A faint red cloud swirled around my leg. The cry of a nearby loon echoed in eerie hysteria, rippling across the lake.

"Over there," Siegfried gestured excitedly, "Something's shining down there."

Ignoring my injury, I followed as we scrambled back into the water and repositioned our masks.

"Deep breath," he said, inhaling a huge lungful of air.

We swam to the bottom in the direction of his find. He began to dig at something partially submerged beneath the sand.

When he finally uncovered an old propeller, he brandished it with a crooked smile. Some poor soul had run right over Big Blue with their boat, shattering their propeller in the process. Siegfried tossed the piece of metal back onto the floor of the lake and shrugged his shoulders. I smiled back at him, almost bursting into laughter, but held it in for fear of inhaling a mouthful of water. I peered over his shoulder at an odd-shaped object looming in the distance. It lay twenty feet beyond Big Blue. My eyes widened and I pointed. He turned and spotted it.

We resurfaced and began to swim in the direction of the find, babbling excitedly. Swimming to the spot, we took another deep breath and dove down.

The item lay on the sandy bed in a crate. Crushed wooden slats enclosed soggy straw that was disintegrating, revealing the telltale shape of a bell. Heart pounding, I swam closer and pulled away the remaining straw. I rubbed the surface of the ancient relic and nearly inhaled lake water when I realized what lay before me. Engraved on the bottom rim of the bell was a signature: *Paul Revere*.

Siegfried motioned toward another shape several feet away. I followed him, flipping my fins rapidly. This carton had broken open when it was lowered into the water. Strewn along the sandy bottom were items that glittered and shone in shafts of sunlight. I reached for one and lifted it up, removing it from a soggy wool wrapper. A small porcelain statue of the Virgin Mary glittered before me, its gemstone-studded base twinkling in the watery light. Siegfried grabbed an item and pointed up. I nodded and we resurfaced together.

"This is it!" I gasped, raising the statue into the air. "It's the stuff they stole from the churches. That bell is from St. Stephen's church in Boston. The one Paul Revere cast."

We swam toward the boat and clambered over the side, looking at the items we'd found. Siegfried unwrapped his treasure, revealing a filigreed gold candlestick. We looked at each other; our mouths dropped open in shock.

"*Scheisse*," Siegfried swore under his breath, "*Ich verstehe nicht.* (I don't understand.)"

"I know. Why the heck would they hide the stuff underwater? It doesn't make any sense."

Siegfried switched back to English, his voice thick with his German accent.

"Maybe they planned to hide it in that shack - the one Adamski burned down around you. Then, when the police started searching for him, the area became too hot. They needed to lay low until they shipped it out of the country. They probably planned to hide it in those shipments of wool fabric. Remember you saw him wrap up that scepter? They could wrap the small stuff inside the bolts, and then bury the large crates in the back of the truck behind the rest of the material."

"It makes sense," I said. "I guess no one would search for the stuff under water. When the heat dies down, they'll probably come out at night and lift it up into a boat. Maybe they'll use a larger boat, and a crane. If they drive down one of those logging roads on the west side, no one would even see them."

"*Ja*," Siegfried said, his analytical brain working overtime as he turned the candlestick around in his hand.

"What should we do?" I asked, deferring to his superior intellect.

"I think we should get as much into the boat as we can, for proof. No one will believe us if we don't have evidence."

I nodded in agreement and we went to work.

Fifty-four

We worked for over an hour, repeatedly diving to the sandy bottom as we retrieved the treasures. I'd taken a deep breath and resumed my attempt to open a third crate when the thrum of a motorboat sounded nearby. I looked up as the shadow of a large boat darkened the water. Siegfried was topside, unloading an armful of goods into the Starcraft. The large shape pulled alongside our boat. I assumed Siegfried was explaining our find to our visitors and continued pulling the slats from the roughly fashioned crate, removing a heavy silver platter from a cloth wrapper.

As I marveled over the find, I heard Siegfried jump back into the water. I turned to face him and was astounded to see the ugly face of Frank Adamski through the lens of Siegfried's mask.

Horrified, I dropped the platter and pushed away, using my fins to propel myself backwards. Adamski's hand closed around my right ankle. I struggled to kick free and finally loosened his hold enough to escape. Swiveling around, I swam for my life, pushing through a thicket of weeds. He pulled on my left fin. I kicked maniacally until the fin worked free. With one fin remaining, I swam frantically through the weeds.

Adamski caught up to me and grabbed my arm, pulling me to him. I started to run out of breath, and panicked as his hands approached my neck. His eyes bulged large and angry through the glass and he clamped thick fingers around my throat. I tried to pull back and bumped against something soft.

Frantic, I tried to duck out from his stranglehold against a background of long golden wisps of fine blond hair waving in the water beside my face.

Sharon Adamski's dead eyes stared at me, her face frozen in a surprised watery mask. Another splash sounded from above. Blackness edged my vision as Siegfried torpedoed down and looped the anchor rope neatly around Frank Adamski's throat.

The last thing I remembered was the blurry vision of Adamski as he struggled to free himself and the firm pressure of my friend's hands under my armpits when he dragged me back to the surface.

Fifty-five

"Gus? Sweetheart, wake up."

I lay in bed and swallowed, my eyes sealed shut and my throat sandpaper dry. Willing myself back to sleep, I ignored the insistent, soft whisper of my mother's voice.

"Gus? You have company."

I remained silent, tucking myself back into safe blackness. I slid in the darkness, inside the songs of loons, atop the safety of the gentle waves lapping beneath the floorboards of my room.

Another voice joined the chorus. It sounded familiar: small and frightened. A wisp of curiosity spiraled through my brain and I wondered to whom it belonged.

"Gus? It's me, Elsbeth. Why won't you wake up?"

Her voice trembled, full of fear. I sighed inwardly, realizing the inevitable had come to pass. It was time.

Summoning every ounce of strength, I dragged myself through the mire and cracked opened my eyes. The bright light of the sun stung when my eyelids fluttered to a half-open position.

"*Gluck mal!* He's waking up."

Siegfried rushed to my side, joining Elsbeth and my mother as they gathered around my bed. I heard my mother instruct someone to get the doctor, and pulled myself into the conscious world. Lifting my right hand to my neck, I moved my fingertips gingerly over the swollen welts forming a hideous necklace around my throat. The memory of Frank Adamski's strangling grip flooded back. I looked nervously toward the lake.

"Don't worry, Gus. He's gone. He'll never bother you again."

My mother smoothed the hair over my forehead and smiled down at me. She looked tired.

"How long..." I started to speak, but my voice sounded hoarse.

She lifted a glass of water to my lips and helped me sit up. I sipped the tepid water slowly at first, then took the glass and gulped it down.

Elsbeth spoke rapidly, as if she couldn't believe her own words. "You've been sleeping since yesterday. Doc Whiting was here all night. You almost drowned. Siegfried dragged you up from the bottom."

Her voice cracked and her mouth crumpled. She took a moment to control herself, then looked adoringly at her twin. He grimaced, touching a large purple bruise on his forehead, and moved closer to the bed. In his eyes danced the horror we'd shared beneath the water.

"Adamski's dead. He strangled himself on the anchor rope."

I looked up quickly, wondering if he'd told anyone he had wound the rope around the man's neck. I remained silent for a moment, turning the memory around in my mind. As I lay there looking into Siegfried's traumatized eyes, it all came back.

Sharon.

Long golden hair floating in the water.

White, puffy face.

Flat, dead eyes.

"Sharon's dead, too, isn't she?" I asked, my voice trembling.

My mother laid her hand on my arm.

"I'm afraid so, honey. I'm so sorry."

My throat tightened. I stifled the urge to sob. Sighing, I closed my eyes tightly.

What had happened to her? Why had he chased and then killed her? Had she discovered his secret about the stolen church relics?

Elsbeth took my hand in hers and squeezed.

"It's okay, Gus. We're here for you. Blood brothers forever. And don't forget, you guys found the church loot. You're heroes."

I smothered the feelings of despair and opened my eyes, flashing a half smile at her. She pushed a purple-wrapped candy bar into my hand. I recognized the Milka label and smiled. It felt warm and mushy from her fingers.

"It's from my mother, Gus. She wanted you to have it when you woke up."

Several larger forms filled the doorway. My father hurried toward the bed and reached down to hug me, right in front of my friends. "You okay, son?"

I looked up into his concerned brown eyes and nodded.

"Of course he's okay, André. He's a LeGarde. All the LeGarde men are tough as nails, right, Odette?" my grandfather chuckled.

He put his arm around my grandmother's shoulders and puffed on his pipe, winking at me from the doorway. She wiggled her fingers at me, a teary smile creasing her face. I heard voices in the outer room. Oscar, Millie, and William Stone; Betsy, Annabel, and even Mrs. Jones were there. Suddenly I related to Dorothy in the Wizard of Oz.

The crowd shifted in and out as my mother waved Mrs. Jones inside. "Come in, Mrs. Kennedy."

I looked up at her in surprise. "Mom! Don't call her that."

"It's all right, young man. I'm leaving today, so no there's no more need for subterfuge."

She walked to the bed and stood beside me as the twins and my grandparents melted back into the living room. Barney stood tall in the doorway, his ever-present sunglasses in place.

"I just wanted to thank you, my young friend. The church bell that you found is very special to me. I was baptized in St. Stephen's church, you know."

"Really?" I whispered.

She smiled and handed me a photograph. It showed her standing beside the President in the rose garden at the White House.

"I want you to have this, Gustave."

I swallowed hard and looked up at her.

"Are you sure?" I asked, holding the treasure carefully.

She nodded. "Quite sure. I have other copies at home. Besides, I wanted to give you a little something before I left. Thank you for everything."

She smiled at me, patted my arm, and drifted back into the living room under the watchful eye of her guard. Stunned, I murmured my thanks.

My mother looked into the room with a worried frown.

"Honey, can you handle a few more visitors? The Stones are here. They were very concerned about you."

Exhaustion hit me hard, but I nodded anyway. "Okay."

Oscar guided Millie into the room, holding her elbow. William and Betsy held back and waited in the doorway. Millie came toward me slowly, smiling through the pain of movement so obvious from her gait.

"I think he's going to be just fine, Oscar. Look, he has a little color in his cheeks, don't-you-know?"

She kissed her fingertips and touched them to my cheeks, arthritic fingers trembling slightly. Oscar supported her arm.

"I do think you're right, Lady. But the boy needs his rest. We'd best leave him be."

William came forward and placed a large box on the bed. Betsy stood beside him, looking fetching in her pink and white sundress. William smiled sheepishly, then removed the gift from the box.

"Go ahead. Give it to him," she said.

He placed the Thunderbird model on my nightstand. My mouth dropped open. The green metallic paint sparkled. It was perfect.

"Here ya go, squirt. It's yours."

He rubbed one finger over his prominent nose and grinned at me, proud of his accomplishment.

Although I was pleased with the gift, my heavy-lidded eyes started to close and I struggled to thank him. "It's really keen. Thanks."

Betsy leaned down to peck my cheek. "He's tired. We'd better go."

Her voice trailed off and I sank down into a deep sleep.

Fifty-six

Halloween, 1964
East Goodland, New York

"Gus, be sure to wear your jacket."

My mother stood in the kitchen, arranging candy in a bowl for prospective trick-or-treaters. I nodded begrudgingly, not wanting to cover up my costume. My winter long johns had been dyed blue, and my red bathing suit doubled as Superman's trunks. My long-sleeved blue jersey was emblazoned with a large red "S," sewn into place last night.

The temperatures had dropped to the forties, but my red tablecloth cape would be hidden if I wore a jacket over it. I thought for a moment, slipped into the lightest jacket I could find, and tied the tablecloth around my neck. It flowed over the coat and hid it. If I left it unzipped, the "S" would still show.

"Are you sure you don't want me to walk with you, son?" my father asked from behind his newspaper.

He put it down and looked at me with a familiar concerned expression. I shook my head as he exchanged worried glances with my mother. The frequent nightmares had finally diminished, although I still had the drowning dream from time to time. Doctor Anton said I might always have such a dream, but not to worry because it was completely normal. We spoke a lot about what was "normal" in our sessions. We talked about death, evil, and fears.

We discussed Sharon's autopsy results and the shocking evidence that revealed sexual abuse. I shuddered when we covered the topic briefly, trying hard not to think about what Adamski had done to her, and how it related to the false claims Mayella Ewell made against Tom Robinson in "To Kill A Mockingbird." I had imagined her finding out about the church relics and posing a threat that way, but the awful truth was so much harder to swallow. The threat of discovery must have loomed far worse in his sick brain than being accused of stealing statues and bells.

I reached for my Superman mask and held it to my face, pulling the elastic strap around my long hair. It was one battle I won that fall—the elimination of the weekly haircut. Although I hadn't yet approached "Beatle" hair length, I made it at least halfway there and was pleased when the other kids in the sixth grade noticed.

I stood before my parents, breathing through the mouth hole in the stiff mask.

"Well, don't you look spiffy," my mother said.

My father rose from his seat and joined me at the door, handing me a silver flashlight and the paper shopping bag I'd decorated in class that day.

"Looks like he could save the world, Gloria."

I smiled behind the mask and nodded, heading out into the dark night. Running hard across the field that connected our house to the Marggranders', I pounded over the grass while my cape rippled in the breeze behind me. My new school sneakers quickly moistened with heavy dew soaked by stubby pasture grass. The mask eyeholes provided minimal vision, but I knew the path by heart and felt protected behind the face of my hero. I pushed fears of lurking monsters deep into my subconscious and sprinted across the field. Although it was only five-thirty, the sky had darkened to indigo and black. Stars arced bright in the sky, lighting the way to the Marggranders' side door.

The porch lights glowed and candles flickered within pulpy shells of carved pumpkins. Elsbeth opened the door before I knocked and pulled me inside. She beamed at me in a long white dress with attached wings. Mrs. Marggrander had been working all week on the wire and filmy fabric structures. They sparkled with glitter and miraculously hung from her small shoulders. A gold braided curtain tie was fashioned into a halo. It rested on her dark curls, encircling her hair like a garland.

"What do you think, Superman?" she asked as she twirled around.

I looked up as Siegfried and his parents entered the room. He was dressed as a doctor, wearing a long white coat, mustache, stethoscope, and carrying a black bag. He winked at me from behind an old pair of heavy glasses.

"It's beautiful, Elsbeth," I said. "I think you'll win first prize."

Siegfried approached and felt my biceps with his fingers, nodding and pretending to examine me. He put the stethoscope up to my chest and listened as I breathed in and out behind the sweaty plastic mask.

"*Ja, ja.* Muscles of steel and a heart of gold. He *must* be Superman."

Elsbeth hopped up and down in place, giggling as she ran to the dining room table to fetch her JC Penney's bag decorated with black cats and jack-o-lanterns. I noticed with a smile—there were no bats in her design.

We'd been anticipating the Halloween party at the East Goodland Methodist church for weeks.

"Papa? Mama? Can we go now?" she asked, prancing toward them.

Mr. Marggrander wore a rare smile. He zipped up his jacket and spoke in his strong German accent.

"*Ja, ja,* presently. But I have one question for Superman."

He lifted a forefinger to his chin and cocked his head.

"Will you be flying to church or driving with us tonight?" he asked. His mustache twitched.

I looked at him in surprise. I'd never heard him crack a joke before. Mrs. Marggrander smiled broadly, shaking her forefinger in his direction and nudging him toward the door as she grabbed her big square pocketbook from the hook on the wall. The twins linked arms with me and answered their father simultaneously when we headed for the door.

"He's coming with us, Papa." They leaned forward and looked at each other, laughed, and repeated the words in unison. "He's coming with us."

The End

Author Bio

After writing in the early morning hours, Aaron Lazar works as an electrophotographic engineer in Rochester, New York. Additional passions include vegetable, fruit, and flower gardening; preparing large family feasts; photographing his family, gardens, and the breathtakingly beautiful Genesee Valley; cross-country skiing across the rolling hills; playing a distinctly amateur level of piano, and spending "time" with the French Impressionists whenever possible.

Mr. Lazar resides in Upstate New York with his wife, three daughters, two grandsons, mother-in-law, dog, and four cats. Although he adored raising his three delightful daughters, he finds grandfathering his "two little buddies" to be one of the finest experiences of his life.

Contact him at aaron.lazar@yahoo.com, or visit his websites:

www.legardemysteries.com
www.mooremysteries.com
www.aaronlazar.blogspot.com
www.aplazar.gather.com

Don't miss any of these other
exciting mainstream novels

➤ Death on Delivery
(1-931201-60-9, $16.50 US)

➤ Death to the Centurion
(1-931201-26-9, $16.95 US)

➤ The Elixir
(1-933353-03-1, $16.95 US)

➤ The Golden Crusader
(1-933353-91-0, $16.95 US)

➤ The Moon Child
(1-931201-20-X, $15.50 US)

➤ The Vandenberg Diamonds
(1-933353-83-X, $18.95 US)

➤ Unraveled
(1-931201-11-0, $15.50 US)

Twilight Times Books
Kingsport, Tennessee

Order Form

If not available from your local bookstore or favorite online bookstore, send this coupon and a check or money order for the retail price plus $3.50 s&h to Twilight Times Books, Dept. GB-1007 POB 3340 Kingsport TN 37664. Delivery may take up to four weeks.

Name: _____

Address: _____

_____

Email: _____

I have enclosed a check or money order in the amount of

$_____

for _____ .

If you enjoyed this book, please post a review at your favorite online bookstore.

Twilight Times Books
P O Box 3340
Kingsport, TN 37664
Phone/Fax: 423-323-0183
www.twilighttimesbooks.com/